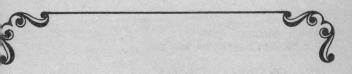

Moved by sudden impulse, the marquess bent his head to brush his lips lightly against hers—only to find that the lips against his held and clung in a full-blooded, passionate embrace as Miss Jean Lindsay gave herself wholeheartedly up to her first kiss.

Swept by an answering passion that shook him down to the soles of his glossy Hessian boots, the marquess broke away, breathing hard as though he had been running.

"Really, Miss Lindsay...you must not...you shouldn't. Hell and damnation!" roared the marquess. "You shouldn't kiss me like that."

Also by Marion Chesney
Published by Fawcett Books:

THE CONSTANT COMPANION
MY LORDS, LADIES & MARJORIE
QUADRILLE
LOVE AND LADY LOVELACE
THE GHOST AND LADY ALICE
THE DUKE'S DIAMONDS
LADY LUCY'S LOVER
THE FRENCH AFFAIR
MINERVA
SWEET MASQUERADE
THE TAMING OF ANNABELLE
DEIRDRE AND DESIRE
THE FLIRT
DAPHNE
THOSE ENDEARING YOUNG CHARMS
TO DREAM OF LOVE
DIANA THE HUNTRESS
AT THE SIGN OF THE GOLDEN PINEAPPLE
FREDERICA IN FASHION
MILADY IN LOVE
LESSONS IN LOVE
THE PAPER PRINCESS
THE PERFECT GENTLEMAN
PRETTY POLLY

REGENCY GOLD

A NOVEL BY
Marion Chesney

FAWCETT CREST • NEW YORK

A Fawcett Crest Book
Published by Ballantine Books
Copyright © 1980 by Marion Chesney

ISBN 0-449-21656-X

Manufactured in the United States of America

First Fawcett Coventry Edition: January 1980
First Ballantine Books Edition: October 1988

Chapter One

It was not the first time that Miss Jean Lindsay had entertained unchristian feelings toward her uncle, the Reverend Hamish. But as she sat in the chill manse parlor, staring at the gold-embossed invitation which he had put into her hands before leaving for the church, thoughts of slow torture, mutilation or just plain murder burned in her heart. Her first ball, and less than twenty-four hours to prepare for it!

"I do not let my mind run on worldly matters," her uncle had snapped by way of an explanation as to why the precious invitation had reposed in his desk drawer for the past two weeks. "And don't expect me to waste good money on finery. There's a trunk full of your mother's clothes in the attic. Find something there."

There had been talk of little else in the village of Dunwearie but the ball to be given by the Duke and Duchess of Glenrandall. The villagers were very proud of living in the vicinity of a real duke and duchess and as proud of Glenrandall Castle as if it were their own. For the castle, perched on a cliff above Loch Garvin, facing down the sea loch to the rocky Atlantic shores of the Scottish West Highlands, was modern, and since the famous brothers Adam who had designed the castle had kept to their policy of employing local craftsmen, the building and maintenance of the great pile brought some small prosperity to the village of Dunwearie itself.

Jean had sadly assumed she was not to be invited, for although her social background was impeccable, her life of drudgery at the manse had not taught her to think much of herself.

Her grandfather, General Sir Duncan Lindsay, had been a famous Far Eastern explorer and had died a wealthy man. He left three sons: Jean's father, Sir Philip, who inherited the bulk of the estate, Hamish and Joseph. While Hamish took holy orders and Joseph sailed to India to seek his fortune, Sir Philip gave up the days of his bachelorhood in his late forties to marry a pretty but feckless and impoverished lady, Venetia Harrington, and then settled back to dissipate his wealth in every gambling hall from Land's End to John O' Groats with the help of his wife.

The spendthrift couple had met their death a few months after Jean was born when their carriage had plunged off one of the treacherous Highland roads into a ravine. Venetia Lindsay had long before alienated the affections of her stiff-necked family who objected to her profligate way of life, Joseph was presumed dead in some tribal uprising in the strife-torn North-West Frontier of India, so only the Reverend Hamish was left to give the baby a home.

The girl would have become little more than a drudge but for the intervention of her godmother, Lady Harriet Telfer-Billington, a childhood friend of her mother. Although Lady Harriet resided in London, she had persuaded the Duchess of Glenrandall to allow Jean to share her schooling with the Duchess's twin daughters, Lady Mary and Lady Bess. Hamish grumbled about the waste of educating a mere girl, but the thought of getting anything at all free was too much for him. Jean was allowed to visit Glenrandall Castle each weekday for two hours to be taught the art of ladylike accomplishments.

Jean's angry thoughts turned from her uncle to her classmates, Lady Mary and Lady Bess. The twins were as pretty and empty-headed as china dolls, forever giggling and whispering in corners and excluding Jean from their conversation. They had prattled on for weeks about the dresses and jewelery they would wear to the ball and speculated about the gentlemen who would be present, but never once had they intimated that Jean was to be one of the guests.

The ball was in honor of Mary and Bess's eighteenth birthday and was to be a prelude to their removal to London the following week where they were to make their come-out. The Duchess of Glenrandall also nourished hopes that the romantic setting of a ball would prompt their houseguest, the Marquess of Fleetwater, to develop a *tendre* for one of her daughters. Jean wished them all success with the marquess. She had only seen him from a distance, and although she allowed him to be extremely handsome, he seemed very cold and proud.

That evening, Jean wearily waited to be dismissed from the dining room while her uncle ranted and raved over the shortcomings of his parishioners, the meager dinner, and the insolence of their housekeeper, Agnes, who had pointed out that it would take another miracle of the loaves and fishes to provide a decent meal out of the beggarly housekeeping allowance.

At last he fell asleep over his brandy, a thin, cadaverous figure in rusty blacks, periwig over one eye, snuff stains overlaying wine stains on the clerical white cravat. With a sigh of relief, Jean picked up her candle and made her way up three flights of dark, narrow stairs to the attic.

Throwing back the lid of an old black trunk, Jean picked out dress after dress, putting aside the ones with great hoops and panniers until she came across one of a

7

simpler cut than the rest. It was of straw-colored satin, scooped low over the bosom but narrower than the others. It had an overdress with panniers *à la bergère* which was surely long out of style, but the heavy sheen of satin felt luxurious to fingers used to serge, cotton and calico. It would have to do. The current mode was for evening slippers of kid tied with delicate ribbons. The only footwear available was a pair of gold shoes with high heels of crimson. She decided that they would not show under the long skirt—and who would ask her to dance anyway!

When Jean arrived at the castle next day, the whole household seemed to be in a tremendous bustle with preparations for the ball. Escaping up the stairs to the comparative quiet of the schoolroom, she found the governess, Miss Taylor, waiting alone.

"Lady Mary and Lady Bess have persuaded Her Grace that they are now too old for the schoolroom, so my job here is finished," said the little governess. "I shall receive a pension of course, but what is to become of you, my dear?" She looked sadly at her pupil and friend.

At seventeen, Jean had grown into a slim, dreamy girl with a heavy mass of carrot-colored hair, slanting green eyes and a small, pointed, freckled face which no amount of Denmark Lotion would leave unblemished. It seemed unfair, mused Miss Taylor, that two such silly chits as her ducal charges had all the wealth and the clever Miss Lindsay none at all.

"I shall manage," said Jean. "I can't think of the future, only of this evening. I shall be wearing a dress of my mama's. It is not the height of fashion but the color is exceeding pretty."

Miss Taylor threw up her hands in horror. "Do you mean your uncle has not bought you a dress for the ball?"

Jean shook her head sadly. "He says 'tis sinfully wicked to be thinking of clothes."

"Well, goodness knows we're far enough away from London," said Miss Taylor bracingly. "I doubt if many of the ladies will be the crack of fashion."

Jean looked moodily out of the window across the sunlit terraced gardens to the loch below. The water, rippling in the chill winter wind, darkened and changed like the expressions on Jean's face. It was hard to remember that in the summer, orange blossoms grew around the urns and balustrades of the terraces and one could pick peaches and apricots in the walled garden.

"It doesn't really matter what I look like," she said, savagely stabbing her needle into the tambour frame. "What man there is going to be interested in a dowerless girl from the manse? Then I never know what to say to people and I keep dropping things and forgetting things."

"You daydream too much," said Miss Taylor. "I should never have encouraged you to read novels. Life does not work out that way in real life. If only your uncle could be persuaded to let you visit your godmother in London, then your chance of meeting a suitable husband would be great. You are not lacking in looks."

"He says that London abounds in fleshpots and hell-rakes and all manner of sinful goings-on," sighed Jean. "He will never let me go."

The night of the ball was clear, frosty and cold. Jean drew her cloak tightly around her as she went downstairs to where her uncle was waiting, attired in rusty black silk, the lace at his throat and cuffs so worn and old, it looked like cobwebs. If he saw the depth of her neckline, she would not be allowed to go or—horrors—be sent upstairs to put on her best Sunday black which was so funereal that the youths of the village danced after her shouting out, "Here comes corbie Jean," and a trifle immodesty was better than looking like a crow.

As they walked up the long driveway to the castle,

Jean felt a lifting of her heart. Perhaps it would not be so bad after all. Perhaps the man of her dreams would be there. "I do not care if your niece is dowerless, Mr. Alexander, I must make her my wife. When I saw her walk into the ballroom. . . ."

"Stop dreaming like a gowk," hissed her uncle. "We're here."

Jean left her cloak in a downstairs room assigned to the ladies and joined her uncle before ascending the staircase to make her curtsy to the duke and duchess.

Characteristically, Hamish's horror at his niece's appearance was not because she looked as if she had stepped down from one of the family portraits in the hall but because the Georgian cut of her dress revealed a good part of two excellent white breasts.

"Ye shameless hussy," he spluttered. "Get your cloak and I'll get you out of here. We'll say you have the vapors."

The fact that Lady Mary and Lady Bess were in uncontrollable fits of the giggles at the sight of their schoolmate's ball gown brought a high flush to Hamish's face. Both girls were in the latest Regency mode of simple, high-waisted silk dresses which also showed a great deal of bosom but that did nothing to allay the minister's wrath. He was such a confirmed old snob that the aristocracy could walk around naked and he would consider it quite the thing.

Jean stiffly made her curtsy, her face flaming as she caught a loud whisper from Bess. "La, what a quiz!" Her prayers that she would suddenly become invisible or that a thunder bolt would strike down the entire family of Glenrandall were obviously not going to be answered. She pushed out her little chin and marched into the room, her antique red heels clacking on the polished floor.

The ballroom was like a fairytale, decorated with masses of exotic hothouse blooms and the walls hung with great swaths of rose silk more in keeping with the duchess's rather florid taste than with the severe classical design of the brothers Adam.

The reverend bowed to various acquaintances and led Jean behind a pillar. "Now stay there out of sight. We will remain but a respectable bit of time. You will then go straight away to get your cloak when I tell you and leave me to make our good-byes as best I can. The shame of it! You did it deliberately. This is what I get for giving a home to a thankless orphan. You are a viper in my bosom. A veritable viper!"

The viper had never felt so miserable in all her life and there was no one to tell her that her outmoded dress was strangely becoming and that the rose silk on the walls turned her hair to a fascinating, deeper shade of red. She moodily stared down at her fan—depicting a Georgian couple, flirting happily, quite unaware in their painted Eden that they were out of fashion—and tried to think of something else.

"Did you think it was a masquerade?" Lady Bess was at her elbow, all mock solicitation. "Well, well, if you stay here you will be all right and perhaps I can persuade Jamie to take you in to supper." Jamie was a distant cousin of the family who did not appear in company much because it was said he was touched in his upper works.

"Look over there," said Bess, momentarily distracted from the delicious game of humiliating her clever schoolmate. "That's John, the Marquess of Fleetwater, who is staying with us. He is said to be a very Corinthian and as rich as Golden Ball. Thirty years and *not* married, my dear. But so handsome for all that he is a trifle old."

Jean looked across the ballroom to the gentleman in question. He was without a doubt the handsomest man in the room, tall with blond hair in a Brutus crop, his cravat a miracle of sculptured perfection and his gray,

11

heavy-lidded eyes surveying the room through a quizzing glass with a fashionable air of boredom. "I don't like his eyes," said Jean. "He could at least pretend to be enjoying himself."

"Oh, hoity-toity, miss," laughed Bess, tossing her butter-colored ringlets. "You're jealous because you haven't a chance of dancing with him. But I have—and a good chance of becoming a marchioness, too." With that, Lady Bess flitted off, leaving Jean to look enviously after her.

For poor Jean was only human. It would be lovely, she thought, to have money, a title, and wear pretty dresses. As was her habit when life seemed too difficult, she began to daydream, leaning her head against the pillar, her dance card empty of names, dangling on her wrist.

The duchess would appear with the marquess at her elbow. "Lord Fleetwater has begged me for an introduction," she would say. The marquess would smile into her eyes, his own no longer sleepy and bored. They would dance. He would whisper in her ear, "I am enchanted by your beauty. We must marry. I can wait no longer . . ."

"Jean!" said the Duchess of Glenrandall imperiously. "I have been trying to present Lord Fleetwater to you for this age. Wake up, girl." Jean blinked her green eyes and brought the ballroom back into focus and realized that the marquess was surveying her but, unlike in her dream, he looked bored and faintly irritated.

"May I have the honor of this dance unless you are already bespoke?" said the marquess, trying not to notice the nervous little hand covering the dance card.

"Yes . . . yes . . . p-please, I'd like to dance," said Jean blushing. "It is the waltz," said the duchess. "I told Lord Fleetwater you are not yet come out but since this is a family party, I see no reason why we should maintain too high a form."

Blessing Miss Taylor who had taught her the steps of the waltz, Jean allowed herself to be swept onto the floor and into seventh heaven. Although the marquess held her the regulation twelve inches away, Jean found it very strange and exciting to have a man's arm around her.

The marquess looked down at the dreamy face below his chin and mentally cursed the soft heart of Honoria, Duchess of Glenrandall.

"Come, John," the duchess had insisted. "You are surely not so high in the instep that you cannot favor one of our local girls with a dance. Now, there's little Jean Lindsay. Yes, yes, I know she's wearing that impossible dress but it's all the fault of that old miser of an uncle of hers and I hate to see the child unhappy."

The child in question floated around the ballroom, her little red heels hardly touching the floor, oblivious of the jealous stares that followed her progress, for in her mind, she and the marquess were already married.

It would be a marriage of equals, she decided. Not like some of the poor bullied slaves in the village. If she did not like any of her husband's orders and he tried to become too masterful, she would put her foot down. And she did. And found herself staring up into the hard, angry eyes of reality.

"You stamped on my foot!" hissed the marquess.

Appalled, Jean heard a malicious whisper from Mary to Bess. "Poor Lord Fleetwater. Mama should never have made him give Jean a dance."

Her eyes full of tears, Jean sobbed, "If you will but return me to my place, my lord. I wish to go home. I have the headache."

But the marquess had also heard the whisper. Compassion was a foreign emotion to him but during his stay he had taken the duchess's spoiled daughters in dislike and considered they needed a set down. He had been the biggest marriage prize in London for many seasons and

13

knew his worth. The company bored him and had it not been for the excellent shooting on the duke's estate, he would have cut his visit short.

"Come now," he said, his voice warm with a sympathy, which surprised him as much as it did Jean, "it is time for supper. I shall escort you and you shall feel more the thing when you have had something to eat." And taking her arm in a firm grasp, he led her toward the supper room, pleased at the little gasp of dismay from the ladies behind him.

He piled Jean's plate high with food but prepared to entertain her with conversation as she nibbled a little of it delicately as was the custom. To his surprise, the odd girl set to with a will and demolished her plateful in what seemed a matter of seconds.

He blinked. "Would you like some more?"

"Oh, yes!" said Jean with delight. The marquess seemed to be human after all. "I'm terribly hungry."

"This will never do in London," said the marquess with mock severity. "I will have you know it is de rigueur for a young lady to pick at her food. In fact most eat a hearty meal *before* coming to a ball or rout so that they can maintain the polite fiction of eating like birds."

"Well, the ladies of your acquaintance do not come from a Scottish manse," replied Jean. She had decided that her social life was obviously going to end with this one evening and it behove her to have as much fun—and food—as she could and forget to bother with the niceties of correct social conversation.

"Anyway," she added, "I have no chance of a season in London. My godmother wishes to have me but my uncle"—she indicated the funereal figure across the room—"will not attend. London, I believe, abounds in fleshpots."

The marquess roared with laughter and Jean realized with surprise that she was a small success. Everyone in the supper room was covertly watching them. Her clothes were suddenly considered quaint but becoming. After all, any girl who could entertain a nonpareil like the marquess must have something.

"I suppose I could have a word with your uncle," said the marquess raising his quizzing glass to look at Hamish and immediately dropping it as the old man started bowing and scraping in his direction, his withered face nearly in his food. "On second thoughts," he mused half to himself, "he might get the wrong idea."

Jean had forgotten the exalted nature of her company. After all, it had been like chatting with Miss Taylor. "Yes, his mind does rather run on sin," she giggled. "He would probably think you meant to offer me a *carte blanche*. Anyway," she stammered, freezing under the marquess's shocked stare, "he would know you did not have any ideas of marriage. I have no dowry."

"*Carte blanche* indeed!" raged the marquess, betrayed into equally bad form by his anger. "I'll have you know, my dear, that should I wish to mount a new mistress, I should look for something more experienced. I do not seduce village girls."

Jean's face was the same color as her hair. "I faith, my lord, if I forgot myself, I am sorry. I had thought we were talking as friends."

"Don't forget yourself again," snapped the marquess, struggling to assume the calm mask of thirty years of social modes and manners. "It was an outrageous thing to say," he added in a kinder tone. "You must never speak like that *again* to any man of your acquaintance."

Feeling like a gauche schoolgirl, Jean was led back into the ballroom to find Hamish waiting to be introduced.

"Will you be long in these parts, my lord?"

Horrible old man, thought the marquess, his pity for Jean again aroused. "No," he said, shortly. "I leave tomorrow."

"Well, now, perhaps you may see my little Jean in London?" said Hamish with an ingratiating leer.

"But I thought . . ." started Jean, bewildered.

"Now, now," said Hamish. "You didn't take any notice of an old man's teasing. I shall write to your godmother on the morrow."

The marquess bowed formally and departed, leaving Jean happy but confused. It had dawned on Hamish that his niece might be able to catch a rich husband and, after all, Lady Harriet Telfer-Billington had said she would frank Jean's season, so it wasn't as if he would have to pay anything.

"Glad to see you doing the pretty with the Lindsay girl," said the Duke of Glenrandall, linking arms with the marquess. "She don't get too much fun. That old curmudgeon of an uncle is too mean. Wouldn't tolerate him around the place but the family's very sound. The old general was a great character, I believe. Before m' time, of course. Knew the girl's father, Philip. Charming but couldn't hold on to a farthing. Bet on everything from flies on the windowpane to geese crossing the road."

The marquess shrugged his elegant shoulders. "Poor thing," he said. "That old-fashioned gown and that terrible uncle. Least I could do."

Lady Bess gleefully heard this aside and rushed to tell Jean. To be an object of pity is a dreadful thing. After one furious, hurt, stormy look at the marquess, Jean gathered the rags of her dignity and informed her uncle that she was leaving.

The following Sunday, the desire for revenge against the whole world in general and the marquess in particular burned in Jean's now sedately covered bosom. She sharpened her quill with savage strokes, dipped her pen in the inkwell and applied herself to her uncle's sermon.

A few years ago when the reverend had taken to his

16

bed suffering from an excess of the duke's brandy, Jean had written his sermon for him and had been landed with the thankless task ever since. Her uncle, she knew, never read her sermons. He merely intoned them mindlessly, being well fortified with madeira before the event. She tore up what she had written and began again.

"Because some among us today have great wealth and rank, it does not mean that they should humiliate those beneath them in social station. They should not be so puffed up that they forget the lowliest herdsman has feelings. The aristocracy of this fair country have become spoiled, vice-ridden and corrupt. Its young men waste their time in gaming halls and its so-called ladies are little better than whores offering their bodies to the highest bidder on the marriage mart . . ."

Jean giggled as she thought of the marquess's face and ended the sermon with one of her uncle's famous sayings. "And so, dear brethren, it is my utmost wish that the increase of such as these shall be given to the worm and that their immortal souls shall burn in hell."

But it would never do. Perhaps it might amuse Miss Taylor. Jean slipped it into the desk drawer and began on what she mentally dubbed the "authorized version" of Uncle Hamish's sermon.

When she had finished, she left for the church to arrange flowers sent over after the ball by the duchess. It was a beautiful morning, bright and fair, all wind and glitter. The old trees around the manse tossed their arms up to the cloudless sky and yesterday's rain sparkled like gems on the smooth grass of the churchyard. Jean had learned that the marquess had decided to extend his stay, and although she was still smarting from his patronizing remark, she could not help looking forward to seeing him again. She chided herself for being impressed with nothing more than a tailored coat and a handsome face.

At the manse, the reverend carefully put down the

17

decanter and made his way into the study to collect the sermon. First he opened the drawer of the desk to look for his snuffbox, which had unaccountably been missing, and to his surprise saw the sermon lying there. Without glancing at the papers on top of the desk, he picked it up and made his way sedately, if somewhat unsteadily, to the church next door.

He frowned at the elaborate display of hothouse flowers which he considered smacked of popery, but he was gratified to notice that the church was filled to capacity, and also that the Marquess of Fleetwater was ensconced in the duke's pew, listening with bored attention to the prattling of Mary and Bess.

Clutching the wings of the brass eagle which supported the bible on the pulpit, he began his sermon. His blurred mind had no thought in it higher than the anticipation of lunch and it was only as he neared the end that he realized that the duke's face was mottled purple, the duchess was looking at him in blank horror and the Ladies Bess and Mary were bridling like startled horses. Out of the corner of his eye, he could see Jean, very white-faced, freckles standing out against the skin. At the final sentence, a deathly hush lay over the congregation, suddenly broken by an enormous roar of laughter, as the elegant marquess doubled up in the pew.

For the first time, Hamish focused blearily on the words he was supposed to have written and, after a quick perusal, held up his hands for silence.

"This is the work of a Jezebel!" he roared. "My thoughts were on God's business or I should have noticed the viper in my bosom, my own flesh and blood, my niece Jean had been at the Devil's work. She placed this . . . this—" he waved the papers—"in my hands substituting it for my own holy work."

He leaned over the pulpit and pointed straight at Jean. "Begone from this church, daughter of Satan!"

Jean turned and walked out, two spots of color burning on her cheeks, and, strangely enough, more hate for the marquess in her heart than for her uncle.

Chapter Two

The daughter of Satan sat on the edge of her bed and watched the light fading from the top of the mountains across the loch. A chill breeze rippled over the gray water and a seagull cried mournfully from the rocks.

A murmur of voices rose from the parlor below but Jean, who had wept until she felt numb, was past caring. There was a timid scratching at the door and it opened to reveal the housekeeper carrying a cheap tallow candle.

"Come, Mistress Jean, ye're wanted downstairs," said Agnes. Heaven help the girl; she looked so white! There was already talk in the village of her being a witch and Agnes's kind heart ached for the girl she had known since a baby.

"It'll be all right. You'll see," she said kindly. "Her Grace is there with the meenister and he will not be ranting and raving in front of the likes of her."

Jean followed the housekeeper down the narrow, dark stairs into the parlor. Ornately carved Jacobean furniture stood stiffly to attention as if awaiting her judgment. The grandfather clock in the corner gave a small, asthmatic cough, cleared its throat and chimed the quarter hour. As Jean moved forward into the room, the peat fire helpfully belched out a puff of black smoke to enhance her devilish image.

"Now, child," began Her Grace and held up her hand as Hamish would have spoken, "that was indeed a terrible business today." Honoria, the Duchess of Glenrandall, felt a mixture of pity and irritation as she looked at the woebegone figure in front of her. A lazy, kindhearted woman, she hated to see anyone unhappy but at the same time felt resentful if she was forced to bestir herself.

"We have decided that it is better if you journey to your godmother's on the morrow with my daughters and myself. I have sent an express to Lady Harriet Telfer-Billington apprising her of your arrival. I know it is short notice but I am sure you have little enough to pack"— with a glare at Hamish. "The clothes you have are not at all the thing, so it will be up to your godmother to furnish you with a suitable wardrobe.

"Miss Taylor will be arriving at any minute to help you choose anything that may be suitable. We shall stay with the Lamonts on the borders to break our journey. Remember always that you are being sent away in disgrace and it is up to you to rectify your errors by behaving modestly and like a gentlewoman. Ah, there is Miss Taylor now."

Jean, still speechless, could only wait as the governess bustled into the room. "My poor Miss Lindsay . . ." she began but was interrupted by the duchess. "No sympathy," she said sternly. "Leave us not forget that the girl has made a shameful spectacle of herself. I have told my daughters not to mention anything of this matter in London, and the Marquess of Fleetwater is, of course, a gentleman. He has assured me that no one will know anything of what occurred. Off you go with Miss Taylor."

"And as for you, Hamish," she said as the door closed

behind the two ladies, "you have only yourself to blame. You should thank your Maker that the duke has decided not to remove you from your living."

Upstairs, Miss Taylor, the only one to hear the true story of the sermon, shook her head over Jean's scanty wardrobe.

"If you give me the gown you wore to the ball, I shall alter it on the journey and then when we arrive at the Lamonts, I shall try my best with the remainder."

United by the common female bond of fashion, the two women looked gloomily at the well-worn dresses hanging in Jean's closet. "I am to be punished indeed!" exclaimed Jean miserably. "To travel all the way to London only to appear an antique dowd in the eyes of the ton. How Bess and Mary will giggle and stare."

As her eyes filled with tears, Agnes hurried into the room panting under the weight of a small trunk. "Your uncle's had this locked away since your mother died," said Agnes placing it in the middle of the room.

"He thinks there might be bits of jewelry in it. He says he hasn't even looked inside, which might be the case since the meenister was awfy smitten with your mama." And with that Agnes hurried off leaving both ladies to stare at each other in amazement at this revelation that Hamish might once have had a softer side to his flinty character.

Jean threw open the lid of the trunk. A faint odor of perfume wafted into the room and floated like an elegant, exotic memory on the chilly air and over the sparse furnishings. A sudden, almost desperate longing for the gay, pretty mother she had never known caught at Jean's throat and she crouched on the floor beside the trunk scarcely hearing the ecstatic cries from Miss Taylor.

"Look, here is a magnificent string of pearls and oh! . . . this darling fan with the ivory sticks. Do look, my dear, it is a veritable treasure trove."

At last Jean turned to the contents of the trunk. Miss Taylor's enthusiasm was infectious and the sight of a set of garnets in an antique, gold setting warmed Jean's feminine heart.

"Look, here are diamond earrings!" gasped Miss Taylor. "The stones are small but I could sell them for you in London and get you some pretty clothes."

Life began to look rosier and Jean plunged happily into a daydream. She would sell the diamonds and buy the prettiest, most fashionable ball gown in all London. She would descend the staircase of the ballroom slowly, her head held high. Waiting at the foot of the staircase would be the marquess, his bored eyes leaping to appreciative life . . .

Another gasp from Miss Taylor and the ballroom and the marquess fled into the mist of imagination.

The little governess had opened a heavy wash leather bag.

"Gold, my dear, real gold! There must be about . . . let me see," said Miss Taylor, her voice shaking with excitement as the pieces cascaded through her fingers . . . *one hundred guineas!* Oh, do not tell your uncle on any account or he will never let you have it."

Jean stared at the gold as if hypnotized. She did not know that so much money existed. It had been dinned into her head at Glenrandall Castle that only tradesmen discussed money, so her standards were those of the Highlanders in the village.

"Why . . . I am an heiress," she breathed.

Unaware that her unworldly charge really believed it, Miss Taylor gave an indulgent laugh and rattled on.

"We are to stay with Sir Edward and Lady Cynthia Lamont and they are said to be exceeding grand, you know. You must have money to give to the servants," said the worldly-wise Miss Taylor. "Servants are *so* important to one's comfort. Give your vails to the housekeeper and butler when you *arrive*, not when you leave, then everything will be made easy for you during your stay."

Jean nodded out of the window of her dreamworld in recognition of her governess's wisdom and then retired back into a land of rosy fantasies.

Miss Taylor clapped her hands. "Enough of this. Let's get your things together, though Lord knows you've only enough for one bandbox."

The morning dawned cold and thick with mist as the duke's carriages paused at the end of the manse drive to take up Jean. The duke himself was remaining behind to attend to estate matters.

In the foremost carriage sat the duchess clutching a vinaigrette and already supported by no less than two abigails. Her Grace detested traveling. In the second coach came Bess and Mary, who would have had it that Miss Taylor should travel in the third coach with the servants but the kindly duchess pooh-poohed the idea. They made room with bad grace.

As Jean climbed in, four pairs of china-blue eyes stared at her contemptuously, flicked over her well-worn plaid dress and shabby pelisse and turned to stare out of the window.

Despite Jean's disgrace, many of the parishioners had turned up to wave her good-bye and press little presents and comforts for the road on her. Jean's green eyes blurred as the carriage rolled off and had it not been for the sight of Hamish glowering through the mist like a demon, she would have broken down completely.

His parting words had been in character. "Remember where your duty lies, my girl, and get yourself a rich husband. The Lord expects it of you. Try to remember to be a credit to me. And here"—searching in a rusty black pocket—"to show you I am a forgiving and generous man, this will buy you some gee-gaws." He counted ten shillings slowly and reluctantly into her palm, seeming surprised that she did not faint from gratitude.

If I marry, thought Jean, it will be so that I don't have to be obliged to that horrible old man again, ever.

After an hour of travel, Bess and Mary started to yawn and stretch with boredom but Jean was enchanted with the novelty of it all and pulled the bearskin rug closer around her legs and nestled her feet on the hot brick placed in the carriage for her comfort.

Two days of travel went by, broken by a brief night's rest at a posting house. When they finally turned into the broad avenue which led to Rowannan Castle, home of Sir Edward Lamont where they were to stay for a few days, even Jean was heartily thankful. Bess and Mary had complained and whined throughout the whole journey and the duchess was nigh prostrate with travel sickness.

Rowannan Castle, set on the Scottish borders, was of mellow gray stone with crow-step gables and romantic turrets. The countryside was green, rolling and gentle, pleasing to Jean's eyes, which were accustomed to the savage beauty of the Highlands. A modern extension with a terrace had been added to the entrance. Jean clapped her hands in delight. "Oh, look. Peacocks!"

"Don't be so rustic, for pity's sake," snapped Bess. "Only yokels leap about as if everything were a carnival."

"That was unkind and unnecessary," remonstrated Miss Taylor.

"Pray remember you are no longer our governess. A fact of which I am exceeding glad," retorted Lady Bess with a toss of her yellow curls. "And were it not for Jean playing the very freak by altering her uncle's sermon, you would be pensioned off and Mary and I should not be obliged to endure any more of your company. Or Jean's, for that matter."

"Faith!" exclaimed Bess, twisting her features into what she hoped was a worldly sneer. "I do so detest provincials."

Jean was saved from replying by the opening of the carriage door. Sir Edward Lamont, who had come down the steps to meet them, turned out to be a portly man in his middle years with a friendly, easy manner. But his wife, Lady Cynthia, made Jean's heart sink to the soles of her shabby boots.

Impervious to the chill of a Scottish castle, Lady Cynthia was clad in a gown of diaphanous green gauze, her hair was dressed *à la Sappho* and her roseleaf complexion was achieved by paint put on by the hand of a genius. To Jean's unsophisticated eyes, Lady Cynthia appeared the most beautiful woman she had ever seen.

"It is good to have female company," said Lady Cynthia, languidly extending a white hand in welcome. "Edward will bore on so about his crops and horses. But it seems we are to have quite a party. The Marquess of Fleetwater is coming tomorrow to stay and bringing two of his friends. He seems anxious to renew his acquaintance." She paused as Bess and Mary giggled coyly. "So we shall be quite gay."

I shall never, never be fashionable, thought Jean. How on earth does she manage to keep her voice on that same tired, languid level?

Bess and Mary immediately started to imitate Lady Cynthia and the die-away airs sat ludicrously on the buxom figures and rosy cheeks. Overtired from the journey and slightly overwrought, Jean began to giggle. A faint flicker of annoyance showed in Cynthia's lustrous black eyes.

"Ah, yes, Miss Lindsay is it not? I think you will wish to retire to your room to change." Cynthia's plucked eyebrows raised a millimeter but it was enough to indicate what she thought of Jean's attire. She turned to the duchess. "Do stay with me a minute, Honoria, with your girls. I am sure you are not in need of such drastic repairs before dinner. You all look charming."

Upstairs, Jean threw her reticule across the room and stared around her with wide, hurt, unseeing eyes. It seemed that a young lifetime of snubs from Uncle Hamish had not inured her to insult. Gradually she quietened and settled down to take stock of her surroundings.

The bedroom was decorated in shades of rose from the thick carpet under her feet to the chintz hangings on the four-poster. It opened into a sitting room designed in the same shades of rose, which in turn led to a small bedroom allocated to Miss Taylor. From her windows, she could look across the rolling beauty of the southern uplands and directly beneath her to the symmetric formality of the gardens, white with winter frost. Slowly the scene faded from her eyes as she escaped to dream country.

The marquess would arrive on the morrow. Lady Mary and Lady Bess would be vying for his attention. She would descend the stairs wearing—the dream faded momentarily as Jean strained to think of what she could wear that would be at all attractive. No matter. The marquess's eyes would narrow. Brushing unseeingly past Bess and Mary, he would seize her hand and whisper . . .

"Good heavens, child! Are you not yet dressed for dinner?" The voice was Miss Taylor's, the hands on the little, gilt French clock ten minutes to five and, despite Lady Cynthia's sophistication, the Lamonts kept country hours for dinner.

Jean's straw-colored ball gown had been skillfully altered to Empire lines by Miss Taylor and pressed by the maid. By the time Jean had slipped it on and teased her red curls into some semblance of fashionable disorder, it was several minutes past five. As they crossed the main hall, Miss Taylor whispered, "Did you give vails to the butler and housekeeper?" Jean nodded and absentmindedly dropped her fan. Immediately four footmen nearly collided their powdered heads in their efforts to be first to retrieve it. Miss Taylor stared. "How much did you give them?" But the double doors of the dining room were already being held open, so Jean was unable to reply.

"Why, how becomingly you look, my dear," said Lady Cynthia, floating toward them with arms outstretched. "So simple and in such good taste. We invited your *dame de compagnie* to join us this evening so that you should not feel strange."

The bewildered governess looked hastily around for the companion and then realized that Lady Cynthia was referring to her. Why Cynthia should be affable all of a sudden was a mystery to Jean but she was pathetically grateful for the warmth of her welcome and found nothing amiss. She could only assume that her first impression of Lady Cynthia had been wrong and that the flattering attention she was receiving from Bess and Mary was because they were copying their new idol.

Poor Jean. She did not realize the furor she had caused in the servants' hall earlier when Wilkins, the butler, spilled out the five golden guineas she had shyly pressed into his hand onto the kitchen table in front of a breathless and admiring audience.

"She must be as rich as creetures," exclaimed the cook.

"Croesus, Mrs. Spencer," corrected the butler loftily. "And she gave three of them golden boys to our good housekeeper who is so faint—her delicate neves you know—she has gone to lie down with the hartshorn."

"But her clothes are downright shabby," protested the lady's maid who had been allocated to Jean.

"Do not let that deceive you," said Wilkins. "That's the quality for you. Them eccentric heiresses is always pertending they 'asn't got it when they 'as," said the Cockney Wilkins, dropping his grand manner along with his aspirates in all the excitment.

"Take old Lady Bellows what was 'ere. Rich as Golden Ball 'er was *and* she made all 'er own clothes. So there!"

Just before dinner, the story of Jean's wealth had permeated to the upper regions, Lady Cynthia having been complimented by *her* maid on her visitor, who was "ever-so unassuming for an heiress." Bess and Mary considered listening to servants' gossip positively plebeian but had nonetheless perfected an act between them capable of winkling the darkest secrets out of the most reticent retainer. They gathered that Jean had been left a fortune by some mysterious benefactor. "And never a word about it," sniffed Bess. "I always said she was sly."

The dinner party passed pleasantly and without incident. The food was delicious, the company pleasant. Jean happily decided that she was going to like fashionable life after all.

At breakfast next morning, Wilkins hovered solicitously over Jean's plate, seemingly oblivious to Bess and Mary for, as he had confided downstairs, "They may be duke's daughters but they've got a clutch-fisted look about 'em and treats me like I was dirt beneath their feet."

Afterward, when the ladies took the air in the bleak winter scene of the rose garden, Miss Taylor found an opportunity to draw Jean aside. "The servants are practically falling over themselves to look after you. How much did you give them?" she asked.

"Oh, not much," said Jean absently, crushing a shriveled, blackened rose between her fingers. "Wilkins looked as grand as a lord, so I gave him five guineas."

"Five guineas!" screamed the little governess. "You must be mad."

"Is it so much?" sighed Jean. "I have a lot to learn. What do we do for amusement here, for example? I am not used to being idle."

"Well, after luncheon, we all retire to the drawing room," considered Miss Taylor. "Let me see: one writes letters or plays on the pianoforte or nets a purse or walks . . ."

"*Walks!*" interrupted Jean. "Where?"

"Why in the drawing room, for genteel exercise, you know. And sometimes one of the gentlemen will offer you his arm and walk with you."

"Faith," sighed Jean. "It all sounds exceeding dull. No wonder it is easy for ladies of quality to look bored."

"Ah, but that is the fashion," explained the governess with a superior smile. "It reached its height at the court of Marie Antoinette where to show the slightest sign of animation or make any sudden movement was considered vulgar in the extreme. The manner was adopted in fashionable circles in London and is still very much the mode. It is quite sensible really. Excessive liveliness causes wrinkles."

Perhaps the dashing marquess would enliven things, reflected Jean. Perhaps he had learned of her visit and had deliberately arranged to visit the Lamonts so as to be near her. Then she laughed at herself. She was in danger of letting her fantasies take over.

As they strolled to the main door of the castle, several smart traveling equipages were being led off to the stables. The marquess and his party had arrived.

The gentlemen were introduced at lunchtime. The marquess's friends turned out to be an ebullient youth by the title of Lord Freddie Blackstone and a slightly older, soberly dressed gentleman called Mr. Harry Fairchild.

All were in high spirits and declared themselves not in the least fatigued from their journey. "Perhaps the ladies would care to join us for a ride this afternoon," said the marquess in his pleasant drawl. All accepted enthusiastically, except Jean.

"Do you know how to horse-ride, Jean?" asked Bess maliciously.

"Of course," replied Jean, outwardly cool and inwardly trembling. "But unfortunately I left my riding habit at home."

Now she really has gone mad, thought Miss Taylor.

"That is no problem," said Lady Cynthia. "Allow me to lend you one of mine."

Jean tried to protest but was overcome by Cynthia, who was determined to be generous to the new heiress.

When the party changed and reassembled at the stables, all the glory of a smart blue velvet riding habit with gold frogging and a dashing shako could not stop Jean from eyeing the horse led up to her as if she were facing the guillotine. Teetering on the mounting block, she gingerly hoisted herself into the side saddle and looked down at the ground, which seemed to be a long, long way away.

"That's my favorite mount," called Sir Edward cheerfully. "Name's Caesar. Gentle as a lamb. Only sorry I haven't time to join the party."

They moved off at a sedate pace until Jean found she was being slowly outdistanced by the rest. "Giddyup, Caesar!" she said to the big roan, who merely flattened his ears slightly and continued at his own slow pace. She racked her brains. How did one get a horse to move? Of course! The riding crop. Jean gave Caesar a smart crack across his glossy rump. Gathering all his resources, the horse lunged forward down the ride in a headlong gallop with Jean clinging desperately to his mane.

"Tally-ho!" yelled Lord Freddie enthusiastically. "Look at her go!"

The marquess said nothing but immediately spurred his own horse to a gallop and raced down the ride after the fast disappearing figure.

Just as Jean felt that every bone in her body had been broken, Caesar slowed to a canter, then to a walk and then stopped dead and started to crop the long grass by the side of the path, leaving Jean, who by some miracle had managed to stay on his back, to slide to the ground with trembling legs. Lowering herself carefully onto the grass, she sat down and cursed the uncaring horse with a fluency that would have amazed an ostler.

"Don't blame the poor animal. It was entirely your own fault, you know," said a familiar voice behind her.

It was the marquess, impeccable and unperturbed as ever. As she blushed and stammered for words, he added gently, "You have never ridden before, have you?" And taking her bowed head for assent, he reached down to help her to her feet. Her trembling legs nearly gave way and she fell against him.

The marquess stared down into the piquant, freckled face and wide green eyes looking up into his from their frame of thick, curling lashes. Moved by a sudden impulse, he bent his head to brush his lips lightly against hers—only to find that the lips against his held and clung in a full-blooded, passionate embrace as Miss Jean Lindsay gave herself wholeheartedly up to her first kiss.

Swept by an answering passion that shook him down to the soles of his glossy Hessian boots, the marquess broke away, breathing hard as though he had been running.

"Really, Miss Lindsay . . . you must not . . . you shouldn't. Hell and damnation!" roared the marquess. "You shouldn't kiss me like that."

Jean made a moue of disappointment.

"Did I do it wrong, my lord? I have had no previous experience. Is it like dancing or horse riding where one must have a certain expertise?"

"No, of course not," snapped the marquess, the angry flush dying out of his thin cheeks as he struggled for composure. "It was meant to be a friendly caress. I did not mean . . ."

"You are trying to say that you were only flirting," suggested Jean helpfully.

"Yes. I mean, no. I mean . . . oh, let us go back and

31

find the others." The marquess threw her up into the saddle and mounting on his own magnificent bay, leaned across to take the reins of her horse and lead her sedately back down the ride.

When they joined the party, the twins, Bess and Mary, avidly took in the details of Jean's flushed face and the marquess's stormy expression. There was obviously going to be little competition from Miss Lindsay when it came to attracting the handsome marquess.

As they retired to their rooms, Jean began to feel a stirring of excitement at the thought of the evening ahead.

"If only I had something special to wear for dinner, my dear Miss Taylor. I am become positively obsessed with clothes. Uncle Hamish would say it is all the work of the Devil and mere vanity."

"Nonsense!" said Miss Taylor robustly. "It is nobody's fault but that old miser of an uncle of yours. And if he were as concerned with his immortal soul as he seems to be with yours, life would be more comfortable all around for his parishioners."

A surprise awaited Jean as she reached her bedchamber. Lady Cynthia's maid arrived carrying armfuls of beautiful dresses, which she proceeded to hang in an enormous William and Mary wardrobe in the corner.

"Lady Cynthia's compliments, miss. Her Ladyship says that as you will be ordering your wardrobe in London, perhaps you would like to wear some of her clothes for the time being. And miss, if you please, I am to dress your hair. My name is McWhirter."

Jean gazed rapturously at the line of robes swaying on their hangers. "I am so bewildered I know not what to choose."

"Leave it to me," said McWhirter. "I select all Her Ladyship's dresses for her. Now this"—laying out an aquamarine silk gown—"will be perfect. But you must hurry, miss. We have only a little time before dinner."

32

Jean glanced at the clock. "There is a full two hours."

"It will take all of that to get you ready," was all the maid would say. Setting the curling tongs on a small spirit stove to heat, McWhirter advanced with the scissors and despite Jean's protests began snipping away busily.

Jean had wondered why the elegant Lady Cynthia had such a robust and countrified attendant but the maid turned out to have as deft a touch as any French hairdresser.

Jean waved away the rouge pot but allowed her face to be lightly dusted with the haresfoot. The aquamarine dress slipped over her head like a sigh and Jean turned to the pier glass to let McWhirter fasten the long row of tiny buttons at the back.

An elegant green-eyed stranger stared back at her. Her hair rioted in seemingly careless curls on top and one ringlet was placed on her right shoulder. The dress was cut low over the bosom with little puffed sleeves, falling in simple Empire lines to the glory of two deep flounces at the hem.

In an ecstasy of gratitude, Jean pressed two guineas into McWhirter's plump hand. "This is an awful lot of money, miss. You must be very rich," said the maid, rocked from her customary tact.

"Oh, I am! I am!" sang Jean, pirouetting around the room. She thought she told the truth, for a hundred guineas seemed a fortune to a girl who had never been allowed a shilling of her own to spend.

Jean bent over to tie the straps of her slippers and two well-endowed breasts popped out of the top of her gown.

"Quick, McWhirter. Fetch needle and thread," cried Jean.

"There, there," said McWhirter. "It's well seen you've been tucked away in those heathenish Highlands. All gowns are like that these days. Just don't bend over."

33

Clutching her gold, McWhirter retired from the room and fled down the back stairs as fast as her motherly bulk would allow and exploded into the kitchen to spread the further news of Jean's wealth.

As Jean slowly descended the staircase, the marquess with Lord Freddie and Mr. Fairchild were chatting in front of a huge fire in the hall. Appreciative murmurs of admiration wafted up to her. As in her fantasies, she kept her head high, a faint other-wordly smile curling her lips—missed the third step from the bottom and collapsed face downward in the hallway.

A concerted rush of guests and servants eager for gold threatened to overwhelm her. "Leave me alone!" she shouted, terrified to be pulled to her feet and find her bosom exposed. She writhed desperately away on her stomach from their outstretched arms.

"Dear God," said the lazy voice of the marquess. "I think the child is having a fit."

Under the company's astonished gaze, Jean wriggled over to the banister and with her back to them, pulled herself slowly to her feet.

"I am so sorry. I am all right now. I am so sorry to have startled you," she said in a tremulous voice. There was a burst of masculine denial and only poor Miss Taylor heard Lord Freddie Blackstone's aside to the marquess.

"Who cares if she's queer in her attic. All that money and a looker too."

As she followed her charge into the dining room, Miss Taylor reflected bitterly on the damage of servants' gossip. She had descended to the kitchen before dinner to scotch the rumor of Jean's wealth only to be disbelieved in general and snubbed by Wilkins in particular. "Wants it all for 'erself," she heard Wilkins say as she closed the kitchen door, defeated.

The long dining room was resplendent with crystal and silver. Miss Taylor was seated well away from Jean who was placed on Sir Edward's right with the marquess on her left and an enormous silver epergne in the center of the table blocking her completely from the governess's anxious eyes.

It seemed almost indecent to eat so much food but Jean set to with a hearty appetite as remove followed remove. As instructed by her governess, she left her wine untouched in front of her.

John, the Marquess of Fleetwater, maintained an easy flow of conversation, making no reference to the events of the afternoon. Jean blossomed under his flattering attention, oblivious of Lady Cynthia's calculating looks from the far end of the table. For Cynthia found the marquess exceedingly attractive and failed to see what he could find so amusing in an unsophisticated chit barely out of the schoolroom.

The marquess was hard put to understand it himself. The girl was pretty but decidedly naïve. He decided her enthusiasm for everything was refreshing and with a rare grace set himself to please.

"Why don't you try some of this excellent claret, Miss Lindsay, and tell me how you came to write your uncle's sermon?"

Blushing and embarrassed, Jean lifted her glass and under His Lordship's astonished gaze, drained it in one gulp. Goodness, it tasted like vinegar. But as a warm glow of confidence began to seep through her, she realized why it must be that people drank the stuff.

"Please do not talk about that awful sermon," she begged. "I don't know what came over me."

"My word as a gentleman," said the marquess solemnly. "No one shall hear of it from me. I confess I landed myself in disgrace by laughing so loudly in church.

"Lady Cynthia tells me you have recently come into a great deal of money."

The marquess knew that he was being ill-bred but his

curiosity was immense. "Oh, yes," said Jean blithely. "I have one hundred guineas of my late mother."

"My dear girl, that very fetching gown you are wearing cost a good portion of that alone," said the marquess, running an expert eye over Cynthia's gift.

Jean laughed gaily and knocked back another glass of wine without pausing for breath. It did not taste as bad as the first. He was only funning. Men naturally did not know the price of gowns, she thought, blissfully unaware that there were quite a few ladies of the demi-monde who had enjoyed the marquess's protection and would have told her that he was able to price everything on her to a penny.

Several glasses of wine later and Jean was dead to the proprieties. An excellent mimic, her sketches of the characters in her home village had Sir Edward and the marquess helpless with laughter and a startled silence fell over the rest of the company as roars of masculine mirth shook the tapestries and set the crystals of the Waterford chandelier tinkling.

Lady Cynthia rose to her feet with a determined glint in her eye. "Shall we leave the gentlemen to their wine?" and without waiting for a reply, sailed from the room. Jean rose to her feet confused and lightheaded. She staggered slightly, and were it not for the marquess's restraining arm, would have fallen into the remains of an excellent syllabub in front of her. She paused for a moment looking down at the marquess's long fingers on her arm and felt as if she were suddenly on fire. This wine was strange stuff indeed!

The atmosphere in the drawing room was decidedly chilly at first but as the cause of it all sat staring at the fire completely unconcerned, the ladies' manner thawed. The girl was young and unsophisticated and the rich must be allowed their foibles.

"I have some of the latest editions of the Ladies Magazine should you care to peruse them, Miss Lindsay," said Lady Cynthia. "They have many of the latest fashions."

Jean kept on staring into the fire with an idiotic expression on her face, so Miss Taylor bravely spoke up from the corner to try to cover up for her pupil's social gaffe.

"It is very good of you, Lady Cynthia," said the governess. "It is difficult to keep abreast of the modes in a place like Dunwearie although we do have a little woman in the village who runs up very good gowns."

"Indeed! She must be small," remarked Cynthia acidly.

"But very *good*—ver' *good* little woman since she only runs up very *good* gowns," said Jean beginning with a giggle and ending with a hiccup.

The stony silence which greeted this inanity was fortunately soon broken by the arrival of the gentlemen. The marquess looked as if he were going to join Jean but Lady Cynthia waylaid him and drew him down to sit beside her on the sofa. Although the marquess considered Cynthia a bored and boring sophisticate, she was, after all, his host's wife and also very beautiful. He forgot about Jean, and basking in the afterglow of Sir Edward's brandy, settled down to enjoy the sort of light flirtation at which he was adept.

They made a handsome couple, reflected Jean wryly. Never in all her fantasies had she envisaged the marquess so much as looking at another woman and, being unpracticed in the art of masking her feelings and more than a little tipsy, she sat staring across at them, looking the picture of misery.

The marquess writhed inwardly under her gaze and cursed himself for having paid her too much attention. This is what became of giving little rustics ideas above their station. Good Heavens, the gauche child might even now be regarding him in the light of a suitor.

Miss Taylor felt that things had gone far enough and rose to her feet. "Miss Lindsay is still feeling the effects of the journey. Come, my dear. Let us retire."

She had not seen Jean drinking wine at dinner and put her odd behavior down to shyness and travel fatigue.

In the morning, Jean kept to her bed with the clothes over her head, trying to block out memories of the evening before. By eleven o'clock, she judged the rest of the company would already have breakfasted and gone about their amusements, and feeling very fragile, crept down the stairs to the breakfast room.

To her embarrassment, the marquess and his two friends got to their feet as she entered. It transpired that the ladies were breakfasting in their rooms and that the gentlemen had only just preceded her to the breakfast table.

She started to chatter nervously and brightly about the fine day and stopped in mid-sentence as Lord Freddie stared at her like a piked cod, the marquess put a hand to his brow and Mr. Fairchild let out a groan.

"We are all feeling rather under-par at the moment, Miss Lindsay," explained the marquess, "but we shall come about presently."

"Wilkins!" Lord Freddie let out a sudden roar that made Jean jump as he pointed with a shaking hand to the apple wood fire which burned merrily on the hearth.

"Do something with that demned thing. Demned hissing and popping and banging away like curst artillery. Oh, my head! Breakfast? Get me anything at all, man."

Wilkins, inured to the delicate heads and nerves of Sir Edward's guests, deftly slid a plate under Freddie's pallid face and backed off at another explosion of wrath.

"What the . . . beg pardon, Miss Lindsay . . . is this?"

"Grilled kidneys, my lord."

"Well, it looks to me like a demned great pile of . . ."

"Lady present, y'know," interjected Mr. Fairchild hurriedly.

"Sorry," blushed Freddie. "Anyway, take the demned thing away. Take everything away in fact and bring us some hock and seltzer."

It was Jean's first sight of the pink of the ton as they habitually appeared at the breakfast table. Although the sun shone brightly outside, the blinds were drawn so that not a chink of offending light could penetrate. In the half gloom, three pale faces watched Jean devour a hearty breakfast and three elegantly tailored pairs of shoulders shuddered in awe.

"Tell you what," said Lord Freddie, revived by two large glasses of hock and seltzer. "I'll race you to the nearest inn. Landlord's daughter's got the biggest pair of . . ."

The marquess kicked him under the table.

" . . . ale glasses in all Scotland," he finished lamely.

The other two agreed enthusiastically to the expedition and hastened off leaving Jean feeling very small and unwanted.

The day seemed long and boring and Jean could not help looking forward to the evening ahead when she would see the marquess again. But at dinner, the seating had been rearranged. She was placed next to Miss Taylor with the marquess far away from her, next to Lady Cynthia. Again, as the gentlemen entered the drawing room, the marquess joined Lady Cynthia on the sofa.

Jean was left to help the Duchess of Glenrandall card her wool. The duchess was an avid knitter of intricately stitched garters which she bestowed on the poor of the village, blissfully unaware that they had no stockings to hold up. As the wool slid between her fingers, a dream began to form in Jean's head.

She could see it all. During the night, she would leave her room to . . . to . . . get a book from the library downstairs. Holding her flickering candle high, she would collide with the marquess who was in the act of stealing from Lady Cynthia's bedchamber.

"Oh, my lord!" she would gasp.

"Alas!" he would say on a choking sob. "Can you in your sweetness and innocence ever forgive me for the terrible thing I have just done? Philandering with mine host's wife! What I have lacked all my life is the love of a pure girl." With that, he would seize her in his arms. But she was not to be so easily won. With one sweeping motion, she would repel him . . .

The occasional table next to her went flying across the room, scattering objets d'art into the far corners. Jean flushed to the roots of her hair as she realized that she had indeed diverted the marquess's thoughts from Cynthia.

Again, Miss Taylor made hasty excuses for her charge, and in the middle of an awesome silence, Jean was led from the room.

As they ascended the stairs, Lord Freddie's voice followed after them like a clarion call. "Foxed again, is she?"

The governess followed Jean into her bedchamber. "What on earth came over you girl," she snapped, sorely tempted to shake the elegant creature in front of her. "You were daydreaming again, that's it.

"Now, look here. We all daydream but you go too far. In fact, Miss Lindsay, any more scenes like the one you enacted this evening and you will end your days in Bedlam. Try to enjoy things as they are and look for a husband but *not* above your station. For," she added shrewdly, "if you are to imagine yourself at the altar with every lord we meet, you will be considered worse than mad. You will be considered *fast* and that means social ruin. I beg of you, cease this nonsense."

"I will, I will," vowed Jean. "I will do anything rather than return to Uncle Hamish. I would rather end my days in a convent."

40

"There you go again!" screamed the much-tried Miss Taylor. "A convent indeed. And your uncle a minister. He would see you in hell first."

She slammed her way out of the room, wondering if a retired life as the duchess's pensioner might not be infinitely preferable to her present situation.

Perhaps Jean might not have attended to Miss Taylor's strictures had it not been for the events of the night.

For an hour, she tossed and turned on her pillow, reliving the embarrassment of the evening. Suddenly, she swept back the covers and reached for her wrapper. She *would* creep down to the library and find something to read to take her mind off her troubles.

Holding her candle aloft, she tiptoed along the long passage—and nearly bumped into the marquess, who was emerging from a room. Lady Cynthia's mocking voice followed him into the corridor, "I am sorry to break up your evening's entertainment but I am indeed fatigued."

For one second, Jean took in the glory of the marquess's resplendent dressing gown.

He was a rake!

Pressing her hand against her mouth to stifle a sob, Jean dropped her candle and fled back down the passage to her room where she buried her head under the bedclothes and cried herself to sleep.

"What's all the commotion?" said Sir Edward, stepping into the passage. The marquess shrugged. "The Lindsay girl wandering around. Must have given her a scare."

"Look at that candle," said Sir Edward angrily. "Could have set the place on fire. Touched in her upper works that's what she is."

"Oh, come to bed," snapped Lady Cynthia peevishly. She joined them in the corridor. "You have both kept me awake prosing on about hunting until my head aches."

She had reason to feel cross. The handsome marquess

had been more interested in her husband's horses than in his wife.

The marquess, who had just spent a pleasant hour in Sir Edward's private sitting room, sighed and ambled off to bed. He thought momentarily of Jean as she had looked at the dinner table with her hair like a flame and her green eyes sparkling.

" 'Tis a pity," he murmured to himself. "So pretty but so Gothic."

The morning of their departure for London was sunny and clear. Miss Taylor was pleased to see that her lecture of the previous night had obviously had some effect on her charge. Jean was heavy-eyed but pleasant and modestly behaved. She made her adieu's prettily and as soon as the heavy coach had lumbered down the driveway, put her head in a book and to all intents and purposes appeared oblivious of her surroundings.

Chapter Three

It was several months before the marquess was to see Jean again. His estates lay in the north of England and there was much to keep him fully occupied. It was not until the Season had been started a full week that he headed for London to take up his place in Society.

After staying with friends in Bath on his journey south and having made a start late in the day, he bowled along in his sporting curricle at a smart pace enjoying the late spring evening and the scent of May from the country fields. He decided to rack up for the night at one of the many excellent posting houses along the road and turned smartly into the courtyard of the Pelican, throwing his reins to the ostler and striding into the taproom, ignoring the bowing and scraping of the landlord.

There was only one other person in the low-raftered room, a pleasant-looking young man whose dress marked him as one of the gentry. Tired of his own company, the marquess made a passing reference to the countryside, and detecting a slight Scotch burr in the other's voice, asked him if he had traveled far.

"From Edinburgh," replied the traveler. "Allow me to introduce myself. My name is Colqhoun, James Colqhoun. I am a lawyer traveling eventually to London on business but I am going to stay with friends in Chelmsford first."

"Why I believe I know your father if it be the same Colqhoun. My name is Fleetwater."

"Ah, yes. We did handle some business to do with Your Lordship's Scottish properties," said Colqhoun sketching a bow. "My father is dead, my lord, and I am now head of the firm."

"You business is certainly widespread if you must travel all the way to London to see your clients."

"Well, now," said James Colqhoun, shaking his head. "I hardly ever have to travel so far afield but this is a very odd case indeed. Why, it's like something out of one of Mrs. Radcliffe's novels."

His curiosity piqued, the marquess said, "Join me for supper. I have bespoke a private parlor. If you can, tell me about it, for I would dearly love some other company this evening than my own."

James looked flustered but gratified. "I shall indeed

43

be honored," he stammered, "and I am sure anything I tell you will go no further." He followed the marquess up the inn stairs to the parlor above.

The marquess kept the conversation on easy social topics but as the covers were removed and the brandy brought in, he lit a cheroot and settled back in his chair. "Now let us hear your Gothic story."

Putting the tips of his long, bony fingers together and clearing his throat, James started to tell his story in a dry, precise voice.

"It concerns a young lady called Miss Jean Lindsay who lives in a village called . . ."

"Called Dunwearie!" exclaimed the marquess. "I know the lady. This is coincidence indeed."

"Then perhaps you have met the lady's uncle? Ah, well —just so. According to the will of the girl's uncle, Joseph Lindsay, who made his pile with the East India Company after many adventures, her uncle Hamish was to receive one thousand pounds per annum, all the money to go to turning her into a gentlewoman and taking her place in society. On her eighteenth birthday in two months' time, she will receive the full bulk of his fortune worth about 100,000 pounds sterling, not to count an annual income from properties in Glasgow and Ayr. Seeing that the event was so close, I decided to travel to Dunwearie to find out what arrangements had been made for the handling of her estate.

"It was late when I arrived at the manse. At first the reverend refused to see me. When he did, he kept arguing that the fortune was too immense for a silly girl to handle on her own and that Miss Lindsay had gone to London to dissipate all the money that he had carefully saved for her. He refused to bed me for the night and I was forced to stay at the primitive bothy they call an inn in the village.

"It was there that the housekeeper from the manse

44

found me. She told me the girl had been kept on poverty rations since she was a babe, and what Hamish had done with the thousand a year, she did not know. The girl had been packed off to her godmother in London because of some disgrace and now, she said, the reverend was ranting and raving around the manse saying the money was rightly his and the girl shouldn't see a penny of it.

"The housekeeper seemed very attached to the girl and begged that I apprise her of her good fortune since it seemed that Hamish was hell-bent on traveling to London in an effort to keep her in ignorance. Evidently, he had not realized that Miss Lindsay would inherit and thought that he would have a cozy income for life.

"Since I had long planned a visit to Chelmsford, I decided to convey the glad tidings of her inheritance to Miss Lindsay personally. And that is my story."

The marquess thoughtfully rolled the amber liquid around in his goblet to catch the light from the fire. A chill wind had sprung up outside and was tugging fretfully at the latticed windows and howling in the chimney. The candles guttered in their sockets and the marquess— a young man not given to fancies—felt as if a sly, menacing presence had joined them at the table. Abruptly, he rang for fresh candles.

"The girl has already the reputation of being a great heiress," said the marquess, "but I believe it's all a hum started by a lot of gossiping servants. Does the old fool mean her harm, think you?"

"I should think not," replied James severely. "He is a man of the cloth."

"He is an evil old miser. I would not be too sure of him."

"Perhaps I should go direct to London, unless, of course, Your Lordship . . . ?"

"In that case, my dear Colqhoun, I shall take care of Miss Lindsay until you arrive. I will not tell her anything of her good fortune because it would please me to catch the villainous uncle if he makes his move."

The new candles brought in by the landlord shone out cheerfully, sending the shadows flying to the corners of the room.

The marquess gave a self-conscious laugh.

"We are probably imagining things. Hamish will fuss and fret but that is all he will do. You'll see."

The marquess would have been hard put to recognize Jean Lindsay after three months of town bronze. Although Miss Taylor's training in etiquette had seemed rigorous, it palled before the long list of "don'ts" to be carefully memorized before taking her place in the ton.

There were easy rules such as never walking down St. James's or staying longer than fifteen minutes in returning a call, but the small ones were the hardest of all to remember. Never cut your thread, always bite it; never sit down on a chair still warm from a gentleman's vacancy; never, never cross your legs even in the privacy of your bedroom; never glance behind you for the chair when you sit down; and never speak to the formidable patronesses of Almack's unless spoken to. The list went on and on.

After a few false starts, Jean had mastered them all and become a small success. Lady Harriet Telfer-Billington, Jean's godmother, was in a quandary as to whether to scotch the rumor of Jean's fortune or stay quiet and pray that the girl would find a rich husband and make the problem of the dowry no matter.

Not given to long and anguished thought on any occasion except in matters of dress, Jean's godmother had decided on the latter course. The girl was pretty enough and to explain that she was penniless would not help her socially. Even wealthy merchants looked for at least a title among the ranks of the dowerless.

As they sat together in the morning room of the elegant

town house in Cavendish Square, Jean eyed her god-mother with affection. Lady Harriet Telfer-Billington was a tiny, brown-haired woman, ever energetic, ever restless, with big eyes like a marmoset. She had seen three husbands to their graves and rumor had it, was seeking a fourth. Jean was at first taken aback and slightly humiliated at being regarded by Her Ladyship in the nature of a new toy to dress and parade but being unused to any affection other than that of Agnes or Miss Taylor, she became grateful for the scatter-brained warmth and generosity of her frivolous godmother.

The day was exceptionally warm for London and Lady Harriet snapped her chicken-wing fan backward and forward while her other prehensile little hand sorted deftly through a pile of embossed cards.

"Ah! Here it is. An invitation to the Courtlands' ball tonight. Very grand. Wear your gold silk with the matching gauze overdress and we will get Antoine to do your hair. I had it from Sally Jersey yesterday that Fleetwater is in town. You know him, I believe?"

The new Miss Lindsay made a murmur of assent.

Lady Harriet gave her goddaughter a penetrating look. "Very rich you know, and quite the handsomest man in London. Any hopes in that quarter?"

A soft murmur of denial.

Her Ladyship's large, dark eyes snapped. "It would be marvelous if you could engage the affections of a man like that. Must I needs remind you again that Lord Ian Percy is a gazetted fortune hunter and, were it not that his mama and I are *bosom beaux,* I would show him the door. Should he ask for your hand, I would be obliged to tell him that you have no fortune whatsoever. Anyway, he is too old."

"He is a mature man of forty, which is *not* too old," said Jean stiffly. "He is a most courteous gentleman and, I believe, likes me for myself alone."

47

"He's as courteous as a ferret and just as trustworthy. Oh, don't look daggers at me, miss! If I thought it would come to anything, I should be concerned. What your uncle . . . why here is a letter from him!"

She rapidly perused the crossed and re-crossed missive which looked as if hundreds of spiders had run riot on the paper. "What abominable writing. So difficult. And what's this?"—pointing to several dark red stains— "Blood?"

"Probably wine."

"His letter reads as if he were a trifle bosky. Good Heavens! He is coming here! 'Cannot be parted from my dear niece much longer.' Sounds like a hum."

"Indeed it must be, ma'am," said Jean. "He has shown no interest in me since I left home."

"He says that by the time I receive this he will already be on the road. Oh, fiddle! I cannot say that your dear uncle will exactly add to your social consequence but mayhap he does not mean to go about much."

Jean tried to imagine her uncle among the gay, frivolous London crowd and failed. What would Lord Ian make of him? She flushed slightly as she thought of the suave, elegant Lord Ian with Hamish.

Jean had met Lord Ian at her first ball at Almack's and had found his conversation mature and his thin, sallow face and world-weary air fascinating. Warnings from Lady Harriet and a scolding from the Duchess of Glenrandall had left her unmoved. She would choose her own friends. And if Lord Ian did not make her heart flutter quite as the marquess had done, well, look where that had led. His sophistication was intriguing and his attentions flattering.

The butler threw open the double doors and intoned, "Lord Ian Percy."

Lady Harriet rose in a flutter of irritation as Lord Ian made his bow.

"It is a fine morning, ma'am," he said. "I am come to persuade Miss Lindsay to drive with me in the park."

Lady Harriet shut her fan with a snap. "We are terribly sorry. I am sure Jean has other commitments."

Jean rose gracefully to her feet. "No, ma'am, I am quite at liberty. Allow me but a few moments to collect my bonnet."

Jean curtsied and left Lady Harriet to eye Lord Ian with ill-concealed disdain. Lord Ian, amused by her scrutiny, crossed to the fireplace and leaned negligently against the mantelpiece.

Lady Harriet came to a decision. "I have tried to convey to you many times my displeasure of your interest in my goddaughter. Contrary to public rumor, the child is dowerless. I have heard from a good source that you are in dun territory but you will find nothing in that quarter to repair your debts."

Lord Ian flushed with annoyance but his hooded lids dropped momentarily over his eyes to hide his anger. "Doing it too brown, Harriet," he said insolently. "The Glenrandall gals told me on their come-out that she's an heiress. Some benefactor up in the North."

"Nonsense!" said Harriet roundly. "The poor child hasn't a feather to fly with. I had it from her governess that she had too liberal a hand with servants' vails on her journey South.

"Bess and Mary are two silly chits who listen to servants' gossip and Lady Cynthia Lamont is no better. I did not counteract the lie for fear of spoiling the girl's season but I will *not* have her waste her time and her future with such as you!"

His eyes blazing, Lord Ian opened his mouth to retort but broke off as Jean entered the room. With a chilly bow he made his *adieu's* and departed with Jean leaving Lady Harriet feeling shaky and sick. "I hope I have done the right thing. Faith, I feel I have just turned over a stone and looked at something creepy-crawly underneath."

The drive in the park was pleasant but Jean noticed that her usually urbane companion was rigid and silent. She was about to ask him what troubled him when he rudely cut across her opening remark.

"Who's the gal in the yaller carriage?" Startled, Jean looked at the girl in question.

"Why, 'tis Amy Jenkins. Her father is a wealthy mill owner from Yorkshire and, although she does not move much in our circles, I have a slight acquaintanceship with her."

Lord Ian glanced down at her with something like a sneer on his face. "Doesn't move in *our* circles, eh? Introduce me."

He maneuvered over expertly until they were alongside Miss Jenkins's landau and Jean effected the introductions. Miss Jenkins was a small, rabbity-faced child of seventeen with an alarming titter, but the sophisticated Lord Ian seemed unaware of it. He was all charm and begged Miss Jenkins's complacent mother for permission to call. After passing ten minutes of exchanging pleasantries and ignoring Jean, he turned the carriage homeward. "Can you alight by yourself?" he asked distantly when they reached Cavendish Square. "I do not wish to leave my cattle standing."

Jean got down and looked up into Lord Ian's stony face. "Is aught amiss?"

"Nonsense. What should be?" And with a vicious crack of his whip, he bowled off around the square at a fast trot.

Lady Harriet watched the drooping figure entering the house and felt like a murderess. She had spent all her courage on Lord Ian and had none left to inform Jean of what she had done.

* * *

At the Courtlands' ball, therefore, Jean felt she had stepped back in time to her first ball. There were uneasy glances in her direction. Several high-nosed dowagers had cut her dead and her dance program was nearly empty.

She was standing listlessly against a pillar when she heard a familiar voice. "May I have the honor, Miss Lindsay?"

It was the Marquess of Fleetwater, resplendent in black and white evening dress with a large diamond glittering in the folds of his snowy cravat. Jean gave a start of pleasure, all bad memories forgotten, as he drew her into the steps of the waltz.

Lady Harriet had done wonders, reflected the marquess. The girl looked quite beautiful. He had already heard the whispered tale that her fortune was all a hum and shrewdly judged that Lord Ian Percy was behind Jean's downfall. When he first saw the lonely figure by the pillar, he was tempted to break the lawyer's trust, but decided instead to use his very high standing with the ton to bring the girl back into fashion.

A light flirtation would not hurt her, he reflected, and then in a few weeks' time, the news of her fortune would be all over London and her future would be secure. For the present, it would be better to keep her safe from prize hunters like Lord Ian.

Jean discovered that her newfound social poise had not deserted her after all and was able to chat easily with the marquess on all sort of subjects including the latest *on-dits*. For his part, the marquess found the girl delightful and reflected it was just as well that he had resigned himself to bachelordom long ago or he might find his heart in danger.

He led her into supper and they found themselves getting along famously. When he returned her to the ballroom, she was again solicited on all sides. The handsome marquess set the fashion and Jean, becoming aware of the fact, decided to make use of him and keep a firm guard on her heart and her fantasies.

Lord Ian had been watching them narrowly. Had Harriet been lying to him? He had no mind to spend more money squiring Jean to balls and routs until he found out the truth. One of Lady Harriet's friends had reported the uncle's visit to London. He would keep on friendly terms until the old man arrived and then try to winkle the truth out of the minister.

All too soon, Hamish arrived. He had traveled by the stage and the morning of his arrival was taken up with his loud lamentations about how he had been fleeced at every posting house and inn on the road. Lady Harriet listened with weary boredom and was relieved when Jean came in from a walk. Immediately, Hamish was all avuncular solicitation. How was his little niece? He had been lonely without her and meant to see a lot of her during his visit.

Jean sighed inwardly and reflected that absence did not make the heart grow fonder. Hamish's mumbling and fond leering were so nauseating, she would have preferred his customary bad temper.

"I am sure you have people in the church to visit, Hamish," said Lady Harriet. "Jean goes around with a very young set of friends and I am sure old people like ourselves would be very much in the way."

Hamish gave an awful smile. "Now, that is where you are wrong, Lady Harriet. A bit of youth is just what my poor old eyes need."

His "poor old eyes" narrowed suspiciously as the Marquess of Fleetwater was announced. That Jean should inherit all the money and catch a rich husband too seemed past bearing. The marquess made a magnificent leg to Lady Harriet but accorded the grinning and scraping Hamish no more than a common bow.

"I am planning an excursion to a mill near Richmond

on the morrow. The Duchess of Glenrandall is going with us as chaperone. Her daughters will be of the party. Lord Freddie Blackstone and Mr. John Fairchild of whom you are acquainted will come with us and it only needs Miss Lindsay to make the party complete. The girls are anxious to try their hand at watercolors, since it is a famous beauty spot."

As Jean was opening her mouth to accept, Hamish sidled forward. "With Your Lordship's permission, I would like to join your group. I mean to see as much of my niece as possible."

The marquess rapidly cast around in his mind for some means of refusal and finding none, gave a chilly nod.

He then took his leave and Hamish, with a coyness terrible to behold, teased Jean about her aristocratic beau until Lady Harriet took pity on her and insisted that the reverend retire to his rooms for a rest.

The party arrived early on the following morning. Bess had already secured a seat beside the marquess in his curricle, leaving Jean, with a flat feeling of disappointment, to travel with Lord Freddie. But the day was fine and Freddie rattled on nonstop about horses and hunting, only expecting an occasional "yes" or "no."

The mill turned out to be as picturesque as promised and, setting up her easel, Jean prepared to enjoy the day, despite the company of Uncle Hamish.

Bess and Mary were both pretty artists and were having a marvelous time demanding that the gentlemen hand them their paint and their brushes. Seeing them all busily occupied on the little hill overlooking the mill, Jean, who had no artistic talent, decided to stroll down and look at the water. A small stand of trees hid her from view and, since the day was warm and humid, she removed her smart chip straw and dangling it by the ribbons, let the faint breeze cool her brow. She perched on a stone at the water's edge and considered the last few days with pleasure. The marquess had squired her everywhere. Lord Ian had been trying to ingratiate himself but Jean had taken him in distaste. Harriet had finally confided her revelations and there could only be one explanation of Lord Ian's coldness at the balll.

She had learned from Harriet that the marquess was famous for his flirtations but that they never came to anything and so decided to enjoy his company for as long as she could.

"Let us make our love fast forever," whispered the dream marquess in her ear. "Will you ma . . ."

Her dream was cut short as a brutal shove on her back sent her hurtling off the rock into the pool. She surfaced, desperately gasping for air, and a glancing blow from an unknown assailant sent her down to the bottom.

Just as she was losing consciousness, she felt herself being pulled to the surface by a pair of strong arms and into the blessed air.

The concerned gray eyes of the marquess looked down into hers. With a convulsive sob, she tightened her arms around his neck and hung on for dear life. "Someone t-t-tried to murder me," she stammered.

The marquess looked down at the terrified, childlike face beneath his and bent and kissed her on the mouth. What started as a kiss of concern and affection grew deeper and more exploring and he felt a surge of answering passion in the slim, wet body pressed so tightly against his own.

"Halloa!" A shout from the hilltop made them break guiltily apart. Lord Freddie came bounding up. "What happened? You both fall in?"

The marquess gave Jean's arm a warning squeeze and replied abruptly, "We were trying to pick water lilies and lost our footing."

"Well, I'll be demned! And you a Corinthian! That

breaks up the party, I must say. Got to get you both back to town."

The duchess produced traveling rugs to wrap the bedraggled pair and insisted that Jean should accompany her on the road home but the marquess assured her that Jean would be safe enough in his curricle.

Bess and Mary tittered with envy. They would not have minded a wetting if the marquess had been at hand. Hamish appeared at the last minute and almost overpowered Jean with his concern.

It was a wet and silent pair that headed for London. The marquess sprang his horses and for a while gave all his attention to the road until the others were left far behind. Slowing to a canter, he turned to Jean. "What exactly happened?"

Jean repeated the sequence of events leading up to her near-drowning. "I swear someone tried to murder me." A bruise was turning purple on her forehead and she was beginning to feel giddy and faint with reaction.

"Yes, I believe someone did," said the marquess slowly.

Jean shivered. "It was probably some footpad."

"Probably," said the marquess. "We will discuss the matter this evening at Vauxhall when we are both recovered."

How could he terrify the girl further with his suspicions of her uncle? When they reached Cavendish Square, Jean smiled mistily up at him. "I have not thanked you for saving my life, my lord."

"Had I not decided to walk in the direction of the pond as well, I should have been too late," said the marquess, leading her to the doorway. He bent his fair head and kissed her fingers. "Until tonight."

Lady Harriet came out of the drawing room and started at the sight of the bedraggled figure in the hall.

"Good Heavens, child! What befell?"

Jean smiled dreamily. "Someone tried to murder me

55

by pushing me in the millpond but the marquess was at hand to save me."

Lady Harriet had been warned of Jean's habit of daydreaming and scolded her roundly. "Don't be silly! Murder indeed! You no doubt fell in the pond and were pulled out by Lord Fleetwater. You must stop these crazy ideas. No! Not another word. Go to your rooms and get changed."

Jean walked slowly up the stairs leaving little pools of water on the marble steps. Miss Taylor, newly arrived, came hurrying after her. She tut-tutted over the bruise on Jean's head but, like Lady Harriet, refused to hear a word about murderous attacks.

"I declare! You've been behaving so prettily since we came to London and now you're getting your head filled with dreams and rubbish instead. It's enough to make one weep!" The little governess stamped her foot in fury. "Lie down on your bed, miss, and try to recover. If I did not know that you were in the habit of indulging in fantasies, I would believe that the blow to your head—which you obviously got from hitting it on a stone—had addled your wits!"

Jean did as she was bid but found it hard to sleep as her brain buzzed with excitement. Whoever the footpad had been, she should be grateful to him for having brought the stately marquess into her arms.

Two squares away, the marquess threw his ruined cravat on the floor and swore roundly. Until recently, his life and thoughts had been cool and ordered. Passion was not foreign to him since he had enjoyed many successful affairs with opera dancers, actresses and ladies of the fashionable impure. But the other emotions roused in him by Jean of compassion, pity and affection were novel and at the moment, unpleasing. Toadied to from his birth and hunted down assiduously by every matchmaking mama in London, the marquess had settled down to view life with bored indifference. As long as his lands were kept in order and his tenants well-housed, he felt he had fulfilled his obligations to Society. He would marry one day, of course, and beget an heir. But it would be to some lady his equal in birth who would turn a blind eye to his bachelor pursuits and not to some green-eyed chit from a Scottish manse.

But as he huddled in his dressing gown, fastidiously wrinkling his long nose at the smell of pond-weed and waiting for his valet to draw his bath, he reflected that his original idea of marriage would simply extend the boredom of his life. If he offered for Jean, he would only need to stoop a trifle. She was of excellent birth and there would certainly be no doubt that she would accept him. What woman wouldn't, thought the marquess cynically. He was not ill-favored, but even if he had been a hunchback, his ancient name, title and fortune were prime attractions.

Certainly, the girl was soon to have a fortune of her own, but that did not matter; give it to her horrible uncle for all he cared. And of course, she didn't know yet that she was an heiress. Her naïve idea that one hundred guineas was a fortune must have vanished after a week in the metropolis, so she would be doubly gratified to accept his offer.

As he sank luxuriously into the warm water, the thought of Jean's gratitude seemed sweet. He would propose to her tonight, he decided, suddenly feeling very good and Sir Galahad-like. He should really obtain her uncle's permission first but to hell with the old fool! If Jean accepted —what on earth was he thinking?—*when* Jean accepted, he would then see the old man on the morrow as a matter of form.

Chapter Four

The party that assembled that evening in the
Marquess of Fleetwater's box at Vauxhall Gardens was
a gloomy one. In order to cover the bruise, Jean's abigail
had been liberal with powder, which only succeeded in
making her look pale and wan, added to which her gown
of white silk, unrelieved by any jewelery, heightened
the ghostly effect. She was very silent, still feeling the
effects of the blow on her head. Lady Harriet had had
more than enough of Hamish's constant company and
was wondering if she would ever have enough courage
to persuade the old man of the benefits of frequent
bathing, since he carried with him a constant and all-
pervading odor of stale wine, snuff and what Lady
Harriet privately designated as "something worse." Lord
Freddie Blackstone was also heartily sick of the reverend
and kept trying to move the bowl of rack punch out
of his reach. Freddie had borne the brunt of many of
Hamish's impromptu sermons when the old man was
in his cups and, as he confided to the marquess, "If
the filthy old ragbag calls me a limb of Satan again, I
swear I'll call him out, demme, see if I don't!"

But soon the effects of the punch and thin wafers of
ham, myriads of lanterns, a balmy evening and the

promise of a stupendous firework display cheered the party. Vauxhall was famous for its entertainment, and when the reverend eventually lurched to his feet and announced that he was going to promenade, the evening looked as if it might be a success after all.

Lady Harriet watched the marquess conversing with Jean, the gold head bent close to the red one, and reflected that never before had she seen him look so animated. His blue silk coat was so beautifully tailored across his shoulders that it must have taken the efforts of two footmen to get him into it. His cravat, tied in the Mathematical, was a miracle of snowy perfection. Now there was a man indeed! It was a pity that Jean was not up to snuff tonight. She should have kept her in bed but the girl was determined to come. Could it be that she had developed a *tendre* for the dashing marquess? Harriet smiled dazzlingly at him as he bowed before her and politely begged her permission to escort Jean to the firework display.

Jean tried to control her fluttering heart as she took his proffered arm and strolled down one of the shadowy walks away from the twinkling lights and the cockle-shell bandstand with the fiddlers in their three-cornered hats sawing away at sentimental airs. Although she suspected that the marquess's intentions to any lady must, in the end, be dishonorable, she was enjoying her brief romance and did not wish it to finish.

The crowd gradually thinned as they walked on in silence, past the hermit in his illuminated grove, past the cockneys in their colorful dress, until they found themselves alone in a small grove of cypress. The marquess turned to face the trembling girl and, for the first time in his life, embarked upon a proposal of marriage. He described his wealth and his lands in great detail, the honors she would receive when she became his marchioness, and how he had decided they would deal together extremely well. Looking up into his assured gray eyes, Jean could detect no glint of love or passion. She had an irritating feeling that she was meant to be flattered. She hung her head as the marquess came to the end of his peroration and waited for a reply.

Thoughts tumbled one after the other. As far as getting rid of a future life as a spinster with Uncle Hamish, this was the answer to her dreams. But how could she, at the inexperienced age of seventeen, cope with a rake who was likely to pass his wedded nights nipping in and out of the bedchambers of various titled ladies? Jean had not forgotten Lady Cynthia. Had he taken her in his arms or mentioned one word of love, Jean would undoubtedly have said "yes." But the silent man before her now seemed a frightening stranger, very much part of the sophisticated London world which only paid lip service to its rigid code of morals. She raised her red head, stared at the marquess, opened her mouth to give an unequivocal "no," when a bullet zipped past her cheek and vanished into the shrubbery.

For one second the marquess and Jean stood frozen with shock, then, springing to life, he roughly grabbed her arm, and dragging her after him, ran as hard as he could. He knew that to linger and search for an unknown in the bushes might give Jean's assailant time for another try. When they reached the box where the rest of the party were assembled, the marquess muttered, "Don't say anything," in Jean's ear and thrust her rudely into a chair before running off again.

Fortunately for Jean, everyone was watching the firework display and the marquess's odd behavior passed unnoticed.

As he approached the spot where he had proposed to Jean, he met Hamish and Lord Ian walking arm and arm.

"Where have you been this past half hour?" demanded the marquess, glaring at Hamish.

"He has been with me," said Lord Ian. "And I must say, I don't care for the tone of your voice, Fleetwater."

"Oh, a pox on you!" said the marquess, rudely pushing past them on the narrow walk and continuing his search. The fact that Hamish was accompanied by Lord Ian seemed to rule him out. Lord Ian had been accused of many petty and vicious crimes but murder had not been among them.

The odd couple watched him disappear.

"Call him out! Call him out!" hissed Hamish. "He insulted you!"

"Shut up, you old fool," growled Lord Ian. "Fleetwater's the best shot in the country and an expert swordsman. There are more subtle ways of harming him. Like putting an end to Miss Lindsay."

"But we must have a plan," said Hamish, thrusting his face into Lord Ian's.

"Faugh! Keep your distance, old man," shuddered Lord Ian, waving a scented lace handkerchief under his nose to dispel the fumes of stale rack punch. "Let me think."

Lord Ian had bumped into Hamish when he had been stalking the couple himself. Seizing the pistol from the old man's hand, he had forced him to the ground and leveled it at his throat.

Terrified and half drunk, Hamish had poured out the story of Jean's inheritance. Lord Ian had kept the pistol cocked as he had run over his financial difficulties in his mind. His funds were in such low water that he could hardly raise the necessary blunt to court Miss Jenkins and he was damned if he wanted to be leg-shackled for life to a family that smelled of the shop. He made up his mind quickly.

"I will remove Jean Lindsay for you for half her fortune, which I suppose you inherit—or I will shoot you dead now," he had threatened, pushing the pistol against Hamish's head. "I can always say I killed you to protect the girl."

Babbling with fright, Hamish had agreed, his ferretlike brain already working out schemes to get rid of Lord Ian once he had played his part.

Now the two conspirators stood in the beautiful surroundings of Vauxhall pleasure gardens and racked their brains as to the easiest and safest way to dispose of one seventeen-year-old girl.

Returning from a fruitless search, the marquess was also deep in thought. He was sure Hamish was involved some way in the murder attempt; probably he had hired some ruffian to do his dirty work. He must get Jean away somewhere safe. But where? He was sure she had planned to refuse his offer of marriage. The marquess's gray eyes narrowed.

Aye, that was the rub. Jean Lindsay had been about to refuse no other than John, the Marquess of Fleetwater. But why? A sudden wave of fury swept him. How dare she! How dare this provincial chit from one of Britain's savage backwaters even consider turning down such a matrimonial prize. To hell with her! Every other woman in England would jump at the chance of sharing his bed and his fortune.

Then a strange feeling crept through the marquess's body. He did not recognize it, for he had never been made to feel small before at any time in his life. But there it was: the voice of humility was telling him that he was behaving like the veriest coxcomb. He had done nothing for the last few days but think about Jean Lindsay, protect her and worry about her.

He sighed and decapitated a rose with his swordstick. Without Jean, life stretched out in its old pattern of boredom, *but* The Most Noble Marquess of Fleetwater would make sure that Miss Jean Lindsay was head over heels in love with him before he proposed to her again. And who better than he at making young ladies fall in love with him? His *amour propre* restored and feeling comfortably like Sir Galahad again, the marquess returned to take his chair beside Jean Lindsay and fight any dragons that might be lurking in the bushes of Vauxhall.

Jean eyed him nervously but he made no reference either to the shooting or his proposal and seemed in such good spirits that she began to wonder if she had imagined it all. She certainly did not want him to press his suit and ruin a pleasant romance, but, on the other hand, she felt he might at least have tried.

The marquess, correctly gauging the thoughts running through her carroty head, smiled to himself. The battle for Miss Lindsay's heart was well under way, but the first step was to get her away to a place of safety. His own estates lay too far north. He eyed Lord Freddie speculatively. The Blackstone estates lay in Surrey, an easy ride from London.

He moved along the box and whispered in Freddie's ear, "Walk with me a bit. I would have a word with you in private."

"Can't walk," said Freddie succinctly. "Rack punch got me in the legs."

"Oh, come *on!*" said the marquess, dragging him to his feet.

Freddie sprang to life. "You put a wrinkle in my sleeve," he expostulated, his head clearing at the injury done to his coat. "Weston made it. Said it was his masterpiece. Treat it with respect, old boy, and stop maulin' the thing about." He huffily followed the marquess out of the box.

"Listen, Freddie," said the marquess, when they were out of earshot. "I want you to ask a party of young people to your home and include me and Jean Lindsay in the invitation."

"In the middle of the Season? You've got windmills in your head," said Freddie, raising his quizzing glass to ogle a ripe matron in one of the boxes. "And why the Lindsay chit? She ain't in your usual line and she's weak in her loft."

"You are referring to the future Marchioness of Fleetwater," said the marquess stiffly.

Freddie's mouth hung open until he recovered his senses and pushed it shut with the knob of his cane.

"And here's me thinkin' *I* was foxed," said Freddie indignantly. "It's that demned punch. Nearly offered for that Friday-faced Chelmshurst girl once after a bowl of it."

"I am perfectly sober," said the marquess acidly. "You know Courtland's matched bays are up for sale at Tattersall's?"

"What's that to do with it?"

"An invitation to your home and they're yours."

"Courtland's bays!" exclaimed Freddie, throwing an arm around the marquess's shoulders. "Tell you what, old boy, you buy me cattle like that and you can bring the whole of Bedlam to m'home. Come to think of it, m'sister's there. Act as chaperone. She'll be glad of the company. About to drop her first."

The marquess smiled. The whole Blackstone family were so horsy that the terminology permeated their speech.

"In foal, is she?" he said sympathetically. "Well, I'll leave the arrangements to you. Tell everyone the Season's exhausted you and you're going to the country on a repairing lease."

"That's the ticket," said Freddie. "I'll leave you to square things with Lady Harriet."

The marquess returned to the attack immediately by drawing Lady Harriet aside.

"Miss Lindsay is looking peaked this evening."

"I think she is finding her first Season rather exhausting," said Lady Harriet.

"Lord Freddie is also feeling the effects of the Season."

"Oh, really," said Lady Harriet sourly. "I thought it was the punch."

"No, upon my honor. He is really feeling weak and is arranging a party of young people to visit his sister. Perhaps you could persuade Miss Lindsay to be one of the party?"

"Gladly. But you must take Hamish with you as well. I cannot tolerate that man and I think I deserve a holiday from his whining and preaching."

The marquess frowned. This was not part of his plan. But to have Hamish under his nose every minute of the day might be a good idea. After all, the only way to put a stop to the affair, without causing a scandal by calling in the Runners, was to catch Hamish in the act. It might work after all. He smiled and gave his consent.

That evening, Miss Taylor stepped into Jean's bedchamber for a comfortable coze before retiring for the night. Jean dutifully prattled on about the firework display, the food and the gowns, while all the time she wanted to cry out, "Someone tried to shoot me and Lord Fleetwater proposed marriage to me!" But the marquess had asked her to say nothing of the shooting and anyway, Miss Taylor would think she had imagined the whole thing.

After Miss Taylor retired, Jean puzzled over why the marquess did not wish her to tell anyone about the attempts on her life. Since she did not suspect her uncle, she did not realize that the marquess was trying to prevent a scandal.

Why did her head rule her heart? Jean was beginning to realize that she would love to be married to the marquess. Oh, if only he weren't a rake. She closed her eyes and drifted off to the altar in her dreams, the sound of the disappointed belles of London, weeping and gnashing their teeth, ringing like music in her ears.

Chapter Five

Blackstone Hall, home of the family since the Crusades, came as a surprise to Jean. She had expected Lord Freddie to live in an elegant, modern Palladian mansion instead of this rambling Tudor pile where one needed a guide to find one's way to the dining room.

Built of red brick with mullioned windows and towering crenellated roofs, the Hall stood virtually unchanged from the days of Queen Elizabeth. The whole place was permeated by a smell of damp, dry rot and dogs. There were dogs everywhere, yapping, pawing and getting underfoot. Bones lurked under rugs to trip the unwary and particularly knobby ones were buried under the sofa cushions.

Everyone talked about nothing else but horses from morning till night. In fact, Lord Freddie's sister, Lady Frances—called Frank by one and all—looked remarkably like a rawboned mare.

The party was made up of the marquess, Lord Freddie, the silent Mr. Fairchild, Uncle Hamish, Ladies Mary and Bess, Miss Taylor and Lady Sally Hawkhurst, a dashing young woman who had made a dead set at the marquess on her arrival.

Lord Herbert Elphinstone, Lady Frank's husband, was abroad on diplomatic service so Lady Frank had deserted her own home in the north of England for her brother's more congenial estate in the South.

All Jean's newfound sophistication fled at the sight of Lady Sally. A wealthy heiress and extremely pretty, she seemed to have all the accomplishments that Jean lacked. She embroidered exquisite tapestry, played the pianoforte like an angel and was said to be a bruising rider to hounds.

Thank goodness it wasn't the hunting season, reflected Jean, who felt she had been put in the shade enough. Were it not for the fact that the marquess insisted she accompany the horsy party everywhere they went, she would have decided that he had forgotten about her completely.

At that moment, Jean was enjoying the peace and quiet of the library. Uncle Hamish had earlier stated his intention of riding over to visit a church in the neighborhood, which was of a low enough Anglican order to suit his Calvinistic taste.

Noticing Jean's shudder at the thought of another horseback outing, the marquess suggested she might like to spend a quiet afternoon at the Hall. Jean seized on the idea with relief, understanding that he meant to join her, and it was with no little chagrin that she watched him trotting off happily with Lady Sally with all the appearance of a small boy being let out of the schoolroom.

Jean poked moodily among the dusty shelves looking for something to read. Lord Freddie's family had obviously ordered their books by the yard from the bookseller and had never looked at them since. With relief, she discovered a copy of Maria Edgeworth's *Moral Tales* and curled up in an armchair. The air was heavy and warm in the noonday sun. Even the dogs had disappeared and a faint aroma of boiling horseflesh indicated that they must be waiting for their meal. Her eyes drooped over the exploits of a villain who rejoiced in the name of Lord Raspberry and in no time at all, she was fast asleep.

The marquess was enjoying a mild flirtation with Lady Sally in an effort to put Miss Lindsay out of his thoughts and nearly succeeding. Lady Sally had hair of spun gold and wide blue eyes like cornflowers. The marquess had just told her that she reminded him of a cornfield in summer and—unlike Miss Lindsay who would have stared at him in a puzzled way and asked "Why?"—Lady Sally dropped her long eyelashes and blushed adorably.

He was just edging his mount closer to hers to continue his gallantries when he espied the distant figure of the reverend flying hell for leather towards the Hall.

Swearing under his breath, the marquess turned to his pretty companion. "Please join the others and forgive me. I must see that Miss Lindsay is all right." And with that, he spurred his horse and disappeared down the road in a cloud of white dust.

Sally pouted. Anyone would think that Jean Lindsay was his wife! However prettily the gentleman flirted, he never once took his eyes off that carrot-headed nonentity. Sally had never been overlooked by any man. She was the reigning belle of the Season and had angled for the Blackstone invitation to be near the marquess. And she was not going to waste her time. She narrowed her beautiful eyes and started planning a campaign to bring the marquess to the altar.

Imagining all sorts of murders from bludgeoning to slow poison, the marquess hurtled into the entrance hall only to be told by the butler that Hamish was resting in his room and Miss Lindsay was asleep in the library.

Finding he had got himself and his horse into a lather for no reason, the marquess let out a peevish oath and strode off to the stables to supervise the rubbing down of his mount.

Jean slept on in the throes of a nightmare. She was at the altar with the marquess but he was about to be wed to Lady Sally and she was the bridesmaid! "If anyone present knows of any just cause why this couple . . ." intoned the Bishop. "I do! I do!" screamed Jean, rushing to throw herself into the marquess's arms. She found herself awake, standing in front of the fireplace, waving her arms. A pretty Dresden ballet dancer was swept by her gesticulating hand onto the hearth where it broke into three pieces.

Jean stared at the damage in horror. The only sign of feminine weakness in Lady Frank, apart from her bulging stomach, was her love of pretty figurines. They were the only things in the rambling, messy, cluttered mansion which received any care or cleaning.

She jumped in fright as she heard the whoops and halloos of the returning party and then the sound of brisk steps in the hall. Grabbing the sharp pieces of china, she stood irresolute, and as the library door opened, she dropped them on the sofa cushion and sat down on them.

As they all poured into the room, chatting and gossiping about the day's ride, Jean felt like an early Christian martyr. The sharp edges of the china were digging through the thin muslin of her dress and shift and into her buttocks. The marquess joined the party and crossed to the sofa to take his place beside Jean.

"How's our bonnie Jeannie," roared Lady Frank, giving Jean a hearty slap on the back. To the marquess's amazement, Jean let out a high, thin scream of pain. The old bastard's gone and done it! thought the marquess. He's managed to poison her. The sudden thought of how much she meant to him pierced his heart and he seized her by the arms. Jean screamed again.

"What's the matter?" queried Frank. "Got a sore tum-tum?"

"A what?" asked Jean faintly.

"She means—have you got a pain in your breadbasket," explained Freddie crudely.

"Oh, no!" said Jean. "I will be all right if only you will all go away and leave me."

"It should be the other way around," said the marquess. "Come. I'll carry you to your room and fetch Miss Taylor."

He bent over to pick her up. She shrank away from him and he lost his balance and fell on top of her. Jean let out a full-blooded scream.

"Tell you what," said Freddie, *sotto voce,* to Mr. Fairchild. "Don't it look like some of them moral pictures? Rape of the Virgin, what?"

The marquess extricated himself and pulled her roughly to her feet and the pieces of china, caught in her dress, plopped one by one onto the floor and rolled across the carpet. Bursting into tears of embarrassment, Jean fled from the room.

Lady Frank was the first to break the shocked silence. "She was sittin' on my china. Sittin' on it and breakin' it with her demned bum!" Bess, Mary and Sally shuddered deliciously and covered their ears.

"Here, here, sis," said Freddie, rolling his eyes desperately in the direction of the marquess. "There's probably a simple explanation."

"Simple, be demned," roared Lady Frank, hitching up her riding habit and bending to retrieve her broken treasure. "You, Fleetwater, you're responsible for bringin' that . . . that . . . Scotch thing here. Maybe it's a social pastime in the Highlands to go around sittin' on Dresden. That's why they wear kilts so they can go around enjoyin' themselves, plankin' their great bums on china like a lot of demned fakirs sittin' on nails."

Freddie, crimson to the roots of his curly hair, hustled the young ladies from the room and then hurried back to drag away Mr. Fairchild, who seemed to have gone into a state of shock.

The marquess, left alone with Lady Frank, eyed her with disfavor.

"Really, Frank, your language is only fit for the stables. The girl probably broke the figurine by accident and tried to hide it. I'll replace it with the best that Asprey's has to offer."

Much mollified, Frank tossed the china fragments into the coal scuttle and plopped herself down on the sofa. "Very decent of you, John," she growled. "But are you sure the girl's all right?"

"She is very young and shy," said the marquess. "And she must be feeling wretched at the moment."

Frank's kind heart was moved. "I'll go up to her and tell her it's all right."

"No. Leave it to me," said the marquess, hurriedly taking his leave.

He knocked on the door of Jean's sitting room and was admitted by Miss Taylor. Jean sat in a chair in the corner, staring out of the window with reddened eyes.

"Look, my dear," said the marquess. "You are taking it all too seriously. Frank has forgiven you and everyone else will have forgotten about it by dinnertime. Come. Walk with me in the gardens and calm yourself." Jean rose, without a word, and took his offered arm and they left the room together, under the speculative gaze of Miss Taylor.

Jean sedately promenaded with the marquess in the weed-choked rose garden. Blackstone Hall was a haven for sloppy servants. A strong smell of ale wafted in the sunny air as the gardener snored comfortably on a bench.

71

One of the undergardeners sat motionless in the middle of a flower bed and stared vacantly into space.

The grooms, the stable boys and the parlor maid who dusted the china were all excellent hard workers. The rest of the army of servants did pretty much as they pleased and Lord Freddie's table was reputed to be the worst in England.

The marquess's gray eyes raked over the gardens, looking for a secluded spot where he could re-experience the interesting emotions aroused in him by kissing Miss Lindsay.

"Coo-ee!" They both turned as Lady Sally came fluttering toward them, a vision in white muslin embroidered with blue forget-me-nots and a poke bonnet with wide, blue satin ribbons tied over her blond hair. The marquess graciously offered Sally his other arm and, as he stared down at her enchanting face, he wondered for the thousandth time why he was so besotted with Jean.

Sally chattered and flirted prettily, making great play with her fan. If she wasn't rapping the marquess on the arm with it in reply to some supposed piece of audacity, she was spreading it open before her face and batting her eyelashes over the top.

"Like a cow looking over the top of a fence," thought Jean bitterly, and then blushed fiery-red as she realized she had spoken her thought aloud. Sally glared and the marquess tried hard not to laugh.

"Tell me, Miss Lindsay," said Sally sweetly. "You puzzle me. You are such a serious sort of girl, I would have thought you would have preferred to remain in your Highlands, helping your uncle with his good works, rather than embarking on a Season."

"I came to find a husband," said Jean in a flat voice.

"And have you found one?" asked Sally, twinkling roguishly at the marquess and inviting him to share the joke.

To the marquess's horror, Jean looked directly at him and said forthrightly, "I am beginning to think so."

For the first time in his life, the marquess blushed. He did not like the sudden feeling of being pursued rather than pursuing, and said acidly, "I hope you find someone worthy of you, Miss Jean."

Jean looked at him in astonishment. "Well, of course you know him better than anyone. Why, it's . . ."

If I were a woman, I'd faint, thought the marquess, as he pinched her arm to keep her quiet. The points of his cravat suddenly seemed too high and too hot. The girl was impossible. No modesty. No finesse. She must learn to appreciate him and be aware of the great prize she was about to receive.

"It is time we changed for dinner," he said and almost dragged both ladies back to the house.

Jean was puzzled and upset. She had thought she had only to go to the marquess and say "Yes" and all would be settled. But now it looked as if he had changed his mind and preferred Sally. Really, she must try to outdo Sally in some way. She must plot.

Unaware that a more sinister plot was being hatched under her nose, Jean prepared for dinner.

Along the corridor, Hamish helped himself liberally from the decanter and mulled over the afternoon's events. Instead of visiting the church as he had said, he had rendezvoused with Lord Ian at a nearby inn. It was decided that until Lord Ian could figure out a plan to get himself invited, Hamish should try to fabricate "accidents" any way he could. A visit to a nearby cloisters was planned for the morrow. He would bide his time and see what opportunities arose.

The company assembled in the Blue Saloon before dinner, the exquisitely gowned ladies fluttering and vying for the gentlemen's attention. Mr. Fairchild seemed to be carrying on a kind of strangulated flirtation with Lady

Mary, Lord Freddie was known to be notoriously petti-coat-shy, so that left Bess, Sally and Jean to fight for the marquess's attention.

Well aware of the fuss he was creating, the marquess stood with one elegantly shod foot on the hearth and lapped it up, his eyes occasionally sliding around to see how Jean was coping with the competition. Her green eyes held a vague, dreamy look and the marquess felt piqued. He did not yet know her propensity for vanish-ing into dream country. Bess and Sally, not knowing that Jean was just asking them sweetly in her mind to be her bridesmaids, flirted on regardless.

He crossed the room to offer Jean his arm into dinner. "I do," she said dreamily and, unaware of his startled glance, drifted into the dining room.

Really, thought the marquess, staring at his plate, how could he tell if Hamish was trying to poison Jean with food like this!

Even Jean's excellent appetite had begun to pall when faced with the Blackstone cuisine. "What's this?" she whispered nervously to the marquess, pushing her food around with her fork. The marquess leveled his quizzing glass at the plate. "Boiled Hessians with a side dish of toadstool, I think."

Jean shuddered as horrible entrée followed even more horrible entrée and was glad when the meal ended and the gentlemen elected to join the ladies, instead of linger-ing over their wine.

Lady Sally went immediately to the pianoforte, request-ing the marquess to turn the music for her and Jean watched them, listening to the perfect, bell-like voice, in agonies of jealousy. She was grateful when Lady Frank let out a stentorian yawn and said, "All this music bores me. Used to have better fun when we was young. Played games like hunt the slipper."

"Why not play hunt the slipper now," said Freddie

enthusiastically. He was as bored by the finer arts as his sister.

The young people agreed and the marquess elected to hide one of his own slippers. Then the party set off, laughing and shouting, along the rambling rooms and corridors of the mansion.

Jean was determined to find that slipper. She could not outshine Sally in anything else, so find that slipper she would. As she wandered farther into the partially unused section of the West Wing, she had the uneasy feeling that someone was stalking her. The sounds of the others were very far away and her candle flame flickered in the draft, sending multiple shadows of herself dancing and racing up into the rafters like so many ghosts.

Just as she decided to turn back, she noticed a thick oaken door of a closet under the attic stairs. Jean decided to take one last try and then give up the hunt. With candle held high, she swung open the door and peered inside. A tremendous shove from behind sent her flying head first into the closet, the door was slammed tight behind her, and the key turned in the lock.

Her candle dropped and went out. Hysterically, she pounded on the door and screamed. Very far away, she could hear Freddie tootling on his hunting horn and the rest laughing. They sounded as if they were in another country.

Jean sank slowly to the floor of the closet, her teeth beginning to chatter with fear. Someone was very definitely trying to kill her and it must be someone she knew. The only person she suspected of actively hating her was her uncle but, as far as she knew, he had no motive for killing her. Perhaps Lady Frank's bluff exterior covered a mad, twisted mind. Perhaps Lady Sally's Dresden face hid the mind of a cunning murderess. The more her frantic brain turned it over, the more the whole of the house party began to look sinister.

Back in the music room, Lady Sally proudly held up the slipper and coyly demanded a kiss from the marquess who eagerly complied, egged on by cheers from the others. He drew back disappointed. Obviously no girl, however pretty, was going to arouse the fierce passion in him engendered by Miss Jean Lindsay. He sighed. Lady Sally taking his sigh to betoken passion, fluttered her eyelashes and cast a triumphant look at Lady Bess, who stuck her tongue out in return. Bess was feeling extremely sore. She had wasted a chunk of the London Season to no account and made plans to leave as soon as possible.

The marquess realized that Jean showed no sign of returning. Hamish had reappeared and now sat in a corner, apparently comatose, over the decanter. The marquess felt the first small flicker of panic.

"I think we shall have another game," he announced. "Find Jean Lindsay." Sally pouted. "She has probably retired." The marquess insisted, leading the way himself. Freddie, slightly foxed, blew a blast on his hunting horn and the party spread out once more, the ladies searching and calling in a very halfhearted manner.

Now, thought the marquess, if I were Miss Jean Lindsay, what hen-witted place would I decide to go. He stumbled through the rabbit warren of a house, occasionally calling her name and cursing her bitterly under his breath the rest of the time. He was about to give up when he thought he heard a faint noise coming from the West Wing. He raced toward the sound and stopped short by the closet. He threw open the door and saw in the flickering light, Jean, white-faced, terrified, her hands bruised and bloody from beating on the door. He put down the candle and wordlessly held out his arms.

Miss Jean Lindsay, in the manner of her favorite heroines, put one faltering hand to her brow and fainted dead away.

Chapter Six

The visit to the cloisters was canceled until Jean recovered from her fright. She lay in bed, drinking her chocolate and nursing her bandaged hands. The marquess had begged her to say that the whole thing had been an accident so that he could try to catch the culprit red-handed. Jean regretted agreeing to the scheme. It left her feeling unprotected at the most and, at the least, like a fool since the rest of the house party considered her hare-brained.

The long, boring day stretched wearily ahead. How on earth can I be so frightened and so bored? thought Jean. Miss Taylor had called in the services of two footmen to move her to a daybed by the window, so she had an excellent view of the marquess and Lady Sally promenading in the gardens with their blond heads close together.

By late afternoon, she declared herself well enough to go down for dinner and stared moodily in the mirror as the abigail arranged her hair.

"My eyes look very small," said Jean fretfully. "They are still puffed with crying."

"I have heard said that the ladies in London use belladonna to make their eyes shine," said the abigail.

"Can you get me some?" asked Jean hopefully.

"Oh, yes," said the abigail. "I think there is some below stairs." She hurried off and returned presently with a vial.

She tilted Jean's head back and dropped a little of the liquid into each green eye. Jean straightened up and stared in horror at the blur where the mirror was supposed to be.

"I can hardly see a thing," wailed Jean.

"It'll wear off after a bit," said the abigail. "But it makes your eyes ever so lovely, miss. They're like emeralds."

"Well," said Jean philosophically. *"Il faut souffrir pour être belle*—we must suffer to be beautiful." She tried to cross the room and fell over a footstool.

"Wait there and I'll get Miss Taylor to take you downstairs," said the abigail.

Miss Taylor sighed when the problem was explained to her. "I keep thinking you have done everything socially wrong that there is to do and you think of something else," she told Jean. "You had better hang onto my arm as much as possible."

As they entered the Blue Saloon, the marquess caught his breath. Never had Jean Lindsay looked so magnificent. Her sea-green gown set off the whiteness of her skin and her eyes shone like huge emeralds.

He wished to whisper compliments in her ear, but Miss Taylor, who had seemed to favor his suit, stayed firmly by her charge's side and showed no signs of leaving.

After dinner, a musical evening had been planned, much to Freddie and Frank's disgust. It had come about that Mr. Fairchild was possessed of an extremely charming tenor voice and made up in his singing for what he lacked in general conversation.

As Miss Taylor was about to take her place beside Jean, Lady Bess called her over to help choose silks, and

Miss Taylor, with the thought of her pension ever in mind, had to comply.

Jean gazed blurrily around the room for the marquess and at last focused mistily on a tall figure in bottle green next to her. The marquess had a very fine evening coat of bottle green superfine so it must be he. Jean decided to give him some encouragement to divert his attention from Lady Sally. Forgetting that the Blackstone servants' livery was bottle green, she reached out and took the hand of the second footman in a warm clasp.

Henry, the second footman, looked down into the green eyes gazing adoringly into his and the sweat started to run down his forehead under his powdered wig. This was his big moment. This is what the older footmen had often whispered about below stairs. That marvelous moment when a lady of fashion falls for you!

"They lets you know they wants you in their boodwars by little signs," the older men had said. "They strokes your 'and or chucks yer chin or gives yer meaning little looks." But never in his wildest dreams had Henry expected the approach to be so blatant.

The marquess glanced across the room and froze at the sight of his beloved handclasped with the second footman. He was getting to his feet when an insistent hand tugged at his sleeve.

"She has belladonna in her eyes. I think she thinks that she is holding hands with you," hissed Miss Taylor.

The marquess marched over and with a flick of his hand and a glare sent the footman from the room and, taking Jean's hand in his, stood prey to a mixture of emotions. How could he possibly consider making this impossible child his marchioness? He would be the laughingstock of society. As Mr. Fairchild's voice soared on the penultimate line of the love song, he looked down into the green eyes and mentally shrugged. After all, he had long planned to retire from Society and spend more time on his estates—and holding the girl's hand in public was tantamount to a declaration.

Jean was apprised of her conduct before going to bed by a very angry Miss Taylor, who failed to tell her that the marquess had taken her hand when the footman was dismissed, so Jean was left to cry herself to sleep, thinking she had held hands all evening with the second footman.

The night was close and thundery and Jean tossed and turned as clap upon clap of thunder rocked the old house, causing the dogs to howl and scrabble at the bedroom doors in hope of human comfort.

One particularly loud crack of thunder wakened Jean from her fitful sleep and, as the echoes rolled away, she became aware of a scratching at the door. Thinking it was one of the dogs, she pulled back the bed curtains and groped her way to the door, damning all four-footed animals under her breath, from dogs to horses. She flung open the door and retreated with a gasp as Henry, the second footman, calmly walked into the room and slammed the door behind him.

Farther down the corridor, Uncle Hamish was receiving frights of his own as a tall figure bent over him and shook him roughly awake. "May the good Lord protect me!" he cried out in fright.

"Call on the Devil, you old hypocrite," hissed a nasty, well-remembered voice. Lightning flashed through the room and showed Hamish the pallid face and glinting eyes of his visitor, standing in the livid glare like Satan himself.

"Lord Ian!" cried Hamish. "What brings you here!"

"I am come to expedite the murder of your niece," said Lord Ian.

" 'Tis not murder, man. 'Tis my rights. I am an instrument of the Lord," babbled Hamish.

"Stow it, you old fool," said Lord Ian brutally. "Or call it what you will so long as it gets done."

"Well, now," said Hamish, lighting a candle. "Let us make plans."

"Enough of plans. We go down the passage into the girl's room, strangle her, and arrange it to look as if someone broke in."

"Could we not wait a bit?" pleaded Hamish. Dreams of gold and murder were one thing, reality another. After his amateurish attempts at drowning Jean, shooting Jean and locking her in the closet had failed, he had hoped Lord Ian would handle the business himself. "I'm giving you half the girl's fortune after all."

Lord Ian opened his snuffbox and eyed the shivering minister with contempt. "We do it tonight. I'll do the deed and you come with me. I'll not have you crying murderer at me so as to keep my share for yourself." He held out his long, bony fingers. "One squeeze and Miss Jean Lindsay breathes her last!"

At that moment, Jean was already fighting for breath as she was pressed passionately to the chest of the second footman and nearly smothered in an overwhelming odor of attar of roses.

"My little darling," whispered Henry. "When you 'eld my hand, I says to myself, I says, ' 'Er is as 'ot with passion as wot I is.' "

"It was all a dreadful mistake," sobbed Jean, trying to push him away. "I thought you were the marquess. There was something up with my eyes." Henry was about to put this down to maidenly modesty when he received a vicious kick on the shin.

"Ouch!" yelled Henry, hurt in body and soul. "That for a Banbury Tale. You have bin trifling with my affections, that's wot." He edged closer again. "But if you was to give me some gold, perraps them wounded feelin's would 'eal."

81

Jean backed across the room pursued by a now very angry Henry. She was about to reply, when they both froze as the door began to creak slowly open and two dark figures crept in and made their way to the bed.

"Ho, Miss Modesty," yelled Henry. "Two of them. A regular turnpike you are, you slut!"

Jean's nerve cracked and she threw back her head and screamed and screamed. The two figures made a dash for the door but there were already cries and lights in the corridor. In the vanguard was the Marquess of Fleetwater, attired only in his nightshirt and clutching a drawn sword. A flash of lightning lit up the tableau and he stopped, amazed, as Hamish was revealed trying to burrow under the bedclothes, Lord Ian, who had him by the leg, was trying to pull him back, and Henry was in the act of sidling out of the door.

The marquess deftly caught Henry by the arm, and, dragging him into the room, held his sword to Lord Ian's throat. "An explanation, gentlemen, if you please."

"She lured me! She lured me!" yelled Henry.

"Enough, man," said Lord Ian, smoothly. "Put up your sword, Fleetwater, and don't be so demned dramatic. I was visiting in the district and my horse fell lame. I did not want to waken the household so I went to ask the reverend for help. We had heard noises coming from Miss Lindsay's room and we found her with this servant."

Lord Freddie and Mr. Fairchild arrived on the scene, waving a dueling pistol apiece. "Servant, Miss Lindsay," said Freddie, sweeping off his nightcap and making his usual impeccable bow. Amid her embarrassment and confusion, Jean could still wonder that the gentlemen had more lace around their nightshirts than she had on her more modest attire.

Freddie suddenly caught sight of the terror-stricken footman. "Hey! That's my dressing gown. Hey, Muggles, demmit—*Muggles*. Where is the curst fellow?"

"H-here, m'lord," hiccupped the butler, Muggles, from directly behind Freddie, making that young gentleman jump.

"Demme, what a household. You've been thievin' my brandy by the smell of you and this fellow's paradin' around in my best dressing gown.

"I'm too easy-goin'," said Freddie righteously. "But it's goin' to stop right now. You, Muggles, will get that skinful of my brandy taken off your wages and you can take that . . . that"—he pointed at the shivering footman —"down to the stables and have him horsewhipped."

"Wait a bit," said the marquess. "I mean to get to the bottom of this. All of you go away and leave me to have a word with Miss Lindsay. I shall speak with you later, Mr. Lindsay, and cease muttering about harlots or I shall call you out."

The party shuffled out, and, leaving the door punctiliously ajar, the marquess turned his attention to Jean, who was laughing hysterically.

"Shut up!" he said pleasantly, slapping her efficiently across the face. As she gasped and gulped, he threw her her wrapper and motioned her to sit down. Like a giant with dyspepsia, the thunder rumbled away in the distance.

"It's all my fault," said Jean. "I put belladonna in my eyes and couldn't see, and this evening I held hands with what I thought was . . . well, never mind. Anyway, it was the second footman all along and he thought . . . he thought . . ."

"It becomes quite obvious what he thought," said the marquess grimly. "I will be back in a minute. It was wrong of the man to borrow Freddie's dressing gown but it hardly merits a horsewhipping." He strode from the room, leaving Jean a prey to jumbled emotions.

Presently he was back, this time warmly wrapped in a magnificent dressing gown. "What am I to do with you, Jean? You have left the schoolroom, you know, and should not keep falling in and out of scrapes like a child."

Jean hung her head.

He drew her to her feet and wrapped his arms around her. "Oh, my dear, we could deal better than this. If only you would learn to behave like, say, Lady Sally, who is a model of decorum."

Jean, who had been trembling in his grasp a moment before, broke away from him in a fury.

"Lady Sally. Hah!" shouted Jean, her temper matching her hair. "Why don't you marry the paragon?"

"Calm yourself," said the marquess. "You are only jealous. You must admit that you are not yet used to how to go on in Society. Miss Taylor is excellent in the schoolroom, no doubt, but you certainly need some lady of fashion to school you. I could suggest . . ."

"Why, you insufferable, conceited coxcomb," shouted Jean, now beside herself with rage and, swinging back her arm, she landed a well-placed blow right on the end of the marquess's aristocratic nose. He howled with pain and raised his hand to strike her and recollected himself in time.

"It is as well that I have found out in time what a termagent you are," he said, gathering the rags of his dignity. "And to think that I was about to bestow my name on an ungrateful little piece such as yourself. You deserve only to be treated like the hussy you are." And grabbing her by the front of her nightdress, he dragged her brutally into his arms and forced his mouth down on hers.

A wave of almost uncontrollable passion swept the two antagonists and they broke apart staring at each other, until Jean let out a sob and, turning about, threw herself on the bed.

The marquess stood stunned for a minute watching her,

his hands at his sides. Then, "A pox on all women," he roared, exasperated, and stalked from the room.

On the road to his chambers, the marquess looked over the banisters and spied a light in the library. He marched down and kicked open the door. Freddie and Mr. Harry Fairchild sat on either side of the fireplace, staring at the brandy decanter.

"Just the man we wanted, didn't we, Harry," said Freddie, winking hideously at Mr. Fairchild. "Harry wants to have a word with you."

The marquess poured himself a liberal glass of brandy and sat down. "This is an evening of surprises, indeed. Silence itself is about to speak. Go on, Harry."

Harry Fairchild rolled his eyes and shied nervously. A few inarticulate sounds escaped his lips. "What he's tryin' to tell you, John," said Freddie, who usually acted as Mr. Fairchild's interpreter, "is that he thinks you're a demned fool."

"Explain," said the marquess coldly.

"Well, it's like this," said Freddie, sighing heavily. "We're all friends, ain't we? Known you since we was all in short coats at Eton. Now, you're thirty years old and have your pick of the gels and some demned fine high-flyers too. Take that little bit of fluff at the opera, calls herself Madame Duvalle, 'cept she's really Maggie Blunt from Clapham, and take Mrs. . . ."

"If you are going to catalogue my love life," said the marquess acidly, "we shall be here all night."

"The point of the matter is the Lindsay girl," said Freddie, ignoring the marquess's glare. "Now, she's a good-lookin' chit, no doubt about that, and a sweet gel, but she ain't for you. Got to think of your family, got to think of your name, got to . . ."

"Fiddle!" snapped the marquess, doubly angry because that was just what he had been thinking himself.

"*And,*" continued Freddie, faint but pursuing, "there's

85

somethin' up with her toploft. What was that footman-fellow doin' in her room?"

The marquess explained about the belladonna. "There y'are," said Freddie triumphantly. "See 'em now pointin' her out at Almack's. 'That's the Marchioness of Fleet-water. That gel over there holdin' hands with the foot-man!' "

"Rubbish!" said the marquess. "I refuse to discuss my relations with Miss Lindsay any longer. But I do need help with another matter . . ." He outlined his suspicions of Hamish and Lord Ian Percy.

"How did Percy get into the house anyway?"

"Demned if I know," said Freddie. "Servants have run to seed, y'know. M'sister doesn't keep a tight enough hand on the reins. Probably one of them just let him in without a question. Do you want me to throw him out? Can't stand the fellow."

"No," said the marquess slowly. "Let's keep them both under observation and trap them when they next make a move. They were probably in her room for some rotten purpose. She'll need a guard. We'll take turns. I'll take first watch."

"Won't it look odd," complained Freddie. "One of us sittin' outside her door like Patience on the Thingummy?"

"Anyone but us outside her door in the middle of the night shouldn't be there in the first place. There's not much of the night left so I'll watch it out." He got wearily to his feet. The two friends solemnly watched him go.

"Y'know what?" said Freddie as the door closed be-hind the marquess. Mr. Fairchild uttered some inarticulate sounds.

"Dashed if you ain't right," said Freddie. "Don't know what I think . . . . !"

In the morning, the storm had blown itself out and the sun shone bravely through the mullioned windows, turning the dust motes to gold and rousing the army of dogs who had been sleeping off their fright of the night before.

En route to the breakfast room, Jean was uncomfortably aware of the furtive, hostile stares of the servants. Henry had been voluble below stairs in his defense and the marquess, that notorious rake, had been espied in the early dawn by the between stairs maid fast asleep outside Jean's door.

Even the usually amiable Freddie gave her a cool stare over the breakfast table and Mr. Fairchild hitched up the points of his cravat and hunched his face down into the wads of linen to escape her glance. The marquess, heavy-eyed and slightly red about the nose, pointedly ignored her. Bess, Mary and Sally darted curious glances back and forth and began to visibly brighten like the day outside.

Lady Sally looked particularly radiant. An exquisite parasol of lace with an ivory handle had been delivered to her rooms that morning with a note from the marquess. She was not to know that the marquess had bought it for Jean Lindsay before leaving town and had presented it to her instead in a combination of pique and fatigue. Anxious to display her treasure in front of the other ladies, Sally piped up.

"Can we not make the expedition to the cloisters today?"

The gentlemen agreed halfheartedly and were discussing the arrangements when Lord Ian entered the breakfast room with Hamish at his heels.

"What in tarnation are you doin' here, Percy?" asked Lady Frank, throwing the remains of her breakfast to the dogs with blithe unconcern for her oriental rugs. Lord Ian explained his mishap.

"We'll lend you another mount and then you can be on our way," said Lady Frank rudely.

"Why don't you stay with us for a few days, Percy?" said Freddie as the marquess nudged him in the ribs.

"I should be delighted, if it is not an inconvenience to Your Ladyship," said Lord Ian smoothly.

Lady Frank gave her brother a fulminating glare. "Too right. Demned inconvenient. Place is crawlin' with people already, crashin' about all night like herds of wild thingies."

"This is my house, sis. And I will invite whomever I want," said Freddie. "You're welcome to stay as long as you like, Percy."

"Charmed," said Lord Ian, trying to bow over Lady Frank's hand but was thwarted when she abruptly rose from the table and marched to the door. The man had a hide like a rhinoceros, reflected the marquess bitterly, as Lord Ian calmly took his seat at the table next to Jean.

Miss Taylor bowed her head over her breakfast and tried not to notice the undercurrents. She gathered that her charge was in trouble again and, with a sigh, decided that she was at last becoming accustomed to it.

By the time the party set out later that morning, everyone was again in good spirits with the exception of Jean. Sally, twirling and flirting with her parasol, had left the company in no doubt about the identity of the donor. Freddie and Harry Fairchild positively beamed at the marquess. Their friend was obviously coming to his senses. Lady Sally—now, *she* was everything that was suitable.

Jean and Sally were taken up in the marquess's curricle, Jean wedged on the outside, listening to their gay conversation, and feeling wretched.

The cloisters, situated a few miles distant from Blackstone Hall, were all that remained of a once great abbey after Henry the Eighth had finished with it. Gothic gray arches sprang from green lawns as if placed there by magic and formal hedges of yew supplied shade for the

88

party. It was an idyllic setting with the fluttering dresses of the ladies and the gay morning coats and striped waistcoats of the men adding color to the scene.

"All it needs is a lake with some swans," said Lady Sally dreamily. The marquess bent over her hand. "The exquisite blue of your eyes is all the decoration this landscape needs."

"Fustian," muttered Miss Lindsay.

"La!" exclaimed Sally, lowering the parasol to hide her blushes. "First presents and now pretty speeches. I declare, you are a hardened flirt, sir. Why, only last evening you were holding hands with Miss Lindsay."

The marquess bent his head closer and whispered something which sent Sally into trills of delighted laughter. Jean turned on her heel and walked away, closely followed by Lord Ian.

"Walk with me a little, my dear," he said, his eyes appreciating the picture she made in her slim, yellow muslin dress and *bergère* hat with matching ribbons. "I have not seen enough of you lately."

"Could it be because you found out from my godmother that I have no dowry?" asked Jean sweetly.

"I have never cared for money. I thought I did," said Lord Ian with mock honesty. "But since your absence from the metropolis, I have discovered that my heart rules me after all. What is gold," he exclaimed, grabbing her small, gloved hand in his, "when I am faced with the wealth of your beauty!"

Jean drew her hand away. "Very pretty, sir. Now could we discuss a more interesting topic?"

But Lord Ian was not to be put off. Why kill the goose with the golden eggs? He would not be averse to having Miss Lindsay and her fortune as well.

He drew her into the shadow of a lichened wall. Shaking out a lace handkerchief, he spread it on the turf and knelt down on one knee before her.

"I cannot be stopped. I must tell you the feelings that burn in my heart. I must . . ."

Whatever else Lord Ian was about to say was drowned by a grating rumble from above as a large stone, dislodged from the masonry, came hurtling down, missing the couple with inches to spare.

Jean screamed and Lord Ian cursed fluently. The marquess headed by the rest of the party rounded the wall, his face as white as Jean's.

As Jean finished stammering out what had happened, the marquess strode back to the picnic table, which the servants had arranged on the grass. Hamish was sitting at his ease, his customary glass of madeira in his hand.

"Where were you five minutes ago?" snapped the marquess.

Hamish slowly took a sip of wine, his vinous, old eyes looking insolently into the marquess's angry gray ones.

"I should not need to remind you, my lord, of the respect due to my gray hairs and my cloth."

"Damn your gray hairs and damn your cloth," said the marquess. "Should any accident befall your niece, Hamish Lindsay, you will have me to answer to. What d'ye think of that?"

"You are talking fustian, my son," said Hamish. "Get down on your knees and cry out to your Maker for forgiveness, for you are such that was conceived in iniquity."

One minute it seemed to the reverend he was sitting comfortably in his chair, the next he found himself held up by his shirt front in the air, his legs dangling, and looking straight into the murderous eyes of the marquess. "You insolent whoreson. Save your cant for your ignorant parishioners. Insult me or my name again and, by God, I'll beat you to a pulp." With that, the marquess threw Hamish from him and he fell backward on the turf like a grotesque doll. He lay glaring at the retreating back of the marquess with ideas of more than one murder burning in his heart.

But his worries were not over. As the Reverend got unsteadily to his feet, he was sent flying again by a blow from Lord Ian.

"Try to kill me, would you," hissed Lord Ian.

Hamish got to his feet and brushed himself down. "Look you, Percy. I know your game. But if you marry my niece, you'll never be alive on your wedding night. Keep that in mind. And should you think to kill me, there is a sealed letter at my lawyers with instructions that it be opened on the event of my death—my *untimely* death, that is. I could have killed you easily just now. That was just in the way of being a wee warning."

Lord Ian thought momentarily of the charms of Miss Amy Jenkins, the merchant's wealthy daughter, and then shrugged and took his place at the table. "Shall we begin anew?" he said coldly. But whatever plans the couple would have embarked on were thwarted by the arrival of the rest of the company, eager for lunch.

The sun sparkled, the wine and food were excellent since the marquess had arranged the treat by hiring the services of the local inn rather than suffer the terrible cooking of Blackstone Hall.

But a shadow seemed to have come over the party. The marquess was preoccupied, Jean was white and shaken. The only happy ones were Lady Mary and Mr. Fairchild, who were holding hands under the table and sitting, staring into space, in silent rapture.

Lady Sally felt that her day of triumph was not turning out the way she expected. Any time the marquess began behaving prettily, something would happen to that tiresome Scotch female and put a damper on things. She would not be defeated. She addressed the marquess.

"John, dear!" She glanced out of the corner of her eyes to try to see how Jean was reacting to her familiar use of the marquess's Christian name. "Could we not have a ball at Blackstone Hall? I confess I am missing the delights of the Season."

"Ask Freddie," said the marquess a shade abruptly. "It's his home."

"Capital!" said Freddie. "We'll have a fancy-dress ball. I like that sort of thing. Like to dress up as a pirate and chase all the ladies, what!"

Feminine giggles greeted this witticism, except for Jean, who said, "Why?"

"What d'y'mean, *why*," said Freddie crossly. "Why do I want to dress up as a pirate or why do I want to chase the ladies?"

"Both."

"Dashed if I know. You'd like it anyway, Lady Sally. Always like fun, don't you?" asked Freddie with a pointed look at the marquess.

"Oh, I am never too serious," said Sally happily. "Not like Miss Lindsay. But after all," she turned to Jean, "you did say your sole purpose in having a Season in London was to find a husband."

"Well, why not?" asked Jean defiantly. "What else are we made fit for. All our accomplishments—needlework, cooking, playing on the pianoforte, playing the harp, singing, etiquette—are they not all put into our mind with one end in view: to entrap a man? Do our families not go to the expense of routs and champagne suppers and balls, jewelery and gowns so that we may be paraded on the marriage mart like so many prize pigs? It is a wonder you gentlemen don't lean over the fence and poke us with a stick!" And with that, she left the table and walked off toward the cloisters.

"Well, really!" said Bess as the others gasped.

"She's only telling the unpalatable truth," said the marquess, lazily eyeing the retreating figure. No, he would not follow her. She was rude and gauche and he felt sure that Hamish had shot his bolt for the day.

Miss Jean Lindsay was off in the cloisters, giving herself the talking to of a lifetime. She had secretly despised the antics of the heroines in the romances she read so avidly—always sobbing and swooning and behaving like regular wet blankets. Love was destroying her sense of humor and making her mawkish. "Forget about the marquess, you silly girl," she admonished herself. "Go back there this instant and be lively and gay."

The company watched her doubtfully as she approached the table, but to everyone's surprise, Jean launched into plans for the ball, outlining the costumes best suited to the characters present. As her suggestions were very flattering, everyone joined in the fun, and, in no time at all, the day was a success with Jean controlling the conversational ball and sending it rolling backward and forward with all the expertise of an experienced hostess.

Freddie began to decide she wasn't so bad after all and volunteered the information that they had trunks full of costumes at the Hall, which had once been used for charades in his parents' day.

It was a lively group who returned to the Hall. The marquess would have been enchanted with Jean had she not singled Lord Ian out for her special attention.

They retired to their rooms in high spirits, promising to meet before dinner in the Blue Saloon and examine the costumes which Freddie had ordered the servants to bring down from the attics.

Once safely back in her bedroom, Jean sank down in an armchair and stared sadly out of the window. For the first time, since coming South, she felt homesick for the Highlands. Everything suddenly felt strange and foreign, the rigid social rules of conduct which governed the gayest outing, stifling. Never had she thought to wish herself back at the manse but that is exactly what she did. Her feelings for the handsome marquess had got out of hand. Either she would need to admit defeat and escape home and try to get rid of the painful sickness called love or stay and battle for the marquess's flinty heart. She suddenly decided that unless she got him to the altar, she would never know a day's peace again.

That evening, as the guests scrambled among the boxes of costumes like children, Hamish and Lord Ian made a leisurely stroll of the grounds.

"The hustle and bustle of the ball would be an ideal opportunity," said Lord Ian reflectively, blowing a cloud of smoke from his cheroot to dispel a malignant cloud of mosquitoes which were dancing above his head in the humid air.

"When is it to be held?"

"It's an impromptu affair. Two days' time."

"Well, then," said Hamish. "What is your plan?"

"What is *my* plan? It's as much your murder as mine, my friend," said His Lordship peevishly.

Both ambled aimlessly in the direction of the home wood, turning over plots and schemes in their heads.

After much thought, Lord Ian said slowly, "She's always doing something silly. If she wandered away from the Hall into the grounds on the night of the ball—far away—and were found dead, it would be blamed on some outside agent."

"Where? How?" demanded Hamish, eagerly seizing the other by the lapel.

Lord Ian distastefully extricated himself from Hamish's clutch.

"What about that ruin thing over there?" He pointed to a folly set on a small hill at the edge of the gardens. It had been built at the height of the Gothic Revival when all the best families had an ornamental ruin to show their guests, the more crumbling the better.

Hamish snorted. "How on earth are you going to persuade her to leave the ball and the fascination of Fleet-water to go traipsing around the gardens?"

"Simple," said Lord Ian. "We'll make the appointment for, say, eleven o'clock. You engage the marquess in conversation. I will already have delivered a note to Miss Lindsay, supposed to have come from the marquess, making the assignment at the ruin."

"Capital scheme," snickered Hamish cheerfully, rubbing his bony hands together and cracking his knuckles. "Now, let us return. This damp air is not good for my old bones and I wish to outlive my niece!"

As they turned toward the house, Lord Ian asked anxiously, "You are quite sure the girl's fortune goes to you on her death?"

"Quite sure."

"In that case, when we return, you will write a note signing over half her fortune to me."

"Now, then. What kind of a fool d'ye think I am to put a thing like that in writing?"

"A treacherous one," said Lord Ian dryly. "Look you —no note, no murder."

Hamish sighed. "Very well, then. Accompany me to my chambers and you shall have it."

Looking out of the window, the marquess saw the couple entering the Hall and frowned. He and his friends could not keep on guarding Jean's door without occasioning remark. He decided to enlist the aid of Miss Taylor and found himself not believed.

"Jean has obviously infected your brains with her romantical notions, my lord. You must forgive me for speaking plain but I am at my wits' end with the girl's troubles as it is. No, not another word will I listen to!" and Miss Taylor whisked herself away to join the party at the other end of the room.

There was a loud whoop as Freddie discovered his pirate's costume and the rest crowded around selecting their outfits. Lady Sally planned to go as Helen of Troy and the marquess, with a mischevious look at Jean, said that in that case he would be Paris to Lady Sally's Helen. Bess had settled for an ornate jeweled mask, which she said would go with her favorite ball gown, and Mary chose a similar one for herself. Lady Frank declared her intention of going as the Spirit of Liberty in a wide, flowing, loose robe emblazoned with the Union Jack, which, she pointed out indelicately, would disguise her condition. Mr. Fairchild made a few choking sounds which Lady Mary, who had taken over Freddie's role of translator, interpreted to mean that he was going to be a highwayman. Miss Taylor declined to go as anything other than herself, and that left Jean, still undecided.

The marquess held up a powdered wig and a box of patches. "I always think of you as being more suited to the last century, Miss Lindsay," he teased.

Wincing at the memory of her first ball gown, Jean was about to refuse when Frank, of all people, waxed enthusiastic.

"I have a ball gown of my grandmother's that would go with that. Lovely with your hair. Come upstairs with me and have a look."

Jean went with her reluctantly, but one look at the gown tucked away in one of Lady Frank's closets changed her mind. It was of black silk with a design of leaves and flowers, cunningly worked in silver thread and seed pearls. It had a panniered overdress and a demi-train at the back.

"I have everything to go with it," said Frank, unexpectedly dropping her mannish role and becoming almost feminine in her excitement. "I declare I haven't had such fun since my come-out."

Jean, who had really wanted a Grecian dress to outshine Lady Sally, realized the futility of it, and settled for the Georgian dress.

Until the night of the ball, the house was in an uproar. Lady Frank had decided for once to work the servants and banish the dogs to the stables. Messengers were sent out from the Hall to the neighboring county families, Freddie himself posted up to Nathan's in Covent Garden to order flowers for the ladies, and the marquess sent for his own chef.

A woodland theme was decided on to decorate the ballroom and the young people changed into old clothes and wandered far and wide collecting wild flowers and branches.

Jean's homesickness began to vanish. Never in her life before had she thought she would enjoy the luxury of being able to wear old clothes and scrambled around the countryside, indefatigably happy as, for two blessed days, the woman disappeared and left the carefree child.

The weather had turned chilly and fires were lit throughout the Hall to heat the rooms. "We should do this more often," said Freddie enthusiastically. He had never seen his home look so clean.

Before the carriages began to arrive with the other guests, the house party gathered downstairs to admire each other's costumes. Jean, who had been feeling very gay and young and happy, suddenly felt the knife of jealousy twist in her heart as she saw the marquess and Lady Sally standing together.

Sally made an exquisite Helen with her blond hair caught up in silver ribbons and her simple, white silk dress falling in classic lines to the floor and showing off her excellent figure. The marquess was magnificent as Paris with his short, white and gold tunic displaying his muscular legs to advantage. He had a silver Grecian helmet on his head with a horsehair crest, dyed scarlet, and carried a spear from the armory.

He caught the fire of jealousy in Jean's eyes and miraculously felt his old urbane self again. He would have that chit down on her knees, begging him to marry her! Not that she didn't look a ravishing picture.

Jean wore her own hair powdered instead of the wig. The dress fitted her to perfection and she wore her mother's pearls, which enhanced her excellent bosom. One black patch was placed at the corner of her mouth, accentuating the dimple. I'll kiss her before this evening's out, thought the marquess, and then there will be no more nonsense out of Miss Jean Lindsay.

Bess sidled up to Jean, her eyes glinting behind her jeweled mask. "Don't they make a handsome couple," she tittered, pointing to the marquess and Sally with her ostrich-feather fan. "Sally has written to her parents to say that she expects to make a match of it."

Jean moved away without answering and set herself to flirt outrageously with Lord Ian, who was dressed as a Turk.

Lady Frank had spoiled the Spirit of Liberty costume by topping it up with an enormous purple turban. Lord Freddie made a splendid pirate—that is if one could believe that pirates wore snowy cravats and polished Hessians with gold tassels. Mr. Fairchild was surprisingly the success of the evening. He looked a most ferocious highwayman and Freddie teased him by saying that the magistrate, Sir Giles Mannering, was to be one of the guests and that Harry would end up on a gibbet before the evening was out. Despite his cutthroat appearance, the highwayman blushed and choked and had to be fortified with champagne.

The house party moved to the ballroom. If the marquess does not take me into supper this evening, I shall die, swore Jean to herself, forgetting all her vows not to behave like a Gothic heroine.

The local county residents, who arrived in droves, turned out to be a noisy, cheerful, rambunctious crowd as the young people were barely out of the schoolroom, their elder brothers and sisters having gone to London to take their places in Society. Jean found it refreshing to be in the company of people of her own age. After all, Sally, Bess and Mary, she thought, had never been young. They had fallen out of their cradles as models of Regency womanhood. Jean romped and flirted with the young bloods of the county and made the marquess feel as old as the hills.

Twice he tried to claim her for a dance and twice she had skipped off before he reached her side on the arm of some young gentleman.

Cow-handed bumpkins, thought the marquess savagely, glaring after them through his quizzing glass. He was further incensed by an outburst of giggles from a party of young misses who shrieked that they had never seen an ancient Greek with a quizzing glass before. Miss Lindsay seemed to be affecting the world with her lack of respect.

Lady Sally drifted up to him and put a hand on his arm. "I confess I weary for the elegance of London. Too many clodhoppers here."

"Nonsense!" said the marquess spitefully. "I find it very refreshing." The supper dance was coming up and the marquess, who had never had to pursue a female in his life before, realized he would now have to do just that if he meant to retain any of Miss Lindsay's fickle attention.

A noisy set of the Lancers came to a stop and Lady Sally pouted as the marquess stepped forward as Jean was curtsying to her partner who held her arm possessively.

The orchestra started up the strains of the waltz and he pulled Jean into his arms, holding her closer than the proprieties allowed. The proximity was too much for both of them and they began to stumble and fall over each other's feet. "I must be fatigued," said the marquess, gallantly taking all the blame. "Let us go into the supper room ahead of the others."

"What for?" asked Miss Lindsay. "To eat rock-hard jelly and hundred-year-old rout cakes?"

"My own chef, I assure you," he said soothingly, leading her out of the ballroom.

He guided her to a table for two in a corner over by the window and told the footman to bring them a selection from the buffet. The footman was Henry and Jean blushed in an agony of embarrassment and wrapped her legs tightly around the leg of the table. Raising her eyes to the marquess's face, she encountered such a blazing look of passion that she blushed again and dropped her eyes to her plate.

Then as Henry arrived and was arranging the selection of food before them, Jean felt the marquess's hand under the table, stroking her thigh. How she contained herself until Henry left, she never knew, but no sooner had he departed than she gave the offending hand a stinging slap with her fan.

"Why so missish all of a sudden," drawled the marquess. "You take delightful liberties with my person, my sweet, and I will take delightful liberties with yours."

Jean stared at him with her mouth open.

"Good God, girl! Don't you know what you are doing."

In sudden confusion, Jean realized that, instead of wrapping her legs tightly around the table leg, she had wound them around a muscular one encased in a Greek sandal.

"Oh, my lord. Indeed I am sorry!" said Jean. "I thought you were the table leg."

The marquess's eyes flashed anger and then his sense of humor saved him. He roared with laughter. "My dear delight. What will you think of next? Shall we start all over again as if we had just met? There are a few things

100

in our acquaintanceship I would like to forget." He stroked his nose. "For example, you have a very punishing left."

Gray eyes met green in perfect understanding. For a few glorious seconds, the ballroom went away as they sat perfectly still at the enchanted island of the corner table.

Then the moment was shattered rudely as the Spirit of Liberty pulled up a chair and plumped herself down at the table.

The marquess groaned inwardly. Lady Frank was obviously in her cups and in that glorious state where she fancied herself a regular buck. Lounging back in her chair with her legs stretched out in front of her, Lady Frank slapped each of them heartily on the back in turn.

"Well, an' if you both ain't smellin' of April and May," roared Lady Frank with the devastating perception of the very drunk. "But have a care . . . have a care!" She wagged her finger roguishly in Jean's face. "This young bucko breaks hearts for breakfast."

Lady Frank pushed back her hideous purple turban from her sweating forehead and knocked back a bumper of champagne as if it were water. "Hey, John! 'Member the time you was up from Oxford with Freddie and there was that very grand Lady Whassername stayin'. Big, high-nosed woman. Very grand. Anyway, she wasn't too grand to creep into your bedchamber at night, hey John?" She nudged the marquess in the ribs. "Then her husband comes gallumphin' along and catches the pair of you, and Freddie and me was laughin' fit to bust and wonderin' if the old boy would call you out."

Memories of Lady Cynthia flooded into Jean's mind. So the marquess not only consorted with beauties but was evidently not averse to philandering with ladies who looked like brood mares.

Under cover of Lady Frank's hoots of laughter, she cast a piteous look at the marquess.

The marquess was savagely regretting that one could not challenge ladies to a duel or land them a facer or do any one of a hundred things that would shut Frank up.

"If you have finished with your tales of my misspent youth, Frank," he said icily, "you might spare a moment for your duties as a hostess. Your butler is about to pass out."

"What!" Lady Frank sprang to her feet and then tottered back to support herself on the table. "Where?"

The marquess languidly pointed his quizzing glass in the direction of Muggles, the butler, who was sitting at the end of the buffet, his head lolling toward a nearly empty decanter of madeira.

"Muggles, c'mere, Muggles," roared Lady Frank. Muggles started to his feet in alarm and tried to approach Lady Frank, who was trying to approach him. Both took three steps forward and two back until they finally met in the middle of the room, advancing and retreating as if performing the steps of the minuet.

Jean looked coldly at the marquess who was doubled up with laughter at the spectacle. She must have been out of her mind to consider even for a minute, tying herself up for life to this rake. Probably his proposal of marriage had been all a hum and he had only been using it to lead her virginal steps into an affair. After all, he had not approached Lady Harriet or Uncle Hamish for her hand.

Suddenly noticing her expression, the marquess stopped laughing. "Come, Jean. You are not going to get upset over the follies of my youth."

"It's not the follies of your youth I'm worried about. 'Tis the follies of your middle age," said Jean coldly. "Take me back to the ballroom. I am beginning to miss the fun of dancing with people of my own age."

"Why must you always go into such a huff over

trivialities," said the marquess furiously, beginning to feel all of his thirty years.

Concerned over Jean's future behavior as the Marchioness of Fleetwater and having drunk a little more than was good for him, he began to deliver himself of a very stuffy lecture on how a lady should comport herself at all times, only to be interrupted in the middle of it by a loud "Fiddlesticks!" as Miss Jean Lindsay got to her feet and marched off to the ballroom, leaving him feeling extremely foolish.

Jean was accosted at the door of the ballroom by Lord Ian who requested a dance. "I have promised the next dance to Lord Fleetwater," said Jean mendaciously, in order to get out of dancing with Lord Ian, who she was beginning to dislike.

Lord Ian moved away from the ballroom with a satisfied smirk on his face, and, as he heard the band strike up a lively Cotillion, he spied Henry standing on duty in the hall, staring vacantly into space, his hands behind his back.

Moving up behind the footman, Lord Ian whispered, "Would you like to make a guinea for a few minutes' work. No, don't turn around."

Henry nodded vigorously. A hand slid a note into his followed by a guinea. "Then give this note to the lady who is dancing with the Marquess of Fleetwater when the Cotillion has ended. Make sure no one sees you."

Henry clutched the note and nodded again. After a few minutes he turned around but whoever had spoken to him could be any one of the slightly tipsy young bloods who were crossing and recrossing the hall between the card room and the dance.

The footman waited twenty-five minutes until he judged the dance would be nearly over and stepped into the ballroom. The marquess was performing the steps of the dance with Lady Sally, watched by an admiring audience of dowagers. They were undoubtedly the handsomest couple Society had seen for a long time.

As Lady Sally made her curtsy, the marquess had his arm seized by Lady Frank, anxious to pour her tale of the butler's iniquities into a sympathetic ear. Henry slid the note into Lady Sally's hand.

Lady Sally took the note to the seclusion of a corner behind some potted palms and opened it.

"Dear Lady," she read. "I can wait no longer to declare my passion for you. Meet me at the ruin in the gardens at eleven o'clock, I beg you. Yrs. Fleetwater."

She had triumphed after all. Lady Sally noticed that it was already quarter to the hour and hurried to her rooms to fetch a warm cloak.

The marquess had finally got rid of Lady Frank and was searching the ballroom for Jean when Hamish caught him by the elbow. "My lord, a word in private with you."

"What about?" asked the marquess suspiciously.

"Well, my lord," cringed Hamish. "I have been speculating upon 'Change and would have your opinion on some West Indian stocks."

"Can't it wait till tomorrow?" said the marquess, his gray eyes raking the room for the sight of a Georgian figure in a black and silver dress.

"No, my lord," whispered Hamish. "I am a poor man and these financial negotiations are pressing on my mind."

"Oh, very well," sighed the marquess. If the old curmudgeon had been frittering away Jean's thousand a year on 'Change perhaps it would explain a lot. More fortunes were lost that way than at the gaming tables of St. James's. He led the way toward a private parlor.

As he was dealing briskly with stocks and bonds, he noticed the old man's eyes constantly straying to the clock, almost hugging himself with suppressed excitement.

Hurriedly the marquess threw the papers on the table.

"I insist on dealing with the rest of this matter tomorrow," he said and, throwing off Hamish's restraining arm, marched from the room.

Henry was lurking outside the door. "H'everything h'all right, my lord?"

"Yes, thank you," said the marquess. Really, the insolence of Freddie's servants was unbelievable. Something in Henry's manner gave him pause. "Why shouldn't it be all right?" he asked.

"I did like your friend said and gave your note to the young lady," leered Henry.

The marquess swore. "I wrote no note. What are you talking about, man? Wait a bit. Whatever was in the note, you read it? Right?"

Henry cringed and babbled. "I just had a peek to see I was doing the right thing and the note said you wanted to meet the lady at the ruin."

"I'll deal with you later, you insolent puppy," hissed the marquess, and brandishing his spear like Paris defending the topless towers of Ilium, he raced from the Hall and out into the night.

Henry moodily decided that he did not like the Quality. In his short time in service, he seemed to be getting blamed for things, left, right and center.

Running through the grounds, leaping over bushes, spurred on by the fear of what he would find, the marquess sped toward the ruin which stood on a hillock lit by the faint rays of a quarter moon.

He could just make out a small, hooded figure in a long cloak and then a taller figure creeping around the corner of the ruin.

"Jean!" he called desperately. "Jean!" Lady Sally heard his shouting, turned and saw a menacing black shape looming over her and let out a terrified scream. Her hood fell back from her shoulders and her gold hair shone bravely in the moonlight. With a curse, her assailant turned and fled, leaving Lady Sally to fling herself into the marquess's arms and faint dead away.

The guests, including Jean, crowded into the Hall to see who was pounding on the door and waited impatiently as Muggles advanced and retreated until his tottering steps led him to the handle.

He flung the door wide and the company gasped as the marquess stood on the threshold with the inert body of Lady Sally in his arms.

"She has been attacked," said the marquess. "Freddie, get Lady Sally's abigail and get the servants out to search the grounds."

Sally gave a faint moan and opened her blue eyes. "It is all right. You are perfectly safe," said the marquess tenderly. Miss Jean Lindsay ground her teeth.

The party immediately began to break up. Since most of the guests were young, their parents were anxious to get them to the safety of their homes. In the bustle of departure, Lord Ian went unnoticed as he slipped back into the house. He felt a fool and his hatred of Jean Lindsay knew no bounds. Now he would look forward to killing her.

Chapter Seven

It was a gloomy group who met downstairs next day. The weather, in keeping with their mood, threw buckets of icy rain against the windows, and all the fireplaces smoked abominably.

The only happy ones were the dogs, released from the confines of the stables, who rampaged through the house, leaping affectionately on any hungover person who happened to be passing; and the servants who slopped around in their old lackadaisical manner, glad that Lady Frank's burst of housekeeping was at an end.

The gentlemen had retired to the billiard room to cool their fevered throats with Mr. J. Schweppe's soda water and to play a desultory game. That left the ladies to return to the seclusion of their rooms to review the events of the evening.

Lady Frank was suffering from a monumental hangover and monumental feelings of guilt about drinking so much champagne the night before in her condition, and having horrid imaginings about presenting her spouse with a deformed heir.

Lady Sally was angry at finding out that the romantic note did not, after all, come from the marquess. Jean was jealous of Lady Sally, Bess was jealous of her sister

Mary, who seemed about to marry first, and Miss Taylor dreamt of a quiet, retired life in a Highland cottage.

When they finally left their rooms and descended to seek the company of the gentlemen, all were elaborately dressed and coiffed and laughed and talked in high, strained, tinkling voices like brittle glass. Sally and Jean were especially affectionate to each other.

Lord Ian and Hamish sat in the latter's bedchamber and accused each other of being bungling fools.

"Her eighteenth birthday is nearly upon us," said Hamish. "Surely you can get rid of her by then."

"You mean, surely *we* can get rid of her by then," snapped Lord Ian.

"Well, *we,* then," said Hamish, scratching his shaven head. He was still in his nightshirt and his wig hung from a stand in the corner of the room. "Keep it simple next time. No secret notes and complicated assignments. Stab her in her bed, for God's sake!"

"Can't do it here. Fleetwater's getting too suspicious. Let's see what today brings."

It seemed as if the day would bring nothing but gloom and torrents of rain. Everyone began to get on everyone else's nerves and the usually amiable Lord Freddie was snappish.

"I'm sick of the whole cursed business," he confided to the marquess. "An' it's all your fault. I could be blowin' a cloud in Cribb's parlor right now 'stead of moppin' and mowin' round a lot of petticoats. I declare I'm surprised at you, John!"

"I'm surprised at myself," said the marquess ruefully. "It's only seven days to go till her birthday and my man of business has had a note from her lawyer. He should be here any day now and then the problem will be solved."

"Well, demmit, man. Get 'em all in here and make a

great, big, whoppin' announcement that she's goin' to be an heiress and if she pops off, the uncle gets it."

"I promised the lawyer fellow I would keep mum till he arrives," said the marquess. "Anyway, wouldn't you like to catch those two villains red-handed?"

"No, I wouldn't," said Freddie roundly. "I'm bored with the whole thing. And if you don't watch, the lawyer will be makin' the announcement over her dead body. It ain't like you, John. Egad, you could have had any girl you wanted. All this Gothic carryin' on is gettin' on my nerves."

"Well, I must admit, a life of celibacy doesn't suit me," remarked the marquess lazily, chalking his cue. "I might post up to town and see what's available at the opera."

"And leave me with m'sister and a passel of virgins! Be demned to you!" said Freddie wrathfully.

Jean heard the latter part of the exchange as she passed the billiard room door and went thoughtfully up to her room.

She had been taught that the way to a man's heart was through gold, a well-run household and ladylike accomplishments. The coarser aspects of the case had never been brought home to her.

Through the talk of the women in the village and overhearing servants' gossip, she had an inkling that "men have certain needs," as Miss Taylor so delicately put it. But those were things that resolved themselves, surely, in the privacy of the marital bedchamber. Jean, like many young girls of her age, had never paused to think of what matrimony involved after the altar.

In a panic, she decided she did not want to lose the marquess, rake or not. If she allowed him to escape to London and to the sophisticated charms of some opera dancer, then she felt sure all would be lost. But how to reanimate the marquess's feelings toward her. He now seemed very splendid, elegant and withdrawn. She decided to see what the day would bring, unaware that the two conspirators along the corridor had already arrived at the same conclusion.

By dinnertime, a watery sunlight had struggled through the clouds and a messenger arrived with a note for Lady Frank.

"It's from Sir Giles Mannering," said Lady Frank. "He's our magistrate for the county, y'know. Wants us all to go over there for dinner tomorrow and stay for a few days."

"Oh, do let's go," said Lady Sally. "I am affeared to go out of doors here in case I get attacked. Even though I have a strong protector." She dimpled prettily at the marquess.

"Capital idea!" seconded Freddie, his good humor returning. "Sir Giles has a cozy manor and an excellent chef."

"Then by all means let us go," said the marquess. His chef had returned to London in tears, saying he could not abide the barbaric conditions of the Blackstone kitchens any longer.

While Lady Frank scribbled off a note of acceptance, the party returned to discussions about the identity of Lady Sally's attacker.

"Probably one of these local young sprigs," said Freddie. "Forgot they were all just out of short coats and gave them too much to drink."

"Perhaps," said Lady Sally modestly, lowering her lashes. "Or could it be some unknown who is passionately in love with me and was jealous because my affections were engaged elsewhere." She looked pointedly at the marquess, who suddenly became intensely interested in the portion of overcooked mutton on his plate.

"What on earth is this, Muggles?" he demanded, poking the offending meat with his fork.

"L'agneau a l'Écossaise," said Muggles, improvising wildly.

"This lamb, as you call it, lived a full, long and athletic life and obviously died quite naturally of old age. Take it away. Honestly, Freddie, all I ever manage to eat here is the sorbet between the courses!"

"You're too fussy by half," grumbled Freddie. "If you were out in the Peninsula with those poor devils, you'd eat anything."

"But I'm not, am I?" remarked the marquess sweetly. "I am sure this would taste delightful after the field of battle but in the setting of an English manor, it's demned disgusting."

The next course was brought in.

"Charlie Roosh," intoned Muggles. A faint rancid odor rose from the creamy confection and even Freddie gave up. The ladies retired to leave the gentlemen to their wine and sat silently in the drawing room, each with her own thoughts.

Long after they heard the claret bell ringing, there seemed to be no signs of the gentlemen joining them. As sounds of louder masculine hilarity began to emerge from the dining room, the ladies began to be pleasant to each other, drawing together, united against the sounds of boorish masculinity from the next room.

Lady Sally started to play the piano loudly and enthusiastically, Bess and Mary sang duets with their arms twined around each other's waists, Lady Frank started an animated lecture on hunting to Miss Taylor and Jean sat absorbed in her thoughts.

Obviously there was a lot about men she didn't understand. The marquess, by the sound of it, seemed to be enjoying himself immensely and showed no sign of rushing to her side. She had been too cold toward him. Her mind searched through the pages of her favorite romances, looking for a solution.

After much thought, she came to a grand decision. Somehow, she would need to sacrifice her virginity if she were to keep the marquess by her side. If he did not intend marriage, then she would become a Fallen Woman. Just what being a Fallen Woman involved, she had only a shadowy idea. It was surely just like being married without the ring. She would have an establishment of her own and find her friends among the demimonde. Perhaps she could start a salon. Writers, artists, people like that were surely not too high in the instep.

The more Jean turned it over in her mind, the rosier the picture appeared. She was just laying the marquess's slippers out to warm on the hearth of their sinful and unfashionable residence, when the gentleman in question entered the room.

She blushed painfully and then blushed again as the marquess crossed to the pianoforte to join Lady Sally. Jean decided to think of a plan of action.

So did two other members of the household. Hamish and Lord Ian remained at the dining table, passing the claret back and forth and discussing the visit to Sir Giles's residence.

"That's where we'll do it," said Lord Ian, his sallow face flushed with wine. "And have done with it for once and for all."

"But how?" asked the reverend.

"We'll stay on here so as to have an alibi. During the night I'll ride over with you, and while you keep watch I'll stab the wench while she sleeps."

"Aye," retorted Hamish. "But how will we know which is her bedchamber?"

"Demme! Hadn't thought of that. Tell you what, we'll ride over during the day. It's about ten miles distant and they've all elected to stay a couple of days because of the cooking being so awful here. We'll pay a call and spy out the lay of the land and then we'll know exactly where to go.

"You tell Jean you want to see her on a private matter. She'll take you up to her rooms and take good note of the situation while you're there."

Hamish agreed and the two, feeling very pleased with each other, retired to bed to gain strength for the act of murder ahead.

The morning dawned bright and sunny, a perfect early summer's day. The Surrey woods were alive with birds and the hedgerows bright with flowers as the cheerful party made their way to the Mannering residence. Everything looked fresh and new and scrubbed clean by yesterday's rain. A warm smell of growing things rose from the meadows and great, white fleecy clouds tugged each other across the sky.

The Mannerings lived in a modern building called Oakley Manor, built in the severe classical style with two graceful wings springing out from the colonnaded central building. The rooms were spacious, sunny and pretty. Sir Giles was a thin, gray-haired man in his fifties and his wife, Lady Carol, a sprightly matron in her thirties. Both were obviously delighted to have company as their two sons were absent, one at Harrow and the other at Cambridge.

Jean settled in happily, feeling that it was the first real home she had ever stayed in, and set her mind as to how to find out the modes and manners of a Fallen Woman.

Like the dogs and horses at Blackstone Hall, she was quick to sense that under Lady Frank's gruff exterior and outrageous manners lay a kindly disposition and a heart of gold.

She accordingly headed for the stables as soon after luncheon as she could and, sure enough, there was

Frank in her inevitable riding dress, chatting with the head groom. Jean waited impatiently as they discussed the bloodlines of various horses with all the enthusiasm of the patronesses of Almack's discussing the latest debutante.

At last Lady Frank moved off with her toward the house and Jean took the plunge. "Pray, tell me, Lady Frank, what know you of Fallen Women?"

"Gawd! Why?" Lady Frank's pale blue eyes were uncomfortably shrewd.

"I just wondered," said Jean. "I was thinking of writing a novel and it's a subject I know little about."

Frank relaxed. "Oh, if that's your reason, I'll try to help but I only pick up little bits from the men.

"Well, a lot of the high flyers look just like you and me. But the lower lot wear a lot of paint and coquelicot ribbons and dye their hair. They wear patches and I believe they . . ." Frank looked around to make sure nobody was listening, "rouge their nipples!"

Jean gasped. "What on earth do they do that for?"

"Beats me," shrugged Frank. "The men seem to like it. Then they wear nothing under their dresses and damp down the muslin so pretty much everythin' underneath shows."

"But how do they behave when gentlemen are present?"

"Better ask Freddie. That's the only sort of woman he has anythin' to do with. Sometimes I think he don't like women at all. Not that he likes men, if you know what I mean . . ."

Jean obviously didn't, so Lady Frank glossed over it and racked her brains for further tidbits.

"Y'are askin' me as if I was in the habit of trottin' in and out brothels in Covent Garden. Anyway, they drink a lot and shriek and flirt and ogle. They sits themselves down on the gentlemen's laps and gets them to drink champagne out of their slippers and things like that."

"Oh, dear," sighed Jean. "It sounds like an awful lot of hard work."

"They get their reward," said Frank dryly. "Anyways, what you worried about? Ain't thinkin' of bein' a Fallen Woman, are you?"

And slapping Jean heartily on the back and roaring with laughter, she went off into the house, leaving Miss Lindsay with a lot to think about.

The domestic picture of warming the marquess's slippers fled before the speculation of what it would be like to warm the marquess's bed.

Her mind shied from the unknown and began instead to weave romantic pictures of them dancing together, laughing together and dining together. The marquess would smile across the dining table in Maida Vale or whatever London suburb was suitable for mistresses. "This meal, cooked by your fair hands, rivals that of the French chef at Carlton House," the marquess would say, laughing gaily.

"Quiet, my dear." She would lay her fingers on his lips. "You will wake our little children."

"Yes, how are the little bastards?" inquired the dream marquess pleasantly.

Jean pulled herself out of her dream. Reality kept creeping more and more into her fantasies these days. No children. Back to the dining table.

"This wine is excellent, my love."

"I am glad the claret is to your liking," said Jean.

"Haven't tried the claret today," said a puzzled voice at her elbow as the real marquess made his appearance. "You ladies been down to the cellars on the sly?"

Jean blushed in denial. The marquess was impeccably dressed as usual and seemed very formidable. She was going to require all her courage to make the first move and choose the correct time and place.

That evening, Sir Giles had invited a trio of local

musicians to entertain the party and when everyone seemed to be engaged in dancing or singing or chatting, Jean sat down next to Lord Freddie on a sofa in the corner.

"I was speaking to your sister earlier about Fallen Women," said Jean, under cover of the noise.

Freddie was slightly foxed or "well to go," as he would have put it, and at first did not think he had heard aright. "Did you say Fallen Women?"

Jean nodded.

"Frank startin' up a charity or what?"

"No. I was thinking of writing a novel and I wanted some information."

"Nice gels don't write novels," said Freddie roundly.

"Oh, yes they do," said Jean earnestly. "Mrs. Edgeworth does, for example. And she is considered to be all that is respectable."

Not having read any of the works of Mrs. Edgeworth or even heard of the woman, Freddie eyed Jean doubtfully.

"For example," pursued Jean. "Do men drink champagne from their slippers?"

"Dashed if I know," said Freddie unhelpfully. "Sounds like a crack-brained thing to me. Got perfectly good things with holes in the top to drink out of, even in the lowest taverns, you know."

Jean's face fell with disappointment. "Do you think you could drink some champagne from my slipper just to see what it feels like?"

"*What!*" screamed Freddie, rolling his eyes around the room for help.

"Oh, go *on,* Freddie," begged Jean. "Nobody's looking."

Freddie sighed. "I ain't drinkin' champagne. I'm drinkin' claret."

"That will do just as well. *Please.*"

116

"Oh, all right," said Freddie huffily. "Hand it over."

Jean slipped off her white satin slipper and handed it to him. He looked at it doubtfully and picked up the decanter. "Well, here goes!"

He poured the claret into the slipper and tried to lift it to his mouth. The wine soaked into the fabric like a sponge and poured down onto his impeccable buckskins.

Freddie jumped to his feet with an oath and brought the attention of the whole room around to them.

"You foxed, Freddie?" asked his sister.

"I think the young gentleman was trying to drink his wine from the lady's slipper," said Sir Giles, with his eyes twinkling.

"It's not my fault," said poor Freddie, hurriedly handing Jean her sopping slipper. "Miss Jean begged me to do it. Wanted to feel like a Fallen Woman. Should have asked you, John. You know more about the breed than any of us."

The marquess sighed. "Never has my misspent youth been cast up to me as much as it has been in these past few days. But yes, Miss Lindsay, I will be pleased to give you the benefit of my extensive knowledge of that subject."

The ladies laughed and Jean, feeling very young and stupid, picked up her ruined slipper and left the room to change.

For the rest of the evening, Freddie darted away like a startled fawn when he saw her coming. Obviously that source of knowledge had dried up and Jean did not want to hear the marquess discussing any woman other than herself.

The party agreed to drive to the nearest town of Barminster on the following day on a shopping expedition, so Jean determined to keep her eyes open for any Fallen Women at the wayside whom she could study.

Barminster was a bustling market town, boasting some

excellent shops, a cathedral dating back to Norman times, and an excellent hostelry to which the party repaired before going their various ways.

The gentlemen went to look at the cattle market and the ladies, with the exception of Jean, departed to look at the cathedral. Jean got rid of her maid on some pretext and ventured into the shopping center to make some private purchases of her own.

They had arranged to meet in the coffee room of the White Hart at five o'clock but Jean found she was half an hour early and decided to wait for them.

There was a couple seated in the coffee room when Jean made her entrance, an elderly gentleman with his hair powdered and tied back with a black ribbon, a pepper and salt frock coat, knee breeches and gaiters. But it was his younger companion who drew Jean's fascinated gaze.

Her olive complexion showed that her blond hair owed all to art and nothing to nature. An enormous black patch representing a carriage and pair was placed at the side of a luridly painted mouth. The blacking on her eyelashes was so thick that they stuck out like a forest of spears and the décolletage of her purple-and-white-striped dress plunged to the point of indecency.

She was shrieking with laughter and making great play with her fan. Could it be? But of course! This was the Fallen Woman Jean had been searching for.

When the gentleman left the room for a moment, Jean moved forward and timidly introduced herself. The lady seemed to give her a somewhat haughty glare but Jean's curiosity knew no bounds. In faltering sentences and blushing hotly, she whispered in the lady's ear what she wanted to know.

The dame looked at her as if she could hardly believe her ears, then threw back her head and screamed before going into convulsions. Her companion came running

118

in accompanied by a younger man and the marquess and the rest of his party followed hard at their heels.

After sal volatile had been administered to the distressed lady and she had ceased drumming her heels on the floor and hiccupping, she turned to her companion.

"I have just been sore insulted, Silas," she howled. "This chit has just called me a whore to my face."

"I'm sure it was an understandable mistake," started the marquess and then could have bitten off his tongue. Before he had time to apologize, the younger man had taken off his glove and slapped the marquess hard across the face.

"Name your seconds, sir! I demand satisfaction for the insult to my mother."

The marquess drew himself up to his haughtiest. "My name is Fleetwater and I do not duel with yokels."

The young man presented his card. "My name is Jack Cartwright, my lord. My father there, Sir Silas Cartwright, is mayor of this town and the lady you have just so crudely insulted is his wife, Lady Emma."

The marquess sighed. "Freddie, Harry . . . will you act for me?" The couple of young men nodded gloomily. "Then I shall escort the ladies home and leave you to make the arrangements."

Jean's apologies and protestations were cut short as he dragged her from the room. The marquess was in the worst rage he had ever been in his life.

On reaching Oakley Manor, Jean rushed to her rooms and cried and cried. She had often dreamed of being the cause of a duel but never in such a ridiculous way as this.

Downstairs, the gentlemen were surly and depressed and the ladies, Bess, Mary and Sally, were in a state of suppressed glee. How that little Scotch upstart had ruined her chances! The marquess would surely now have such a distaste of her that he would not even be able to look at her.

In this, surprisingly, they were wrong. The marquess blamed himself as much as Jean. Had it not been for his ill-considered remark, the whole thing could have been explained away as a piece of young girl's nonsense.

He was not frightened for his own safety since he was an excellent swordsman but if word of the duel should get to the ears of the Runners, he would have to flee the country.

He had fought duels twice before in his early youth, both over females of dazzling beauty, but never did he think he would be obliged to fight because he had be-smirched the honor of a raddled tart.

Freddie and Harry Fairchild had informed him that the duel was arranged for six in the morning in Barnes Field, just outside the outskirts of the town. Jean did not put in an appearance and they all retired early to bed.

Miss Taylor, after several futile attemps to speak to Jean, retired to her own room to pen a letter to the Duchess of Glenrandall.

Jean tossed and turned in agonies of remorse. What if Jack Cartwright were the finer swordsman? He was a younger man than the marquess.

In one of Jean's favorite romances, the heroine had stopped the duel by throwing herself on her lover's adversary's sword. Forgetting that the heroine had sub-sequently died and had taken three chapters to do it in, Jean sprang to her feet. She would save the marquess's life if need be.

At five in the morning, wrapped in a long cloak, Jean crept from the house by the servants' entrance and started to walk the three miles to Barnes Field.

She found a comfortable position in a dry ditch which ran around the edge of the field and settling herself down, she peered through a gap in the bushes and waited for the arrival of the duelists. The first rays of the sun struck through the tall poplars at the far end of the field, sending their long shadows over the grass. The buttercups turned their petals toward the warmth and in a short time, the field seemed to be a blaze of gold interspersed with the blood red of poppies.

Blood! Jean forced her drooping eyelids open and stared wildly around.

No one had arrived yet. The sun's rays grew warmer and Jean battled ineffectually against the effects of a sleepless night.

As the sound of the first carriage wheels was heard in the distance, Miss Jean Lindsay fell sound asleep.

Both participants arrived at the same time. The marquess and his seconds had had to creep quietly from the manor so as not to wake the magistrate and his wife. Sir Giles would have taken a dim view of the proceedings. The opposing parties stood at either end of the field in the glory of a summer's morning and waited for the surgeon to arrive. A lark burst from the grass and soared up to the heavens, its clear song sounding worlds away in space and time from the petty quarrels of men.

At last, they saw a sedan approaching at a leisurely pace being carried by two superannuated chairmen. The elderly surgeon tottered forth as the sedan was set down, slightly the worse for liquor.

"Is that all you could get?" the marquess asked Freddie in disgust.

Freddie nodded. "Dueling ain't fashionable, you know. Ain't the eighteenth century."

Both men shrugged off their jackets and drew off their boots. Freddie and Harry, together with Jack Cartwright's seconds, examined the rapiers and prayed that neither combatant would get seriously wounded and demand the services of the tipsy surgeon.

The marquess and Jack Cartwright took up their positions and then plunged into battle with more finesse than ardor. Both were first-class swordsmen and both did not consider the lady they were fighting over worth the battle now that the clear light of dawn had cooled their tempers.

Jack Cartwright had long been ashamed of his mother's mode of dress and only hoped that this duel would be the means of sobering it. Each realized quickly that their swordsmanship was more at stake than their lives and settled down to enjoy the contest.

The marquess parried, feinted and thrust with a will but, brilliant as he was, found himself several times hard pressed. Mr. Cartwright was small and wiry but the marquess had the advantage of a longer reach. After fifteen minutes, when both were beginning to breathe heavily and sweat freely, the marquess saw his opportunity. He feinted expertly, slid under Mr. Cartwright's guard and pinked him neatly on the shoulder.

"Enough!" he cried, putting up his sword.

"By Jove," exclaimed Jack Cartwright, rushing forward to seize the marquess's hand. "Capital swordsmanship! Capital!"

"You're a master of the art yourself, sir," said the marquess smiling. "Please accept my humble apologies for the insult to your mother."

"Gladly," said Mr. Cartwright happily. "Always telling her she dresses like a tart."

"Damn all women!" cried the marquess. "Let's repair to the White Hart and celebrate."

And with their arms around each other's shoulders, the two men left the field in high good humor.

As the carriages rattled away in the distance, a herdsman, leading his cows out to pasture, spied the still figure asleep in the ditch.

"I urrent going to touch that," he muttered to himself. " 'Er might be dead. I'll tell magistrate. 'Er looks right dead."

After he had seen his cattle safely into the field and shut the gate, he hurried off to the Manor.

When Muggles burst into the breakfast room with the information that a young lady of Miss Lindsay's description was lying dead in a ditch at Barnes Field, the house party started to their feet.

Sir Giles called for his horse and sped off. The young ladies shrieked with delighted dismay, Miss Taylor had hysterics for the first time in her placid, well-regulated life, and the only one to appear genuinely upset, since the gentlemen were absent, was Lady Frank. She was fond of Jean and, after fidgeting nervously for a few minutes, ran to the stables, her swollen stomach bouncing in front of her, calling for her horse. "The old tart's probably run her through with a hat pin," she muttered anxiously.

Sir Giles arrived on the scene first and breathed a heartfelt sigh of relief when he realized the girl was asleep and unharmed. He woke her gently, shaking her by the shoulder.

Jean jumped to her feet and looked around wildly. "Is he dead? Is he hurt?" she cried.

"Who?" asked Sir Giles.

"She's been dreamin', ain't you?" said Lady Frank who had arrived on the scene and transfixed Jean with a warning glare.

"Ye-es," stammered Jean, remembering in time that Sir Giles must not know of the duel. Her eyes ranged frantically over the meadow looking for signs of bloodshed and found none.

Sir Giles helped her up onto his horse. "What on earth were you doing there?"

Jean looked wildly at Lady Frank for help but Frank was staring between her horse's ears into the middle distance.

"I . . . I couldn't sleep," stuttered Jean. "So I decided to go for a walk and I must just have fallen asleep."

Sir Giles took a deep breath and gave that young lady a blistering lecture on the evils of footpads, highwaymen and even young bloods. Really, he thought to himself, he had discounted Freddie's occasional remarks about Jean's being not altogether in the head as pure misogyny, but it certainly seemed as if the child were slightly weird.

Jean was silent. All she could think of was, "Is he dead? Why am I always in disgrace? Is he dead?"

When they arrived at the Manor, there was the marquess waiting for them, large as life and twice as elegant, only a hectic gleam in his eye and a heavy drooping of the lids indicating that he had celebrated over-heavily and over-early.

It was quite obvious from his manner that he had surmised that Jean had gone out to watch the duel and so had not worried in the slightest. So instead of casting herself into his arms with heartfelt gratitude, she moved past him with her head averted and went into the breakfast room to enjoy her solitary meal.

Hamish and Lord Ian rode over at noon and invited themselves to lunch. Jean looked across the table and caught her uncle staring at her and hurriedly glanced away.

Why, she thought, I believe he hates me. Hates me enough to murder me!

It was the first time she had spent away from Hamish in the settled routine of a normal, happy home. Now in the charming setting, the old man seemed an evil, twisted thing, something out of the Middle Ages, something from an older, darker time of lawlessness. Instead of an irascible old fool, perpetually carping and complaining, he suddenly seemed to Jean to be something more and someone to be reckoned with. Could he be responsible for the attacks on her life? If so, why? Gold was all the old man cared about and all he might kill for, and she had none of that, her small store of guineas being already greatly depleted.

Lord Ian noticed the exchange of glances and gave Hamish a warning kick. "Jean, my dear," said the minister, "I came over especially to have a wee chat with you. Perhaps we could retire to your rooms after lunch?"

The marquess, who was pouring madeira on the top of the champagne he had had for breakfast, frowned and put down his glass. He had better sober up if he meant to keep a guard on Jean.

As the minister and his niece entered her private sitting room on the second floor, the marquess crept to the door and placed his ear to the panel, ready to rush to the rescue at the first sign of attack.

But the minister's "wee chat" turned out to be a long and lengthy sermon on how Jean was ill-prepared for the afterlife with all this frivolity and that she should start thinking of her immortal soul.

"Really, Uncle Hamish," teased Jean. "Anyone would think you meant to dispatch me to Heaven as soon as possible, the way you go on."

"Show respect! Show respect!" spluttered Hamish. "Or when we get back to Dunwearie, I'll take the rod to your back."

Jean winced at the memory of previous occasions when the old man had beaten her and strengthened her resolve to attach herself to the marquess's protection any way she could.

When he heard Hamish rising to leave, the marquess darted down the stairs and into the safety of the library. Now, what was the point of all that, he wondered. He shrugged mentally. Probably pangs of Calvinistic conscience.

He watched until he saw the minister ride off with Lord Ian and went in search of Jean.

"We have both had an exciting morning, Miss Lindsay,"

he said. "Perhaps you would care to walk with me in the conservatory?"

"Gladly," said Jean, taking his arm. "I had better wake Miss Taylor from her nap and tell her."

"Let her sleep," said the marquess. "You do not need a chaperone. Lady Carol is awake and about somewhere. You are not afraid to be alone with me?"

"No-o," said Jean, eyeing him doubtfully. He was as impeccable as ever in a coat of blue superfine, striped waistcoat and tight-fitting buckskins. His Hessians shone like glass; his cravat was spotless. But Miss Lindsay could not help but feel that there was a decidedly raffish air about him.

She took his arm and they walked sedately down the stairs and through the silent, summer rooms to the conservatory. Everyone else seemed to be abed for an afternoon nap, thought Jean, except for herself and the marquess.

The marquess ushered Jean into the conservatory and slammed the door behind them, leaning his broad shoulders against it.

"What a lot of plants," said Jean nervously.

"Yes, there are, aren't there. Come here to me."

"What!" said Jean, starting, and taking several steps away from him.

"I said, 'Come here,' " said the marquess with a wicked gleam in his eye. "You said you wanted to know how Fallen Women go on and I, my dear Miss Lindsay, am about to instruct you."

Jean eyed him dubiously. It was one thing to dream about being a Fallen Woman, another to take the necessary step.

"Couldn't we leave it till later. We both have had an exhausting day," said Jean timidly.

"Not as exhausting as we're about to have, I hope," said the marquess taking an unsteady step toward her.

He was feeling the enervating effects of having fought a duel, not to mention the effects of a mixture of madeira and champagne, and, in some obscure way, he felt he deserved a reward.

Jean took two steps toward him and stood with her hands at her sides and her eyes screwed shut. Courage! she admonished herself. It's now or never.

"Come now. You are not about to have a tooth extracted," said the marquess, taking her hand and leading her over to a marble bench.

He drew Jean onto his lap and started to kiss her ruthlessly, his hands caressing her slim body and his senses reeling with passion and alcohol. How far they would have gone, they never would know, for with a crash the door swung open and Lady Frank stood on the threshold, her eyes like pieces of ice.

"To your room, Miss Lindsay," she snapped. "Fleetwater! A word with you."

She stood aside as Jean hurried past her with her head bowed. Then she turned to the marquess.

"Since no one else seems to have an eye to that gel's future or morals, it had better be me," said Frank. "Although we're at the Mannerings, she's still my guest, you know. So just what are your intentions, Fleetwater?"

The marquess, his thin face flushed, rose somewhat unsteadily to his feet. "Well, look now, Frank, I mean to marry the girl. If only she would learn how to comport herself properly."

"Well, she ain't goin' to learn it from you by the looks of things," said Frank roundly. "You know what I think?"

"I don't and I would rather not," said the marquess pettishly, getting up to leave.

"I think," pursued Frank regardless, "that if her bloodline weren't as good as it is, you'd seduce her. You feel then you must marry her but what holds you back is you're ashamed of her!

"So hark on, Fleetwater, she may tumble into more scrapes than most young girls but that's because of her awful upbringing with that dismal old miser. There's nothin' up with that gel that a secure home and a bit of genuine love wouldn't cure. I said 'love,' mind you. Not a tumble in the hay.

"Fact is, Fleetwater, you're a demned snob and always have been. Likable chap but spoiled rotten with all these toadies you've been consortin' with. Should have heard yourself the other day at the White Hart. 'My name is Fleetwater and I do not duel with yokels.' Faugh!

"So while Jean Lindsay is my guest, you will observe the proprieties at all times until you get to the altar."

With that, Lady Frank departed, leaving the marquess to curse the plants and tell that uninterested audience what a cursed lot of complicated, devilish puzzles women were.

But Lady Frank's barbs had struck home. He felt like an utter fool. With a groan, he headed to his bedchamber to put his uneasy conscience to sleep.

Meanwhile, Jean walked in the gardens, prey to a jumble of emotions. She was glad Lady Frank appeared when she did. Or was she? Things had been getting quite exciting and interesting before she was interrupted. What I need is a mother, thought Jean sadly. Someone to prompt the marquess to propose. Not a horrible, old uncle who would probably rejoice in her downfall.

Unaware that ten miles distant her uncle was plotting her death, she returned to the house.

Hamish was busy sketching out a plan of Jean's rooms for Lord Ian. "They mean to stay another two days. Let's make it for, say, tomorrow night."

"Done," said Lord Ian. "There is a play being performed in Barminster. We'll show ourselves there to establish an alibi for part of the evening at least."

"There is a wrought iron balcony at her window which

is on the second floor," said Hamish. "It should be an easy matter to climb up."

"I am not one of those muscle-bound Corinthians like Fleetwater," pointed out Lord Ian languidly.

"Aye," agreed Hamish sourly. "And you'd better find yourself a suitable pair of breeches instead of these canary yellow Inexpressibles you've got on.

"Speed is of the essence," the old man went on. "We will return late from the theater to the Manor, pretending to have drunk too much wine. . . ."

"Make sure you *are* pretending, for once," interrupted Lord Ian with a sneer.

"As I was trying to say . . . we'll look as if we are in our cups and send all the servants off to bed. That will give us a bit more of an alibi. Even if Fleetwater suspects anything, he will have no proof."

At that moment, the Marquess of Fleetwater had awakened from his afternoon nap and was lying, staring sightlessly at the canopy of his four-poster. Frank was wrong, he decided. He was not a snob. Certainly, it was wrong of him to try to go so far with the girl but that was not because of her lack of social standing. After all, thought the marquess, he was an easygoing fellow. But Frank could not expect him to go around hobnobbing with every yokel he came across. However, the barb still rankled. He decided to try it out on Freddie.

Accordingly, when the ladies had retired after dinner and he was left with Sir Giles, Freddie and Mr. Harry Fairchild, the marquess put down his glass, and fixing Freddie with an intense gaze, said, "Freddie, I'd like to tell you something."

"Go on, old man," said Freddie goodnaturedly.

The marquess took a deep breath. "Freddie, you're a snob."

"I know," said Freddie, calmly refilling his glass.

"And doesn't it bother you?"

"Demme, why should it?" asked Freddie practically. "We all are, dear boy. It's the way of the world. Why do all us old bachelors trot up for the Season? 'Cos we belong to the elite—the gilded few, an' what, by the deuce, is the demned point of belongin' to the gilded few if we can't rub some upstart's face in it, heh?"

"I'm beginning to find the whole charade of the London Season pointless and hollow," said the marquess, drooping his heavy eyelids in a world-weary manner.

" 'Course you do!" said Freddie happily. "Get that way m'self when m'liver's on the turn. So back to the jolly old estates where everyone scrapes and bows even more and the yokels tug their forelocks. An' we say to ourselves, 'What ho! The simple life of the country and all that rot.'

"Fact is, dear boy, we're stuck with it. 'Cos the world is full of snobs an' if you so much as try to be equal with everybody, 'fore you know it, your house is packed with demned upstarts and Cits and shopkeepers from the cellars to the attics, all fawnin' like mad. So where are you?"

"Halfway down the decanter," said the marquess gloomily.

Sir Giles coughed. "If you won't object to the advice of an older man, I think you will find you are doing your duty if you are a good landlord. And a gentleman is never patronizing, you know."

"In that case," said Freddie blithely, "there ain't a lot of gentlemen around. Stop hoggin' the decanter, Fleetwater."

Mr. Fairchild delivered himself of a few choked mumbles.

"Harry says you're beginnin' to sound like a Frenchie. Cheer up, Harry, it's just the ladies gettin' John down. He ain't goin' to march you to the lantern yet."

Meanwhile, the air in the drawing room was electric.

Lady Mary announced that she and Mr. Fairchild had "an understanding" and that the happy couple were traveling to London in the morning to obtain the Duchess of Glenrandall's consent to the marriage. Bess was quite frankly in the sulks and blamed her spinsterish state on the visit to the Blackstones and on Jean in particular. Lady Sally had an uneasy feeling that the marquess was slipping from her grasp and Jean was no longer sure of her feelings in that quarter.

At times—especially times like the one in the conservatory—she felt like throwing away a lifetime's Calvinistic training and becoming his mistress. At others, she resented the feelings of jealousy, rage and unhappiness he arose in her and longed to escape and start all over again.

If only she were rich, then she could take her sorrows abroad. She would sit in some elegant piazza, sipping her wine, aware of the speculative glances and comments from the Cosmopolitan set. "Egad, who is that beautiful woman who is always alone? Methinks she nurses some dark, secret sorrow," some devastatingly handsome man would mutter as he came to sit beside her and try to woo her troubles away. The handsome man would have hair as dark as night and sapphire blue eyes. No—he would have chestnut hair and laughing brown eyes . . . he would have cold, gray eyes and blond hair, Jean decided wearily, wondering if she would ever banish the marquess from her thoughts.

By the time the gentlemen joined them, Bess had decided to leave for London with the happy couple in the morning and Lady Frank was enthusiastically arranging an outing for the rest to the River Barnes.

Jean was heartily glad that Bess was leaving. Romance had mellowed Mary so much that she had become a happy, lighthearted girl. But Bess was still so full of venom and jealousy that she had made Jean's stay in the pleasant Oakley Manor most uncomfortable, making spiteful remarks and watching her as closely as a cat watches a mouse.

Bess insisted that Miss Taylor accompany her on the journey despite that good lady's protests that the Duchess of Glenrandall had employed her to be a companion to Jean.

Chapter Eight

The diminished house party met in the hall in the morning, preparatory to their outing, in high spirits. Sir Giles and Lady Carol had elected to stay behind since they had other duties to attend to and, with Bess's oppressive personality removed, it was with a feeling of holiday that they set off. Even the fact that Lady Frank insisted Jean accompany herself and her brother in their carriage, leaving the marquess and Lady Sally to ride together, could not dampen Jean's spirits. No Bess to mar the day with her malicious barbs, no Miss Taylor with her anxious looks of sorrowful concern, no Lord Ian and, above all, no Uncle Hamish.

As the carriage swept out of the drive past huge banks of rhododendron at the lodge gates and out onto the country road, Jean felt, for the first time in her life, as if she were on holiday. Frank was a jolly companion, the countryside was alive with birdsong, lilacs, may blossom, early roses rioted in the hedgerows and the sun blazed down from a cloudless sky.

For his part, the marquess was preoccupied, much to the annoyance of Lady Sally. He decided that his treatment of Jean Lindsay had been shameful. He would treat her with kindness and courtesy and find a suitable opportunity to propose to the girl and have done with it. If only she weren't so damned incalculable. What if she refused?

Well, if she did, he would settle down with a young female of impeccable birth and beget heirs. He was getting too old for all this useless merrymaking.

The River Barnes, swollen by the recent rain, was in full spate. It hurtled through the placid meadows, foaming and sparkling like beer in the morning sun, sweeping the long branches of the weeping willows along with it as if it would pull them down into the water and carry them off to the sea.

They settled on a pleasant grassy spot next to a pile of huge boulders and under the shade of a stand of alders. The party sprawled around on the grass, watching the servants from the Manor setting up the picnic table and chairs and opening the hampers.

Jean settled back against the sunny warmth of a large boulder and, in her mind, the grim memories of Dunwearie, the London Season, and the attempts on her life dwindled away, leaving only the delicious peace of the present. The glossy leaves above her rippled, turned and shone in the light breeze and a thrush poured out the full-throated glory of his summer song to a comforting if mundane accompaniment of clinking glasses and dishes.

Her reverie was interrupted by Sally's tinkling voice. "John, dear. Could you escort me a little way along the stream. It's so magnificent, I would like to get a closer look but I am afraid of falling in and I need the strong arm of my protector."

"With pleasure." The marquess got lazily to his feet and offered his arm. Lady Sally was wearing a filmy dress in rose-colored muslin, embroidered with tiny rosebuds, which the breeze whipped around her body, displaying her excellent figure and leaving little to the imagination.

"I declare I don't know what's come over young gels these days," said Frank, getting to her feet and gazing after the couple. "She ain't even got a camisole on an' it's Carlton House to a Charlie's shelter, she's wearin' one of them new scanty petticoats and little else!"

Jean's new blue silk suddenly felt as heavy as serge. How could she compete with Sally, who had all the ease of great wealth and a title. It was "dear John" this and "dear John" that.

Frank glanced at Jean's downcast face out of the corner of her eye. "Shake a leg, Freddie," she said, stirring up her brother with her foot. "Walk with Jean for a bit and keep an eye on Sally. If she don't get raped by Fleetwater, she'll catch her death of cold in that rig. Here! Throw a shawl over her."

Grumbling, Freddie got to his feet, clutching the shawl and then, remembering his manners, offered Jean his arm and led her along the river bank toward where the marquess and Lady Sally could be seen walking in the distance.

Freddie looked down at the sad little face next to him and tried to think of something to say. "Lovely day, what?"

"Lovely," said Jean dully.

"Hear all those birds? Used to imitate them when I was a boy. I say, would you like to hear some?"

As she nodded, he let out a long screech like a barn door being opened.

"Now, what's that?"

"An owl."

"An owl! That was a rook, clear as anythin'. Hey, you ain't very good, are you? Try this one." He delivered himself of a long, dreary, wailing sound.

"A lesser-crested grebe with its foot stuck under a rock," said Jean acidly.

"No, no. A curlew. Plain as day. No need to be sarcastic, you know. Here's another." Freddie cackled loudly.

"I haven't the faintest idea."

"It's an easy one. Here, I'll do it again." Exquisite in faultless morning dress and gleaming Hessians, his curls combed carefully into fashionable disorder, Freddie stood up on a boulder and cackled happily, flapping his arms up and down.

Jean began to giggle. "It's a duck in a fit."

"No, don't be funny. This is a good 'un. Look, this is its wings." He spread Sally's lace shawl wide over his shoulders and went into even more frantic antics until Jean, with the tears of laughter rolling down her cheeks, begged him to stop.

"All right, Freddie," she gasped. "I give up. What is it?"

"It's Freddie Blackstone's cure for gettin' Jean Lindsay out of the dumps," he grinned, jumping down from the rock.

"Oh, Freddie. You and Lady Frank are so kind to me!"

"Yes, ain't we just," said Freddie amiably, "and mopin' after a certain gentleman is bad for your looks.

"Tell you what—we'll throw this demned shawl over Sally—m'sister's right, you know. Her mama would have a fit if she saw her in that dress, and we'll go off and explore. Everythin's too serious around here lately."

As Jean happily agreed, he hurried her along the bank

135

to where the couple stood engaged in conversation. Lady Sally stood with her hand resting on the marquess's arm. In her clear, bell-like voice, she was outlining her plans for the future, how many children she would like to have and the type of establishment she would like to set up. She was rudely interrupted by the arrival of Freddie who threw the shawl around her and said irrepressibly, "Frank says you'll catch cold in them scanties," and turned to lead Jean away.

"Wait a minute, Freddie," said the marquess. "Lady Sally was giving me her views on the running of an establishment and, as I know it's a subject close to your heart, perhaps you would like to hear her views while I escort Miss Lindsay."

"Fustian," said Freddie cheerfully. "My establishment's the worst run in the county and I couldn't care less. We won't interrupt your *tête-à-tête*. We're goin' to explore. C'mon!" And seizing Jean's arm, the pair of them ran off.

Lady Sally coughed delicately to catch the marquess's attention. "Really, I have never seen Miss Lindsay quite so animated. Come, John. Let us leave them to their hoydenish games."

"I must agree," said the marquess. "I have never seen Miss Lindsay look better. The fresh air has brought a good color to her cheeks." And with that dampening remark, he turned to escort her back to Lady Frank, vowing to have a word with Freddie later.

But Freddie showed no signs of hurrying back to the party. From thinking that Jean Lindsay was a poor sort of choice for the marquess, he had rapidly changed his opinion. He decided she was too good for him.

Freddie had at last found a female companion who was prepared to indulge his boyish enthusiasm for throwing stones in the water and looking for birds' nests. Accustomed to walking long distances over rough country

136

n the Highlands, Jean was as indefatigable as he and ound she was enjoying herself immensely. The world of ealousies, social manners and correct form was left far ehind as the pair ranged far and wide and finally showed p at the picnic table, breathless and happy.

Jean was swinging her straw hat by the ribbons and vearing a crown of wild roses in her hair. "How very ural," said Lady Sally. "No doubt you were taught to veave those sylvan wreaths for your hair in that little illage—Weariesome or something—that you hail from."

"Oh, no," said Jean innocently. "Freddie made it for ne."

"Freddie!" said both the marquess and Lady Frank in horus. Freddie blushed and made a few choked sounds worthy of his friend, Mr. Fairchild, and buried his face n a tankard of champagne to get away from the gaze of the others.

Lady Frank was looking at him speculatively and hinking that if Freddie was deciding to run after a petti- coat, she would rather have someone like Jean Lindsay is a sister-in-law than Lady Sally or any of her breed. Lady Sally was delighted at the unexpected match that seemed to have sprung up. The marquess was furious.

He had had the day nicely planned. He had meant to walk Jean Lindsay off to a secluded corner and propose. He had foreseen no obstacles in his way. Now it looked as if he would have to reckon with that well-known misogynist, his best friend, Freddie. Freddie, of all people!

Freddie surfaced from his tankard.

"Have some champagne," he offered Jean. "It's great after all that runnin' around."

"I am sure Miss Lindsay would much prefer a glass of ratafia," said the marquess repressively.

"But I would love some champagne!" Jean held out her glass, giggling, to Freddie who grinned back. The marquess suddenly felt like a stuffy, aged parent.

The sun shone through the trees. The champagne sparkled, Jean sparkled and the Marquess of Fleetwater was bitterly jealous. Well aware of the fact and enjoying every minute of it, Jean encouraged Freddie to play a game of tongue twisters with the loser paying forfeit by draining off his or her glass.

"Can't you stop them?" the marquess whispered to Lady Frank.

"Why? They're havin' fun. If she gets a bit tiddely there's no one here but us, and I'll take her home in the carriage. Poor little thing, I don't know when I've seen her so happy," said Lady Frank indulgently. She was as tired as her brother with the Gothic undertones of the past few days and considered Jean more at peril from the attentions of the marquess than from any tipsy play with her brother.

"Look at those boys fishing," said Lady Sally, anxious to turn the gentlemen's attention elsewhere. "Will they catch anything, do you think?"

Two boys were perched on boulders farther up the bank.

"Shouldn't think so," said Freddie. "The current's too strong."

Even as they watched, one of the boys missed his footing and plunged headlong into the stream. He struggled frantically against the powerful rush of water and, for a moment, it looked as if he would make it to the bank. He grasped frantically at a dead branch sticking out from the shore but it broke and he was swept down the stream, his head disappearing under the foaming water.

It all happened so quickly that the party at the table sat frozen like a pastoral tableau.

Then the marquess leapt to his feet and, tearing off his jacket and cravat, ran down the bank to where the boy had disappeared and dived into the water. Freddie and Jean raced after him, tripping over stones, branches tearing at their clothes. The marquess's head had reappeared and he swam strongly downstream and dived again. After an agonizing wait which seemed like hours, he surfaced again farther down, clutching the boy to him and striking out for the shore. Again and again the river swept them farther away.

"Jump in and help them," screamed Jean. "I can't," yelled Freddie above the noise of the rushing water. "Can't swim."

Jean and Freddie, beside themselves with fear, ran on down the bank of the stream after the fast-disappearing figures.

The banks of the river grew more wooded, the undergrowth thicker as the stream narrowed before it plunged headlong into the falls. Jean, her dress in rags, ran on, praying under her breath, "Please, don't let him die! Oh, please!"

Just before the falls, the marquess managed to wedge his shoulder against a rock and rested, holding the boy's head above water. He saw Freddie and Jean. "Get a rope!" he called.

The couple turned and scrambled back headlong the way they had come, calling frantically for help. When they had nearly reached the picnic spot, they were met by Lady Frank with several of the servants and, sobbing and gasping, they shouted for a rope. One of the servants miraculously produced a thick coil and back they all rushed, Frank, unaware of her pregnancy, loping along with great strides.

When they had reached a clearing before the falls, they stopped in amazement. For the marquess was approaching them slowly with the unconscious boy cradled in his arms.

Jean would never forget how he looked as he stood there, smiling in triumph, his gray eyes sparkling, the sun shining on his blond hair and the whipcord of his muscles showing through the thin, wet cambric of his shirt. He looked like a young god. She fell so much more in love with him that she realized there could be no going back, no flirtations with Freddie to ease the pain. She would love him completely and absolutely until the day she died.

Unaware of the final victory over his beloved's heart, the marquess beamed on them. "The boy will be all right. I pumped some of the water out of him. Not bad for an old man, eh, Freddie?"

Freddie slapped him enthusiastically on the back. "Demme, if you ain't the greatest Corinthian that ever was. You went into that water like a demned cod."

"Come, come, Freddie," teased the marquess. "A Poseidon, a merman, a seal, but spare me the cod."

The boy moaned and opened his eyes and the marquess placed him gently on the ground. He looked up at the circle of concerned faces, the marquess in his dripping clothes, the servants in their livery, and began to wriggle away.

"Hey, wait a bit," said the marquess. "We'll take you home."

But the boy like many of his class had learned to distrust the whims of the Quality. One minute they could be smiling at him, the next they could be horsewhipping him for polluting the river. He squirmed away from their helping hands and ran off. There was no sign either of his earlier companion.

"Let him go!" said Lady Frank. "I'll find out his direction from the vicar and see that he is all right. Let us all go home and get changed. You're soaking, John, and Jean and Freddie look like ragbags."

But the marquess had caught the look of adoration in Miss Lindsay's eyes and suddenly wished that all the boys in Barminster would fall into the river so that he could rescue them.

"Nonsense!" he said roundly. "The sun is warm and we are *en famille* so to speak. Let us finish our lunch."

"Talkin' about bein' *en famille* reminds me that I'm goin' to drop this brat before its time if you lot get up to any more shenanigans," grumbled Lady Frank, making the servants laugh and Jean blush.

As they approached the picnic table, Lady Sally, who had been told of the rescue, got prettily to her feet and, letting the shawl slide from her shoulders, raised her glass to the marquess. "My hero," she sighed, smiling mistily up at him.

"You mean you just sat there as calm as cucumbers," raged Frank. "Your hero, as you call him, was nearly down the falls and into his grave."

Lady Sally looked scornfully at Jean's torn dress. "I have been brought up to behave like a lady at all times, no matter how strong the emotion."

"Well, in that case," snapped Frank, "don't get married 'cause you ain't goin' to be much fun in b . . ."

"Frank!" yelled Freddie, outraged.

"Oh, well, anyway," said Frank huffily, "I'll join Jean in a glass of champagne."

"Y'know," said Freddie, "I'm beginnin' to have fun. All this rustication was a good idea of yours, John. Don't care if I never see another ballroom."

"Are all our pretty dresses to stay locked in our trunks," pouted Sally.

"If you don't think you're all too grand for a local hop, there's a dance at the Assembly Rooms in Barminster tonight," said Frank.

"Oh, please let's go," pleaded Sally. The ballroom was her battlefield and the one setting where she was sure she would outshine Jean Lindsay.

"What do you think, Jean?" asked Frank. "I've seen the Master of Ceremonies and put our names in the book so we can go any time."

Jean thought of her beautiful new ball gown which had been sent to her by her godmother and, as yet, unworn.

"I would love to go."

"That's settled then," said Frank. "As long as John don't go around fightin' duels over any old frumps. I've had enough excitement for one day."

After a lazy lunch, the party started to head back to the Manor to have a nap and refresh themselves for the ball. The marquess deftly swept Jean off to his curricle, leaving Lady Sally to travel with Frank and Freddie.

The marquess debated whether to propose on the road back and decided against it. The mood would have to be perfect and he was feeling exhausted after his swim. He contented himself with holding her hand and the pair returned, slowly and speechlessly, in a state of silent ecstasy.

Jean did not go to sleep. She was too excited and meant to spend every single minute preparing for the evening ahead. Curl papers had to be put in her hair, Denmark Lotion on her face, fan, shoes, shawl and reticule to be chosen with care, and dreams to be dreamed.

She was sure the marquess would never offer her a *carte blanche*. He showed all the signs of a gentleman on the edge of a proposal. Her birth was impeccable, she must not forget that. "We will be married by special license," said the dream marquess. "I can wait no longer. . . ."

Jean frowned. The dream marquess was always saying that he could wait no longer and the real life marquess seemed to be taking his time coming to the point, blowing hot one minute and cold the next.

Chapter Nine

The marquess was lost in a happy daydream of his own. He intended his proposal to be a masterpiece of elegance. There had been enough of the hurly-burly life in the past few weeks. He would dazzle Miss Lindsay with his address so that she would fall gratefully into his arms. He selected a fresh cravat from his valet and proceeded to sculpt the linen with his fingers into one of his famous works of art.

Both Lady Sally and Jean were late in making their appearance in the saloon that evening, both wanting to make an entrance, and it was with little pleasure that they met at the top of the stairs. Sally was wearing a gown of rose-colored slipper satin trimmed with seed pearls and her golden hair was topped with a dainty tiara of diamonds of the first water, Jean, who had felt she looked magnificent in the privacy of her bedroom, began to lose confidence. Sally had never looked more beautiful or more ethereal. Instead of making the grand entrance she had planned, Jean followed very crestfallen in Sally's wake.

She did not know that she herself had never looked more attractive. Her hair burned like a flame in the candlelight of the green and gold saloon. She wore a dress of gold silk, cut low over the bosom, with an overdress of gold gauze edged with bugle beads and her mother's garnet necklace around her neck.

The marquess moved forward to congratulate the ladies on their appearance. He looked every inch the aristocrat, thought Jean, the severe black and white of his evening dress relieved by the brilliant sparkle of diamonds. There were diamonds in his snowy cravat and on his long fingers. The marquess privately thought that he had overdone it a bit but Jean thought he looked magnificent. Freddie was impeccable as ever and Lady Frank stunned them all by appearing in a huge, forbidding turban studded with an enormous ruby and topped up with a waving ostrich plume.

"If I'm goin' to sit with the dowagers, I may as well look the part," she laughed. Sir Giles and Lady Carol, who had opted for a quiet evening at home, were taken aback by the splendor of their guests.

"It's only a local dance," said Lady Carol, eyeing them doubtfully. "We don't boast a spa like Bath or Tunbridge Wells, you know. Our dances are not very grand."

"Then, we'll make 'em grand," said Freddie, holding out his arm to Jean who hesitated, looking shyly toward the marquess. But his fair head was bent over Sally and he did not seem to be paying attention. With a little sigh of disappointment, she allowed Freddie to help her into the large, closed coach and had the doubtful pleasure of subsequently facing the marquess and Lady Sally who were sitting side by side.

Flambeau sputtered and flared from sconces in the wall outside the Assembly Rooms. A number of guests were arriving on foot across the square led by the bobbing lanterns of the link boys. How Bess would sneer, thought Jean.

Jean could hardly contain her excitement as she heard the musicians striking up. This, she decided, was to be the most memorable evening of her life. She would enjoy the dance, the marquess would propose, and the rest of her life stretched before her without a shadow.

Freddie claimed her for the first dance, leaving the marquess to dance with Lady Sally. Jean suffered Freddie's exuberance for the next half hour, looking forward to the moment when the marquess would be able to lead her to the floor.

But no sooner had the country dance finished than Lady Frank introduced her to the son of a local squire who led her off into a rowdy set of the Lancers. And no sooner had that exhausting dance finished than the broad back of the marquess was seen retreating into the card room.

Jean bit her lip and, refusing the offers of several young gentlemen, went to sit beside Lady Frank who was in close conversation with a terrifying-looking dowager. Some of Jean's expectancy began to fade and, as Freddie led her off to the supper room and she caught a glimpse of the marquess in the card room with Jack Cartwright—both engrossed in a rubber of piquet—she began to feel bewildered. The marquess had shown all the signs of a man deeply in love. By rights, he should be sitting across the table from her, gazing into her eyes.

"When I was last in Scotland, I shot a green-spotted deer with pink antlers and six feet," remarked Lord Freddie conversationally.

"How nice," said Jean vaguely.

"Thought you wasn't attendin'. Anythin' the matter?"

"Oh," Jean dragged her thoughts away from the card room. "Sorry, Freddie. I was dreaming."

Freddie eased his cravat and leaned across the table. "You know, since I met you, I've got to thinkin' about settlin' down."

Jean started nervously to her feet. "I hear the music starting up. We had better get back." She began to move and there was a tearing sound. Her thin overdress had caught under Freddie's foot.

"It's all right," she assured that blushing young man, glad of an excuse to get away. "I'll go and mend it and it will look like new." And before he could reply, she hurried off.

She found an empty anteroom and, opening her reticule, drew up a chair behind a draft screen and prepared to repair the damage.

Female voices sounded in the passage outside and then the door of the anteroom opened. Peering through the hinges of the screen, Jean saw two elderly dowagers exclaim over a slight tear in one of their dresses.

"My dear, Mrs. Belfort-Fawcett, let me stitch it for you. I am said to be extremely handy with a needle. These wretched chairs. All nails and splinters, I assure you. The whole Assembly is going to rack and ruin, rack and ruin, and so I told the chairman."

"We have distinguished enough company, this evening, Mrs. ffollett," remarked Mrs. Belfort-Fawcett.

"Yes indeed," remarked Mrs. ffollett in a booming voice. "The dear marquess. So handsome. But do you know what they are saying at Almack's, Mrs. Belfort-Fawcett? Our dear Lord Fleetwater has been ensnared by that red-haired chit who was dancing with Lord Freddie Blackstone this evening."

"No!" An appreciative gasp from Mrs. Belfort-Fawcett.

"Yes, indeed. And I hear that the girl, a Miss Lindsay, is very strange. Why, the Duchess of Glenrandall's girl, Lady Bess, told some friends of mine that she is reputed to be a witch in her home village in Scotland. And Lady Cynthia Lamont says she *drinks*."

"No! How terrible," said Mrs. Belfort-Fawcett with relish. "Surely dear Lord John cannot be considering matrimony, although she is said to be the granddaughter of General Sir Duncan Lindsay."

"Of course marriage is out of the question," replied Mrs. ffollett. "Her birth may be all right, but, my dear, her reputation! Furthermore, she is penniless. If anything is in the wind, it is no more than an *affaire*. Should she return to London, the patronesses of Almack's are considering withdrawing her vouchers and no one can have any claim to the ton after that."

"I think she is very pretty," ventured Mrs. Belfort-Fawcett timidly.

"Nonsense! Those fey Highland looks may have a certain charm for the gentlemen but, for my own part, I think she looks positively *farouche.*"

They both left the room and Jean sat still as a statue behind the screen with her face burning. The malicious tongue of Lady Bess had obviously been busy before they left for the country and what further gossip she must be spreading now that she was back in town, did not bear thinking of.

Jean's first thought was to run away. But where?

On their return to town, Uncle Hamish would hear the gossip and then it would be back to a long life of spinsterhood and drudgery at the manse. So John, the Marquess of Fleetwater, would not consider matrimony with such as herself? Then she would put herself under his protection. She had no reputation left anyway.

Having come to this decision, Jean got to her feet only to sink back into her chair. She had no courage to go back and face the ballroom now that she knew what everyone was saying about her. She was to remember that evening for the rest of her life.

From time to time, voices called her name, several times people came into the room searching, but no one thought to look behind the screen where one young lady sat as if turned to stone. Gradually the music died away, a lackey came in and snuffed the candles, footsteps receded, good nights were called, horses stamped outside and then all was silence, except for the high quavering voice of the watchman calling the time. As she heard the great doors of the Assembly Rooms bang shut and the last footfalls echo away in the distance, Miss Jean Lindsay sank down on the floor beside her chair and cried and cried.

By three in the morning, the anxious house party met together in the library of Oakley Manor. Sir Giles, the marquess and Lord Freddie were exhausted, having ridden all over the countryside.

Lady Frank snatched off her turban and threw it on the sofa. "Maybe she heard what those damned tabbies were sayin' about her at the ball tonight."

Everyone stared.

"Bess has been very busy. She has spread some story about the girl being a witch and sent to London in disgrace and something about her gettin' drunk at the Lamonts."

The marquess flushed uncomfortably, remembering how he had encouraged her to drink.

"I don't think it's all her fault either," said Lady Frank. "Never knew a gel surrounded by such spite and jealousy and supposed gentlemen."

"Hey!" expostulated Freddie.

"I ain't thinkin' of you, Freddie," said Lady Frank, staring at the marquess.

There was a silence while everyone looked at the marquess and the marquess looked at the fire.

Suddenly there was the sound of a soft football from the floor above. "She's back!" shouted Freddie, rushing upstairs with the marquess.

Without any concern for the proprieties, they flung open Jean's bedroom door. The windows over the balcony stood ajar, the silk curtains fluttering ghostlike in the night breeze.

"There she goes!" yelled Freddie, leaning over the balcony.

"That's a man!" said the marquess. "Quick! Get our horses and we'll ride to Blackstone Hall. We'll catch them yet!"

They ran to the stables, yelling for fresh horses, cursing the sleepy ostlers. When they arrived at Blackstone Hall, there was a light shining in the library.

"They could have cut across the fields," said Freddie.

The marquess swore. "You didn't tell me there was a way across the fields."

"Didn't think of it until now," said Freddie woefully. He hammered on the door. "Muggles! Demn you. Muggles!"

Cursing at the delay, the marquess smashed a rock against the hall window and despite Freddie's protests, opened the latch and climbed through.

They burst into the library and the marquess paused for an instant on the threshold, taking in the scene. Hamish and Lord Ian were sprawled at their ease in front of the fire before a table strewn with cards. His quick eyes took in the scratches and mud on Lord Ian's boots.

With one bound he was across the room, jerking Lord Ian out of his chair.

"Where were you tonight, dammit," growled the marquess, shaking Lord Ian like a rat.

Lord Ian gasped and spluttered, his normally sallow face white with fury.

"Unhand me this instant," he choked and, as the marquess dropped him unceremoniously on the rug, he lay glaring up at his adversary with murder in his eyes.

Hamish uncoiled his cadaverous length from the armchair and roared, "Heathen! Mohawk! We have been at a play at Barminster this evening and the servants can confirm that we have been here since then. I demand an apology!"

Muggles, the butler, stood swaying in the doorway, roused by the commotion.

"Ask the butler," yelled Hamish, pointing in his best pulpit manner at the unlucky Muggles.

Muggles, who had been allowed free run of the cellar when the couple left for the play, stammered, avoiding Freddie's eye, "The gentlemen have been here these past four hours."

"I haven't even asked you to give them an alibi," said the marquess suspiciously. "Look you, your niece Jean Lindsay is missing. If she is found harmed in any way, I will come back and murder you both."

With that, he stormed from the room, dragging Freddie after him.

Hamish and Lord Ian eyed each other uneasily as the sounds of the marquess and Freddie searching the Hall from cellar to attic filtered through to them.

"Here's a coil," muttered Hamish. "If we ever do get rid of the girl, we'd better be out of the country on the next boat."

"He'll never prove anything," snarled Lord Ian, getting to his feet and brushing himself down. "With any luck some footpad may have done the job for us. I wonder where she can be. . . ."

It was a gloomy breakfast party at Oakley Manor in the early hours of the morning. No one except Lady Sally had felt like sleeping late. The marquess and Lord Freddie were tired and crumpled, having slept in their clothes, ready to leap to the saddle at the first sign of news.

Lady Frank broke the silence. "I've bin thinkin'," she said wearily. "If I was a young sensitive thing like Jean and maybe heard what these tabbies were sayin', I'd want to run away."

"The stage!" Reanimated, the marquess rushed from the room and could shortly be heard outside, calling for his horse.

Freddie eyed his sister over his mug of beer. "She ain't got any money with her, Frank, and you said there was nothin' missin' from her room."

"True," commented Lady Frank, looking at the dregs of her chocolate. "Maybe she just sat down somewhere too ashamed to move."

Brother and sister looked at each other with dawning hope. "C'mon!" yelled Freddie. "Let's go!"

Frank shook her head wearily. "I'm done for, Freddie. Can't move another step. You go an' bring her back. Tell her she can make her home with me as long as she likes."

Freddie, moved to a rare demonstration of affection, hugged his sister warmly. "You're a trump, Frank. The gel's too good for Fleetwater anyway," and unconsciously giving his sister a lot to think about, he hurried off.

A thin mist was rising over the spires of Barminster as Freddie rode into town. He saw the marquess's horse tethered outside the coaching inn but did not check. All was fair in love and war, thought Freddie, spurring his horse on to the Assembly Rooms.

The great doors were opened wide as the servants went about their duties of cleaning up the debris from the ball the night before.

Freddie stomped through the echoing halls, hallooing at the top of his voice. He was about to leave in disgust, when he strode into the anteroom and saw the edge of a reticule peeping out from behind the screen.

He strode around the screen and stood looking down at Miss Jean Lindsay. She was fast asleep, crouched on the floor with her tearstained face lying on the seat of the chair. She looked all of twelve years old.

Freddie gently picked up a lock of red hair and said quietly, "C'mon, Jean. It's time to go home."

"Yes, John dear," she murmured in her sleep.

"I say, it ain't 'John dear,'" said Freddie crossly. "It's me. Freddie. Wake up!"

Jean opened wide her green eyes and looked up at Freddie's friendly, concerned face. "Oh, Freddie," she sobbed. "I'm so glad it's you." And with that she threw herself into his arms.

Never before had Freddie felt so tall or so gallant. "I'm takin' you home," he murmured into her hair. "No runnin' away again. M'sister says you can stay with her —long as you like. Honest!"

As a proposal of marriage trembled on Freddie's lips, a voice like ice came from the doorway. "What a charming picture."

His face drawn with fatigue and anger, the marquess leaned against the doorjamb.

"Just comfortin' her," said Freddie defiantly. "And don't start rippin' up at me, John. Let's get the girl home."

Jean's hand flew out toward the marquess but he had already turned away, his thoughts hidden behind his usual urbane mask.

"I will ride back to the Manor and have a carriage sent for you directly," said the marquess stiffly and strode off into the sunny morning, grabbing the reins of his horse from an ostler and cursing the fellow roundly because he dared to mention some inanity about it being a fine morning.

Freddie of all people! The marquess ground his teeth. Then let the ungrateful jade *have* Freddie. No female in all the length and breadth of the country had ever spurned the Marquess of Fleetwater before. He would leave for London as soon as possible and be damned to her!

A few miles distant, the conspirators were in an equal state of rage. An early messenger brought Uncle Hamish a note from Mr. James Colquhoun saying that the lawyer would be calling on Miss Jean Lindsay on the morrow to apprise her of her good fortune.

"Hell and bedemned," muttered Lord Ian. "Send a servant to Oakley Manor directly and see if the girl has been found. She must be dispatched today without fail."

"Fleetwater will murder us," said Hamish.

Lord Ian shrugged. "There's nothing he can do if the deed is done without any witnesses. We are not living in the eighteenth century when someone like Fleetwater could take the law pretty much into his own hands. The very presence of the magistrate will protect us. It might look suspicious but then look at all the odd things that have happened to her lately. A little murder will only be a seven days' wonder."

Jean had been put to bed and ordered to rest by an unexpectedly maternal Lady Frank. "We will discuss your future when you wake," said Lady Frank, tucking her in and moving quietly over to the windows to pull the shutters. "In the meantime, *don't* worry."

Jean sighed and snuggled down into the bedclothes but sleep would not come. Long after Frank left, she lay wide-eyed, thinking only about the marquess and wondering if he still loved her. No sisterly love from Frank, no affection from Freddie, could ever replace him. At last, having come to that sorrowful decision, she fell asleep.

Before dinner, Freddie essayed several times to strike up a conversation with the marquess and was snubbed for his pains. The marquess was again the urbane leader of London fashion, seemingly secure and impenetrable behind a mask of chilling manners and impeccable dress.

Jean's timid approaches to him were met with calm, brief replies and the marquess turned to give all his attention to Lady Sally.

Freddie, for his part, found he could only elicit polite little comments of "yes" and "no" from Jean and finally gave up and stood moodily kicking the fire, and ruining a brand new pair of Hessians.

Lady Sally was looking her best in a gold sarcenet gown with no less than five deep flounces, drawn from her seemingly bottomless wardrobe. Lady Frank sat scratching her hair under her turban with a long knitting needle and wished them all to the Devil.

Uncle Hamish and Lord Ian arrived to swell the general gloom. Fortunately, Sir Giles carried the conversation at the dinner table, describing an unsolved series of murders in the district, which he considered were done by the same man.

"There's enough death these days with footpads and highwaymen attacking innocent wayfarers," said the magistrate, "but this is something out of the common way. This felon has been breaking into respectable households and stabbing the occupants as they sleep. Nothing is taken. It almost seems as if he simply enjoys killing."

Lord Ian nudged Hamish. This was a blessing indeed!

"It could be a lady," tittered Lady Sally with a malicious look at Jean. "Some women do the strangest things."

"They do indeed," said Lady Frank roundly. "Like makin' silly, nasty, little remarks that no one wants to hear."

"Well, really," breathed Sally as both women glared at each other from across the table. "Are you referring to me?"

"If the cap fits, wear it," snorted Lady Frank.

Sally bridled. "I have never been so insulted in my life."

"Then it's high time you were," snapped Lady Frank.

With quivering lip and tremulous voice, Lady Sally turned to her hostess. "I thank you for your unusual hospitality, Lady Carol, and take leave to tell you, I shall be leaving on the morrow for London."

The marquess shifted slightly in his chair. "May I offer you my escort, Lady Sally? I too shall be leaving."

Jean gave him a stricken glance which went unnoticed since the marquess had addressed his remark to his wine. Freddie brightened considerably and Hamish and Lord Ian exchanged gleeful glances.

"The Lord obviously means us to do this deed," muttered Hamish under his breath.

Lord Ian shuddered and drew away. The old man was obviously as queer as Dick's hat band.

At last, Lady Carol rose to lead the other ladies to the drawing room and leave the gentlemen to their wine. She sighed to herself. What an uncomfortable house party. Lady Frank was snorting like a warhorse, Sally was chilly and Jean was looking white and pinched.

Outside the dining room, Lady Carol's courage deserted her. "If you will excuse me, I must see the housekeeper directly." Lady Sally also paused.

"I shall not be joining you," she said icily, addressing Lady Frank and Jean. "But I would like to take this opportunity of saying . . ."

"Don't," snapped Frank.

"What?"

"I said don't say what you was goin' to say," remarked Lady Frank, eyeing Sally with distaste. "I ain't landed a woman a facer yet but there's no sayin' I might not start. So I'm tellin' you now, Sally, up those stairs you go at the double or I'll draw your cork!"

Sally picked up her skirts and fled, reflecting that at least she had her triumph. She would have the marquess all to herself in the morning. And what lovely gossip it would make for Almack's—Jean asleep all night in the Barminster Assembly Rooms and Freddie's terrifying sister threatening to punch her.

Frank put a comforting arm around Jean's shoulders and led her into the drawing room.

"These itsy-bitsy girls always diggin' away with spiteful remarks. Can't bear 'em. It's why I don't like livin' in London. Now, about you, m'dear. Like to come and live with me? Lead a quiet life, you know, but we do have some parties and balls and things like that."

Jean burst into tears.

"Now then," said Frank, embarrassed. "No need to be in such a takin'. Think on it. Best thing, y'know. See things in a different way when you get away from 'em."

"But I love him so," Jean sobbed.

"Who? Freddie?"

"No. Lord Fleetwater."

"Wastin' your time there, m'gel. Much too snobbish. Hey—but don't you start thinkin' about settlin' for anythin' else. Fallen Women indeed. It won't do, you know. Lead an awful life."

But I should be with him, thought Jean. The bewildering happenings of the last few days had knocked her off center and she clung desperately to the one stable fact that she loved the marquess and meant to live with him in any capacity whatsoever.

Lady Frank eyed her thoughtfully and pulled the bell cord. "Get us some brandy," she informed the startled servant, and, turning to Jean, "Now, let's repair your face. Nothin' puts a man off more than a waterin' pot."

Jean smiled weakly and dabbed at her face with a wisp of handkerchief and then swallowed the goblet of brandy that Frank pressed on her. A warmth began to seep through her and by the time the gentlemen had arrived, she had downed several and was able to chatter away in an unconcerned manner, leaving the marquess feeling savage and Freddie hopeful.

A crash at the window made everyone jump. Sir Giles peered through the curtains. "Gad, what a tempest," he exclaimed. "That must have sprung up suddenly. Sheets of rain coming down and branches flying all over the lawns. I've never known such erratic weather. I had better see my steward in the morning. The Bar is going to flood if this continues."

"Do you get much flooding in this area?" said the marquess lazily.

"Not a bit of it. Not since the great rains of 1872. But by the way this is going on," said Sir Giles, letting the curtain fall, "it looks as if it could happen again. You'd better stay the night," he added, waving his hand to Lord Ian and Hamish who nodded in agreement.

Lady Frank got to her feet and stretched in a most unladylike manner.

"Well, I'm deuced tired. C'mon, Jean."

Jean cast a shy glance at the marquess but he was studying the toe of his boot with an abstracted air and even when the gentlemen rose as the ladies left the room, he turned his gaze to the Louis Quatorze clock on the mantelpiece as if he had never seen anything like it before.

She trailed up the staircase in the wake of Lady Frank and decided to go into action that very night. Frank pottered around Jean's bedroom for what seemed an age, rattling on about what a gay time they would have in the north of England, little realizing that her young companion was only listening with half an ear. At length she left and Jean hurried over to a closet in the corner of the room where she had hidden her secret purchases from Barminster.

Downstairs, Uncle Hamish and Lord Ian left the room together and Sir Giles, after one or two attempts to break the silence, decided to call it a day. Lord Freddie and the marquess eyed each other across the fireplace.

After a few minutes, the marquess rose to his feet and said coldly, "Forgive me for retiring early but I must make an early start in the morning."

"Sit down!"

"I beg your pardon."

"I said, sit down," remarked Freddie, his boyish face unwontedly stern.

The marquess drew a lace handkerchief from his pocket, brushed an infinitesimal speck of dust from his gleaming Hessians, and stared at Freddie through his quizzing glass.

"Put away that demned eyeglass, John," said Freddie. "Your Bond Street airs ain't goin' to shut me up. I want to talk about Jean Lindsay."

"Ah, yes," drawled the marquess. "I believe I am to wish you happy."

"Stuff!" said Freddie roundly. "I ain't asked her yet but I'm goin' to, soon as I get the chance. You ain't betrothed to her yet, you know, and from the way you've been goin' on I don't know whether you're interested in Sally or Jean. Now 'cause I want her, you're like a demned dog over a curst bone. Well, it won't fadge. We've bin friends for years and I never thought to see the day when you couldn't take a bit of competition."

The marquess smiled ruefully and sat down. "Forgive me, Freddie, but ever since I set eyes on that girl, I'm all to pieces. I've been behaving like a sixteen-year-old. At one point I thought she was in love with me and now I don't know."

"Well, runnin' off to London ain't goin' to solve a thing," said Freddie. "Let's both fight it fair and square." He held out his hand.

The marquess grinned and shook it warmly. "I never thought to see the day when you would give me a dressing down, Freddie. Yes, I'll stay . . . and I'll stay here right now and broach another bottle of Sir Giles's excellent claret to celebrate our battle."

Freddie assented and the couple chatted on into the night, their former friendship renewed.

Upstairs, Jean Lindsay surveyed the finished effect by candlelight. She thought she looked the complete Fallen

Woman. A transparent nightrobe of virulent green stopped short at her knees and showed her rouged nipples. On her feet were high-heeled silk slippers with large rosettes. Her face was painted and rouged and her eyelashes daubed with Warren's boot blacking.

Shivering with fear and excitement, she laid her bolster along the bed under the blankets to look like a body and put the powdered Georgian wig, relic of the Blackstone ball, on her pillow. There! If any inquisitive servant looked in, it would appear that Miss Jean Lindsay was safe in her virginal bed.

For a moment her heart misgave her, then, thinking of life with Uncle Hamish, she squared her shoulders, snatched up her wrapper and, like a young, untried soldier going into battle, prepared to seduce the marquess.

Unaware of what was to descend on him, the marquess paced his sitting room, still fully dressed. His thoughts were in a turmoil and the ferocious noise of the tempest outside made the idea of sleep seem impossible. With a weary sigh, he picked up a book and threw himself into a high-backed chair by the fire.

There was a sudden lull in the storm and he heard faint sounds from the bedroom beyond. He was about to leap to his feet, when the bedroom door opened and there, in all her glory, stood Jean Lindsay. She closed her eyes, threw back her head, and waited.

There was a long, shock-filled silence. Then as the tempest outside started to howl anew, she thought she heard a faint snicker, followed by a stifled giggle. It couldn't possibly be! Stoically she kept her eyes closed and waited for the marquess to fling himself passionately across the room.

Again a lull in the storm and weird choking noises could be heard distinctly. Jean's eyes flew open wide. The marquess was doubled up in his chair, helpless with laughter. He choked, he sobbed, he howled. Jean felt a blush rising from the soles of her feet to the top of her head and a wrenching pain in her heart.

Her ensemble, which had looked so wicked and alluring by candlelight, was now exposed to the full glare of two modern oil lamps. She caught a glimpse of herself in the mirror and nearly fainted. She looked tawdry and ridiculous. With an almost animal cry of pain, Jean fled from the room, pursued by the marquess, who was hiccuping with laughter.

They reached the door of her rooms at the same time. The marquess caught her in his arms to try to explain his odd behavior when, at the same moment, both heard someone in her bedchamber.

The marquess flung open the door. By the light of a single candle which Jean had left carelessly burning on her dressing table, they saw the tall figure of Lord Ian, a dagger in his hand, stabbing again and again at the dummy on the bed.

With one bound, the marquess was across the room. He grabbed Lord Ian as he sprang for the window and, with a crackling blow of his fist, floored Jean's would-be murderer who fell and lay as still as death, half in and half out of the long windows, while the fury of the storm hurled rain and branches into the room.

Freddie came rushing in followed by Sir Giles and two of the servants. In the commotion, Jean held on to her wits and struggled into her wrapper and scrubbed the paint from her face with the rain-soaked edge of one of the curtains.

Quickly the marquess explained the situation, omitting the fact that Jean had been in his room. He said that she had expected something like this to happen and had left a dummy of herself in the bed to trap the murderer.

"You've really knocked him out," said Freddie, bending over the body. Then he yelled, "The old man! The uncle!"

The marquess swore and dashed to Hamish's rooms to find the old man already gone. As he ran out into the storm in the direction of the stables, he could dimly make out a figure on horseback racing down the drive.

Soon he was mounted and hot in pursuit. It was a hideous night, full of the sound and fury of tearing branches and howling, buffeting gusts of wind and rattling sheets of rain.

Near blinded by the storm, the marquess thundered out of the drive and along the Barminster road. All around him, the great trees at the edge of the estate heaved and groaned as the great gale threatened to pull them out by the roots. Several times, the marquess's horse staggered as a ferocious buffet of wind tried to hurl rider and horse from the road.

Suddenly, the slashing rain abated and a thin, new moon raced between the black clouds. One glimmer of fitful light showed the road ahead. The marquess was gaining on Hamish and above the sound of the wind, he could hear the old man cursing and praying to whatever demon possessed his soul. Then all was plunged into blackness again.

The road curved, leading to the bridge over the Bar and at that moment the moon raced out of the clouds. The marquess cried out and savagely reined in his horse so that it reared and plunged. For the Bar was roaring in full spate and the timber bridge had been swept away. The figure of Hamish in front tried desperately to check his mount but it was too late. The terrified goaded beast plunged into the river, taking Hamish with it and both horse and rider were swept from view.

Still fighting against the wind, the marquess dismounted and began to pick his way cautiously along the bank. About half a mile downstream, the wind died as suddenly as it had arisen and the moon shone out.

In a quiet pool, guarded by two rocks from the rushing

current, lay the broken body of Hamish, his old, white face turned up to the sky, his eyes gazing blindly at the racing clouds. The marquess heaved him out onto the grass and turned wearily in the direction of the Manor to look for help.

Lights were blazing from the Manor when he left his exhausted mount in the stables. Everyone seemed to be awake and talking at once. Jean was crying quietly in the corner of the library, being comforted by Lady Frank. The marquess drew Freddie aside and told him the news of Hamish's death.

"Good riddance to bad rubbish," said Freddie gloomily. "But Lord Ian's escaped."

The marquess swore and hurled his riding crop across the room. "How in hell and damnation did that happen?"

"Looks like he wasn't unconscious after all," growled Freddie. "Just playing dead. Moment me back was turned, he was out that window and across the park like a hare. We searched for him of course.

"Look," he added kindly, taking in the marquess's exhausted appearance and the white lines of strain around his mouth, "ain't nothin' we can do now. He'll never show his face in the country again. Sir Giles'll have the Runners after him. We searched his room and found this." Freddie held out Hamish's damaging letter, promising Lord Ian half of Jean's fortune on her death.

"Well, that's that," said the marquess heavily. "Jean, my dear." He stretched out his hand but the sobbing girl shrank from him and clutched onto Lady Frank's dress like a frightened child.

It was Freddie who drew the marquess aside and, kneeling down in front of Jean, told her in a quiet voice of her uncle's death. Then Lady Frank led her from the room.

The next day dawned gloomy and humid. Great shrouds of mist rolled around the elegant manor house which was hushed and still with only the sound of dripping water from the great trees in the park breaking the silence.

Jean was awakened timidly by her maid who informed her that a Mr. James Colqhoun, a lawyer from Edinburgh, was awaiting her in the morning room. She dressed slowly and painfully, feeling as if she were suffering from an accident, instead of a broken heart. With a white, set face, she made her way to the morning room, too tired and anguished to even speculate about the nature of Mr. Colqhoun's visit.

The lawyer was sitting with Sir Giles and both men rose to their feet as she entered the room. After a few hushed condolences on the death of her uncle, Sir Giles left her alone with James.

As if in a dream, Jean heard the lawyer stating in his dry, precise voice the vast amount of her fortune. She shook her head in bewilderment. "Then I am really an heiress," she at last exclaimed faintly. One of her cherished dreams had at last come true. She could travel, build herself a splendid house, buy land and marry well. She spread her hands out in a gesture of appeal. "I don't know where to begin, Mr. Colqhoun. Since I came South, there has been shock after shock."

"Take my advice," said James Colqhoun briskly, "and return to London and finish your Season."

Jean faltered. "But there has been much scandal talked of me in London. There is no point in returning . . ."

James Colqhoun smiled cynically. "My dear Miss Lindsay, a young lady of marriageable age who commands a fortune such as yours, will immediately be hailed as a delightful creature. Minor scandal only sticks to the penniless."

He raised his hand as Jean would have protested. "Do believe me, Miss Lindsay. You are very young and should at least have some balls and parties before settling down

163

to the responsibilities of your estate, although that will be the task of your future husband."

"I shall never marry."

"Tish, tish, lassie," said James, patting her hand in an avuncular manner. "You are now eighteen and the world does not end at eighteen, although it may feel like it."

Overcome by the kindness in his face and the Scottish burr in his voice, Jean began to cry dismally. She made no sound. Only the large tears welled out of her green eyes and rolled unchecked down her cheeks.

James felt nonplussed and mistaking her grief as being sorrow over the death of her uncle, pointed out, in what he hoped was a rallying way, that Hamish had been little more than a murderer. Since his words seemed to have no effect, he ran the bell and, summoning Jean's maid, advised her to go and lie down.

Jean retired in disorder to her room and, overcome with emotion, fell into a dreamless sleep. It was well into the afternoon before she again awoke, still feeling a dull pain in her heart, but readier to cope with life. She would employ Miss Taylor as a constant companion and, with her newfound wealth, they would travel abroad—somewhere which was still free of the presence of Bonaparte.

She would dress only in black and, heavily veiled, would tread the streets of some foreign capital while the Cosmopolitan world speculated on the nature of her sorrow. As this romantic but dreary picture formed in her mind, Jean began to brighten. She was eighteen years old and an heiress. Perhaps life was not so bad after all.

As she searched her wardrobe unsuccessfully for funereal gowns, Jean began to weave dreams about the immediate future. She would treat the marquess with cool, mysterious dignity. Not for one minute should that cruel, laughing, unfeeling rake know how badly he had hurt her.

Having decided on her plan of action, she rang for

her maid and was assisted into her prettiest gown of pale blue sarcenet. Her mourning dresses would need to wait until she got to London and was able to order a fresh wardrobe. After an hour with the curling irons, she felt brave enough to meet the world.

The first person she saw as she descended the staircase was Freddie, who whispered to her mysteriously that he wanted to speak to her in private. He ushered her into the library and closed the door.

Jean watched in amazement as Freddie carefully selected a cushion, placed it on the floor and dropped to his knees in front of her.

Seizing her hand, he began, "Miss Lindsay, I have long admired you and enjoyed the tender feelings you arouse in me. I . . ." He broke off in confusion and then said in his old manner, "Oh, Jean. I do love you awfully. Say you'll marry me."

Still holding her hand, he got to his feet, gazing at her with a very earnest, serious look on his boyish face.

"Oh, Freddie, I can't. But I wish I could," said Jean hugging him impulsively. "I'm very, very fond of you. But I can't think of you in that way. Only as . . ."

"As a brother," Freddie finished gloomily.

Jean felt a great rush of affection for him. "Look, Freddie. So much has been happening to me, I don't know what to think. Perhaps when things have settled down and I have time to consider . . ."

"That's the ticket!" said Freddie joyfully, kissing her on the cheek. "Well, when are we going to be married?" he teased.

The marquess, who had opened the library door in time to see the embrace and hear Freddie's last sentence, closed the door and stood in the hallway, staring at the fire, uncertain what to do. He suddenly felt young and lost and terribly vulnerable. So Jean Lindsay was to marry Freddie. He thought of his laughter of the night before

165

and cursed himself for an insensitive fool. But she had looked so funny and he had felt so sure of her. With a weary sigh, he mounted the stairs and ordered his valet to begin packing.

Chapter Ten

Jean found the renewal of her Season in London much as the shrewd lawyer had predicted. Cards and invitations poured into the elegant town house in Cavendish Square.

Lady Bess and Lady Cynthia Lamont had ceased their malicious gossip after finding that they had lost their audience.

"Nonsense! The girl is charming. A hundred thousand pounds, I hear. Perfectly charming!" was the general view of even the highest-nosed dowagers.

A great deal of the magic had fled from London, Jean considered, now that she was socially acceptable everywhere. She was subjected to the most blatant advances from the town's notorious fortune hunters. Her fortune caused impoverished younger sons to send her flowers and sonnets and ancient roués to beg her to go driving in the park. Jean preferred Lord Freddie's company above all, since at least he knew where he stood and the marquess watched their growing friendship from afar with a jaundiced eye and wondered why the betrothal had not yet been announced in the *Gazette*. No one expected Jean Lindsay to maintain a state of heavy mourning in the circumstances. He avoided both Lord Freddie and Jean and flirted with all the prettiest debutantes in London and felt perfectly miserable.

Sometimes, in all the glory of her newfound wealth, Jean would consider that she had successfully got over the marquess. Then he would walk into a drawing room or ball and her heart would give a painful lurch. For never before had the marquess been more elegant or charming. If he was forced to meet Jean face to face, he merely exchanged a few pleasantries in a cool, bored voice and made it plain to the rest of society that he found the new heiress uninteresting. Where previously this would have meant social ruin, it now did nothing to alter Jean's impeccable social position. As a wealthy heiress, she was invited everywhere.

At last she had learned to mask her feelings and the marquess tried to persuade himself that he was well rid of a heartless flirt. Gossip had informed him that Miss Lindsay meant to retire to Scotland at the end of the Season and, with a heavy heart, he decided to join the Prince Regent's set in Brighton and forget all about her in the summer round of royal gaiety. Unaware that Freddie had almost managed to persuade Jean to spend some time in Brighton before going north, he moodily watched her animated face one evening down the length of the Glenrandall's dining table and wished he were dead.

The affair was a small dinner party given by the Duchess of Glenrandall at the ducal town house to celebrate Jean's new fortune. All the familiar faces were there. Ladies Bess, Mary and Sally, Lord Freddie and Mr. Fairchild, Lady Frank—who had joined her brother in London because it was all so "demned dull" after they left—Miss Taylor, looking positively pretty now that Jean had secured her financial future, the marquess, Sir Edward and Lady Cynthia Lamont.

The footmen were pouring out the wine and the marquess smiled dryly to himself as he remembered how drunk Jean had got at the Lamonts. He noticed idly that the livery of the footman who was refilling Jean's glass was a different shade of scarlet from the others and that he looked more like an ex-boxer and was patently in need of a shave. The marquess watched the footman leaving the room rather hurriedly and turned back to watch Jean, who was in animated conversation with Freddie, raise her glass to her lips.

A horrid feeling of danger flashed into his mind. Jean was too far down the table to snatch the glass from her hand. He grabbed an orange from the epergne and, blessing his cricket days at Eton, hurled it down the table. The orange struck the wineglass dead center and sent its contents flying over the Brussels lace cloth.

Everyone sat in shocked silence as the marquess ran from the room in search of the mysterious footman.

The duchess was the first to break the silence. With an imperious wave of her hand, she signaled for the butler and asked him in a loud whisper if the marquess had been drinking heavily. The butler, in a more discreet whisper, answered that the marquess had hardly touched his wine.

"Well!" said the dutchess dramatically, "I suppose he must be suffering from the sun. It has been uncommon hot lately and you gentlemen will drive in the park in these open carriages."

At that moment, the marquess returned, looking very grim. "Forgive me. But the footman who poured Miss Lindsay's wine did not belong to this household. I fear the wine may have been poisoned."

"But this is ridiculous," spluttered the duchess, calling

forward her butler again. "Strangers can't just come in and wait on table."

The butler coughed nervously. "The footman in question arrived this morning with a letter from His Grace saying as how we were to give him immediate employ. I can fetch the letter now, Your Grace."

The company waited in silence until he had returned and handed the letter to the duchess. She glanced over it. "But that is not my husband's handwriting and it is certainly not his seal!"

"Oh, dear," groaned Lady Frank, echoing the thoughts of all the guests. "Here we go again."

"Can it be anything to do with Lord Ian Percy?" asked Freddie. "I mean, it can't, can it? He won't get a penny now if anything happens to her."

"I think it could well be," said the marquess. "I always considered Lord Ian an unstable sort of fellow. He simply wants revenge."

Jean began to feel sick and faint. The marquess got to his feet. "I myself shall go directly to Bow Street to report this and I suggest, Miss Lindsay, you allow me to employ a bodyguard for you, unless of course," he added smoothly, "you consider it your responsibility, Freddie?"

"No, go ahead," said Freddie cheerfully, unaware of the marquess's startled expression. "You know better than anyone where to get the right sort of fellow. I must say," he added callously, "Miss Lindsay certainly livens things up. Season was beginning to look awfully dull."

Reflecting that Freddie's behavior was unloverlike to the point of idiocy, the marquess made his adieus and took himself off to Bow Street.

The fact was that Freddie was finding being in love a dead bore. The memory of the lively girl who had chased around the countryside with him was beginning to fade as he was daily confronted by a new, quiet Jean Lindsay who always seemed sad and abstracted.

169

But feeling obscurely that he should make some protective gesture, he urged Jean to accompany himself and his sister to Brighton on the following week.

"Smaller place," he explained. "Know everyone who's comin' and goin'. Sea breezes'll put a bit of pink in your cheeks."

Jean made up her mind to go. Lady Frank was a good, uncomplaining friend and her godmother, Lady Harriet Telfer-Billington, was beginning to show signs of tiring of her new toy. It was one thing to play fairy godmother to a Cinderella but boring to chaperone a wealthy heiress who could now move freely in Society and showed every sign of having an excellent dress sense of her own. Also, Lady Frank was the only one who knew Jean was still pining for the marquess and, although she did not lend a very sympathetic ear, at least she was prepared to listen.

Lady Sally bit her pretty lip and eyed Jean speculatively. The Duke of Belmont showed every sign of proposing but he was elderly, fat and overdressed. Every time he bent over her hand, his Cumberland corsets creaked appallingly. Should she risk her time in Brighton chasing the marquess? Oh, if only someone *would* murder Jean Lindsay.

Lady Bess was thinking much the same. "I wonder what goes on in that carrot top of hers," she thought viciously. "There has just been an attempt on her life and she sits there smirking."

Jean had taken refuge in dreamland again. After all, it was a much more comfortable world than the real one. In her dream, the night was black and thundery and the landscape strewn with Gothic ruins and sinister cloaked figures and Lord Ian raced off into the night, holding her a bound prisoner on his horse. She was gagged and could not cry out. But she smiled in her dream for she knew the marquess would rescue her. Lord Ian dragged her

170

into a ruined farmhouse and, watched by a consortium of rats and bats, he tore the gag from her mouth.

"Now my fair wench," he hissed. But those were the last words he said. A blade flashed and the villain crumpled to the floor of the farmhouse where the rats formed themselves into two lines and began dragging him off.

The marquess, her hero, stood laughing in the moonlight. And laughed and laughed and laughed. "What's so funny?" Jean asked the dream marquess.

"Why you are," he giggled helplessly.

"You silly clown! You popinjay," yelled Jean—and found herself glaring straight into the eyes of the real marquess, who was bending over her chair.

The marquess, who had just spent half an hour at Bow Street and who had expected a warmer welcome, retreated a pace and snapped, "If that's all the thanks I get for wasting my valuable time trying to prevent you from being murdered, I wash my hands of the whole business."

Jean blushed miserably to the roots of her hair. "I was thinking of Lord Ian," she lied quickly. "If only I were a man!"

"Well, you're not," said the marquess, still ruffled. "I shall call on you tomorrow morning to discuss what steps we should take for your protection. Freddie will accompany me of course."

"Why?" asked Freddie blankly.

The marquess groaned. "Are you all mad or am I?"

He signaled the footman to fill his glass and turned with relief to Lady Sally who started to prattle on happily about the gossip of the Season.

He could not help comparing her with Jean. She was so exquisitely beautiful and, although she never said anything very witty or amusing, her behavior was correct at all times. He must see to Jean Lindsay's protection and then put her firmly from his mind.

Jean dressed particularly carefully the next morning

and had even sent for Antoine, the court hairdresser, to arrange her hair in the most flattering style. James Colquhoun had arranged a draft for her at Coutt's bank and set up a business manager to handle her bills. Still overawed by the extent of her fortune, Jean had, as yet, spent very little on herself. She had employed Miss Taylor as a permanent companion at a generous salary and had given extravagant presents to Lady Frank, the Duchess of Glenrandall and to her godmother.

Her bedroom window overlooked the square and she had an excellent view of the marquess and Lord Freddie riding up to the entrance. They did not seem to be very much in charity and Lord Freddie's amiable features were marred by a scowl.

The morning had started off well for the two gentlemen. They had met at Gentleman Jackson's saloon at 13 Bond Street to ask the famous boxer for the direction of any former pugilist willing to act as bodyguard. Mr. Jackson promised to see to the matter himself and, well satisfied, the two friends set off to Cavendish Square.

"We're early," remarked the marquess. "Let's take a turn in the park. I want to talk to you about something."

Freddie wriggled uncomfortably. All his life people kept leading up to unpleasant lectures with "I want to talk to you about something."

They were early enough for Hyde Park to be fairly deserted but Freddie rolled his eyes around, looking for a diversion. The marquess reined in under a tree. "Now, Freddie," he began.

"Now what?" burst out Freddie. "Thought you was my friend and you're sittin' there glowerin' like m'father."

"I just wanted to know when it will be in order to offer you my congratulations," said the marquess smoothly.

"On what?" asked Freddie blankly. "Ain't bin racin' or cock fightin' or anythin'."

172

"I meant—when is your betrothal to Miss Jean Lindsay to be announced?"

"Don't know," said Freddie, taken aback. "I mean . . . is it?" he added inanely.

"Good God man," said the marquess. "I saw you in the library at Oakley hugging and kissing the girl and planning the wedding."

Lord Freddie blushed. "I don't know if it's any of your business, old man. But she refused me."

What an absolutely splendid day it was, thought the marquess. What gorgeous trees, what splendid birds, what snowy sheep, what . . .

"She did say, however, that she might change her mind if I gave her time," added Freddie gloomily.

What a dreary, dusty-looking park, thought the marquess as a cloud crossed his sun.

"Of course, there's a problem," Freddie went on. "Fact is, old man, I don't know that I care that much for gettin' married."

The marquess felt almost personally insulted. If he couldn't have her, then at least his best friend should be the natural substitute.

"How dare you play fast and loose with the poor girl's emotions," snarled the marquess.

"Here! Here!" said Freddie, much incensed. "If there is any fast and loose business goin' on then Jean Lindsay's the one that's doin' it. I've danced attendance on her since we came back to London. Have I been at Cribb's? No. Have I been at Watier's? No. Have I been at the Cocoa Tree? No. Have I . . ."

"Stow it Freddie," said the marquess rudely, getting tired of the catalogue of bachelor establishments that Freddie had given up visiting.

"Well, anyway," huffed Freddie, "all I ever get is . . . 'How *kind* you are, Freddie. Just like a *brother*.' Faugh! Women!"

"Then you retire from the lists?" asked the marquess.

"If you mean, am I not goin' to marry her should she want me, I don't know. Don't know at all," said Freddie vaguely.

"Oh, make up your bloody mind," howled the marquess.

"Don't speak to me like that either," snapped Freddie. "If I want to dither, I'll dither." And both gentlemen, very cross with each other, made their way to Cavendish Square.

Both were warmly welcomed by Lady Harriet. The shrewd monkey eyes took in all the impeccable glory of marquess's morning dress. Although he had behaved in a very distant manner toward Jean, Lady Harriet sensed there was a stronger feeling hidden behind the fashionable front which the marquess presented. On hearing that he was removing to Brighton, she had encouraged Jean to go. It would be pleasant to have her goddaughter so well married without having gone to any excessive trouble to bring it about.

She watched Jean closely as the girl came into the room, a slim, breathtaking figure in sprigged muslin. But Jean made her good mornings in a cool, correct manner, showing no undue warmth to either gentleman.

Lady Harriet sighed and then mentally shrugged. As far as money was concerned, the girl's future was secure and she felt the gentlemen's efforts to find her a bodyguard extreme to say the least. She had heard the story of the dinner party and thought the company had taken the matter far too seriously. Lord Ian Percy would not dare show his face in England again.

Jean thanked both men prettily for their efforts on her behalf and, at the end of their call, reminded Freddie that she was to go shopping that morning with Lady Frank.

"We are both in need of new summer clothes," explained Jean. "I fear it has become prodigiously hot."

"Told you—Brighton's the very place to get some fresh air," said Freddie.

"I have decided to join you in Brighton after all," said Jean, "if it will not be too much trouble for you and Lady Frank."

"Nonsense!" said Freddie bracingly. "Got bags of room. House on the Steyne, y'know. We'll all be cozy together."

"Perhaps," interrupted the marquess, "Miss Lindsay and Miss Taylor would prefer to set up their own establishment. My agent could find you a very suitable place."

Jean frowned. "I already consider Lady Frank and Freddie as my family and look forward to sharing their home."

The marquess bowed, gave her a mocking look from under his drooping lids, and took his leave.

Infuriating man! thought Jean. Why, she could swear that he had been trying to put her off from sharing a home with Freddie and his sister. She could not see the point of it at all.

But as the dusty traveling carriage rolled to a stop in front of Lord Freddie's house in Brighton a few days later, she began to have an inkling as to why the marquess wished her to choose an establishment of her own.

The sun was sparkling gaily on the rows of mansions on the Steyne with the exception of Lord Freddie's, which was set back from the rest and overshadowed by the buildings on either side. Jean's heart sank as she saw the familiar figure of Muggles weaving on the doorstep and Henry, the footman, already helping to carry in the luggage.

She followed Lady Frank into the cavernous hall and stepped back with a shriek of alarm. A huge stuffed elephant dominated the center of the hall, a tribute to the taxidermist's art. It had obviously been shot while on the rampage and had been stuffed accordingly. One huge foot was raised menacingly, the huge ragged ears were

175

spread, enormous yellow tusks curved up to the ceiling, and wicked, red glass eyes glared down on the visitors.

"Marvelous, ain't it," said Freddie, appearing around its rump. "Rented the place from a nabob and the whole house is full of great stuff."

Jean gazed in awe at the assortment of dusty palms in brass bowls, tiger skin rugs complete with heads, glaring eyes and sharp yellow teeth, and elephants' feet placed at strategic points to hold a plethora of walking canes and polo sticks. Various Indian deities spread their many arms in the gloom and the heads of every type of Indian animal stared down from the walls.

"The old boy was a great traveler. Spent some time in China and the Far East as well," explained Freddie as he led the way into the drawing room which was so crowded with Buddhas of various shapes and sizes that there was little room left for human company. "That's his portrait over the fireplace." He pointed to a picture of a very stout gentleman with huge military moustaches who was mounted on a horse, waving a saber and obviously putting down a whole Indian mutiny single-handed.

Jean sank down onto a sofa only to leap up again. She bent down and unearthed a knobbly bone from under the cushions.

"Oh, didn't Frank tell you she'd got the servants to bring the dogs," said Freddie somewhat shiftily.

A burst of joyful yelps and barks from the hall bore out his remark. Lady Frank seemed to be borne into the drawing room on a wave of happy dogs, rolling and scampering about her skirts.

"Well, I must say, all this is very cozy," said Frank, sitting beside Jean and looking about her with a pleased air.

Jean breathed in the familiar Blackstone air of damp dog and cabbage water. "Did you bring your own chef?" she asked Freddie timidly.

" 'Course I did," he said cheerfully. "Can't leave all the servants eatin' their heads off at Blackstone Hall. Don't know why people are always complainin' about his cookin'. He cooks good, plain English food. Can't stand that foreign muck although he's goin' to try and give us some curry since we're livin' in a bit of India so to speak."

Jean repressed a shudder and asked to be shown to her room. She followed the housekeeper up the staircase, lit by a square stained-glass window on the center landing, which cast dim harlequin diamonds of color onto the zoo in the hall below.

The housekeeper threw open the door of her bed-chamber and sank to the floor in a curtsy from which she was unable to rise without Jean's help. The aged retainer then stumbled off downstairs, leaving behind a strong odor of spirits. Jean viewed her bedchamber and wondered how Freddie's staff managed to channel any liquor at all above stairs.

The room was a nightmare of chinoiserie with fiery oriental dragons rioting over the hangings of the four-poster and little, yellow-faced men bowing from the window curtains. Various ivory figurines crowded the mantelpiece under a portrait of the nabob's lady who had been painted in her best black silk against an exotic Eastern setting which, from the sour look on her face, she obviously despised.

The hangings of the bed began to move although there was no draft and Jean stood paralyzed with her hand to her lips. The thought of Freddie, Lady Frank and an army of servants close at hand gave her courage. She pulled back the curtains and found herself face to face with an enormous Irish wolfhound who had just been in the act of burying a bone beneath the pillows.

Lady Frank walked in as Jean was trying to pull the dog from the bed. "I see you've met Cerberus. That's m'favorite. He has taken a fancy to you," said Frank, plumping

177

herself down on the bed beside her dog. "Pull back the curtains and let's see what kind of view you've got."

Jean complied with her request and stared out of the window in delight. The sparkling blue sea seemed to spread to infinity, hundreds of bathing machines added their bright colors to the shore and a fashionable crowd were promenading up and down the red-brick pavement outside.

"The Prince Regent's in residence at the Pavilion," said Lady Frank. "We'll probably get invitations to one of his evenings. He's a friend of Fleetwater."

"Can I go sea-bathing?" asked Jean.

" 'Course you can," said Lady Frank, smiling at her enthusiasm. "But rest up this afternoon. We're havin' a quiet dinner at home tonight. Freddie's persuaded John to come."

At the mention of the marquess's name, a shadow crossed Jean's face. "Don't worry," said Lady Frank hurriedly. "He didn't want to accept. Had the cheek to ask Freddie if our cook was goin' to serve up that elephant in the hall."

Lady Frank left as Miss Taylor entered the room. "Really, Miss Lindsay," breathed her companion. "What a bizarre house! But I declare we shall be quite comfortable as long as we do not die of starvation.' "

"We shall dine from home as much as possible," said Jean firmly.

"I do wish we did not have to take Hoskins with us every step we go," said Miss Taylor. "Everyone does stare at him so. He does not look in the least like a footman."

Hoskins was Jean's bodyguard, an ex-boxer who had had the distinction of fighting the great Molyneux. His days of greatness were obviously over as he shambled after Jean like some great shaggy gorilla with his livery threatening to burst at the seams. But Jean had to admit she found his constant presence comforting.

"The Marquess of Fleetwater will be dining with us tonight," continued Miss Taylor tentatively. "At one time I really thought he was in love with you."

To her horror, Jean's eyes filled with tears.

"Tell me about it," said Miss Taylor gently, putting her arms around her in the way she used to when Jean was a child.

The sympathy was too much. The nightmare of that night had long been burning in Jean's soul. The horror of the attack on her and the subsequent death of her uncle were as nothing compared to the memory of the marquess's mocking laughter. Burying her head in Miss Taylor's ample bosom, she choked and sobbed and poured out all the terrible disgrace of that night at Oakley Manor.

Miss Taylor listened, stricken with horror. The only faint comfort she had was that the marquess would never talk about it.

"We should never have come to Brighton," exclaimed Miss Taylor. "Every time you look at him you must be remembering . . ."

"Let us stay just a few more days, Miss Taylor," begged Jean. "Then we will return to Scotland and I will never see him again."

This dismal pronouncement brought a fresh burst of tears. But it was a relief to Jean to confide in someone at last. As she finally dried her eyes, she felt considerably better and, with the callousness of youth, did not notice that her poor companion was rigid with shock and embarrassment.

Dinner was a nightmare. Carried away by his surroundings, the Blackstone cook had produced a curry, a great, steaming casserole of burning hot gristle. They were fortunately saved from sampling it by Jean's bodyguard, Hoskins, who carefully tasted the concoction first from the dish on the sideboard and, with a loud cry of "pisen,"

179

threw open the long windows of the dining room and threw the curry into the garden to the delight of the fashionable crowd walking on the Steyne. Choking and gulping, the poor bodyguard leapt after it into the garden and the bemused party could hear sounds of him being violently ill in the shrubbery.

It was left to the marquess to explain to Hoskins that the Blackstone cook had merely been producing one of his usual culinary delights and not trying to poison Jean. He then suggested that they all repair to the Ship Inn for dinner instead.

The incident had served to thaw out the chilly formality of the party, the night was calm and starry with a fresh breeze blowing in from the ocean, and the marquess and Jean were able to chat unself-consciously for the first time since Oakley Manor. Jean began to sparkle, her green eyes shining, the long fringed ends of her shawl blowing around her in the summer breeze. She was young, she was rich, she was on her first seaside holiday and the most handsome man in the world was walking with her.

For his part, the marquess felt his hopes rising. The old spell which Jean Lindsay always seemed to weave about him seemed stronger than ever. He felt protective, happy as a schoolboy and about ten feet tall. He caught the appreciative glances a group of cavalry officers were casting in Jean's direction and took hold of her arm possessively. Immediately a strong current of emotion flowed between the happy pair and they entered the Ship Inn with all the banners of love bravely flying.

Miss Taylor positively beamed on the pair. After all that had gone on between them, the marquess *ought* to marry Jean Lindsay.

Happiness is infectious. Lady Frank was at her most outrageous, telling jokes, laughing loudly, her great turban bobbing over her plate of prawns. Freddie chattered away, talking nonsense, and even Hoskins, on guard behind

Jean's chair, creased his gorillalike features into an indulgent smile. The marquess and Jean said one thing and said the other and communicated what they really meant to say in the manner of lovers by side glances and inflections of voice.

After dinner, they walked over to view the Pavilion, built by Mr. Henry Holland for the Prince Regent. Jean thought the building with its green-roofed domes and minarets looked like a fairy tale but the marquess damned it as vulgar. "The whole thing is a monument to bad taste," he drawled. "Although the interior does have a certain florid magnificence. You will probably be invited to one of Prinny's musical parties, so you will have an opportunity to view it for yourself."

The marquess took his leave on the doorstep after begging permission to take Jean to Donaldson's circulating library in the morning.

Jean went to bed in a happy daze. As long as the marquess smiled on her, she would forgive him anything.

The next few days had a dreamlike quality and Jean bathed in the ocean, bobbing around happily in a flannel bathing dress and oilskin hat, took walks along the Marine Parade, attended assemblies at the Ship Inn and actually had her hand shaken by no less personage than the Prince Regent himself at one of the Royal musical parties in the Pavilion.

She was popular. Cards and invitations flowed into the house on the Steyne and that gloomy residence was brightened by the bouquets of Jean's admirers. Lady Sally and Lady Bess had followed the fashionable crowd to Brighton, only to find the Marquess of Fleetwater dancing constant attention on Jean Lindsay. Jean and the marquess, although never alone in each other's company, felt they were more in love than any couple had been since time began. The marquess, his normally severe aristocratic features lit by happiness, broke more hearts at the assemblies than he had ever done before and Lady Sally chased after him so blatantly that even Freddie remarked that she was making a cake of herself.

The only cloud on Jean's horizon was that the marquess had not yet declared himself. After returning from a ball at which he had unaccountably been absent, she was about to retire to her room, when Henry handed her a note. She dismissed him and took it into the drawing room where the lamps were still lit.

The note was brief and to the point. "My darling," she read. "Come to the Hove end of the beach. I must see you alone on an important matter. I have enclosed a map. Meet me there at two in the morning when we can be private. Do not fail me, John."

Jean glanced at the clock on the mantel. It was just on midnight. Two hours to wait. Anyone less in love would have been suspicious but to Jean there was no fault in the message. She had had no opportunity to be alone with the marquess. There was always Miss Taylor or her ever-present bodyguard, Hoskins.

She had forgotten about Hoskins. As she crossed the hall to mount the stairs to her room, he detached himself from the shadows and asked if she would be needing him further.

"No, Hoskins, you may go. I am going to retire for the night."

She saw the bodyguard looking at the note crumpled in her hand and shoved it hurriedly into her reticule.

Hoskins refused to move. "Henry says you got a message, miss. Strange this late at night."

"Just a silly little billet-doux," laughed Jean, moving past him.

Hoskins stood his ground. "I thinks you ought for to let me see it. His Lordship said for me to look for suspicious letters."

"Nonsense! This is my private correspondence,"

182

snapped Jean and then gasped as one hairy hand neatly twitched her reticule from her fingers and Hoskins extracted the note and ponderously started to read it.

"How dare you!" raged Jean, trying to snatch her precious note from him. "The Marquess of Fleetwater shall hear of your behavior."

"His Lordship says I wus to look for anything suspicious-like," repeated Hoskins doggedly.

"Well, and are you satisfied? That message is from Lord John and, believe me, I shall see you are dismissed on the morrow."

With that she flounced up the stairs, leaving Hoskins to lean against the elephant and look moodily into space. With a shrug he took himself off into the night to drown his sorrows.

The marquess, who had been on a curricle race with Lord Freddie and several young bloods to Worthing, was returning to town in high spirits. He had won his race, the night was fine, and he would see Jean Lindsay on the morrow.

On the outskirts of Brighton, Freddie spied a small tavern and called to the marquess to stop. "It doesn't look very salubrious," said the marquess doubtfully. "Let's ride on till we get to the Ship or the Anchor."

"I'm demned thirsty and you're too nice in your choice of taverns," said Freddie cheerfully. The marquess sighed and followed him into the dingy tap room, noticing thankfully that it was deserted apart from a drunk asleep in the corner.

After they had got their mugs of ale from a surly landlord, they turned to survey the room which was dimly lit by cheap tallow candles stuck in bottles. The figure in the corner groaned in its sleep and the marquess, who was going to suggest to Freddie that they leave and find a more cheerful establishment, suddenly noticed that the drunk was dressed in familiar livery. With an oath, he picked up the candle from the bar and crossed the room and found himself looking down at the sleeping figure of Hoskins. Freddie followed him.

"Leave Jean's gorilla alone," said Freddie. "He deserves some time off."

The marquess ignored him and rudely shook Hoskins awake. The bodyguard looked at him blearily from red-rimmed eyes, tried to get to his feet, and collapsed back into his seat again.

"You ludship's got no right to make asig . . . asig . . . meetin's with the young lady without a-tellin' me."

The marquess felt suddenly sick and shook Hoskins harder to keep the man awake.

"What assignation, dammit! I made none."

Hoskins sobered with fright.

"You sent 'er a lovey-dovey note sayin' as how she wus to meet you at the 'Ove end o' the beach at two of the clock. You sent 'er a map an' all."

With a curse, the marquess dragged him to his feet. "Quick man," he howled. "Come with us and show us the place. Freddie, oh, my God, Freddie! She's in danger."

Supporting Hoskins between them, they hurried out to the carriages and sped off into the summer night.

Hoskins was not to know that Miss Jean Lindsay was already regretting his absence. Her dress covered in a long cloak and her bright hair hidden by a hood, she slipped out of the house only to find that the Steyne was still thronged with late night revelers, several of whom seemed inclined to chase the solitary female figure.

Thankfully, she reached the beach unmolested and with a beating heart set out in the direction of Hove.

Large waves curled and thudded on the beach and a lonely seagull cried from the rocks, making her start with fear. The bathing machines, which had seemed so bright and cheerful during the day, looked dark and sinister as

184

if each one hid a menacing figure. Stumbling along across the pebbles, she soon left the lights of the town behind and, as the darkness of the summer night closed about her, she began to wonder at the marquess's folly in asking her to venture out so far alone. Had the note come from anyone else, she would immediately have been suspicious, but her great love for the marquess had clouded her wits and she could only think how happy she would be to see his tall figure waiting at the end of the beach. The moon slid behind the clouds and the darkness seemed almost tangible.

She heard the sound of footsteps on the shingle and darted behind some rocks. The moon shone out again and revealed a couple of ragged beachcombers, searching in the pebbles for trinkets or money that the wealthy bathers may have dropped during the day. They seemed to take a long time to pass and Jean waited behind her rock until she could hear their footsteps no more.

A small jetty, the place of assignation, had been marked on the map. After walking for what seemed miles with the sharp pebbles and rocks cutting through her thin half boots, she rounded a small promontory and, in the fitful moonlight, saw the jetty ahead at the end of a stretch of beach and could dimly make out a dark figure waiting on it. Breathing a sharp sigh of relief, she started to run and, as the figure left the jetty and came toward her, she flung herself thankfully into his arms, sobbing and laughing at the same time, "Oh, my dear, of all the stupidest things to do. I was half dead with fright."

"Good," said the voice above her cynically. "Then you have only halfways to go."

She stared up into the sneering face of Lord Ian Percy. Desperately, she tried to break away but was held even tighter.

"Did you think I would skulk abroad and leave you to enjoy your wealth?" said the hateful voice. "By the time

185

I'm finished with you, Jean Lindsay, you'll be praying for death."

She opened her mouth to scream but found it silenced by Lord Ian who thrust his mouth brutally down on hers and shoved his tongue between her teeth as an effective gag.

Fighting against faintness, Jean bit Lord Ian's tongue as hard as she could and he reeled back with blood dripping from his mouth and smacked her savagely across the face. She fell to the ground and he threw himself on top of her, tearing at the bosom of her dress but it was a credit to the Parisians and its seams remained stubbornly intact. Jean opened her mouth again to scream and felt the point of a dagger pressing against her neck.

"Now, Jean Lindsay," sneered Lord Ian, "you will do just as I tell you and you will enjoy every minute of it. Get to your feet."

Her eyes wide with terror, Jean stumbled to her feet and stared at the naked blade of the dagger as if hypnotized.

The wind had risen and was whipping her long cloak about her body. The air was full of the sound of the wind, the crashing waves and their own heavy breathing. Great black clouds swept across the face of the moon and far-off thunder rumbled. It seemed to Jean as if all light and laughter belonged to some other place and century and she felt alone, out of time, on some alien, primitive shore, faced with death.

The noise of the oncoming storm had drowned out the sound of any approach and Jean's hypnotized eyes suddenly saw long, white fingers clutching Lord Ian's shoulder and a beloved voice say, "Turn about, Lord Ian. We will settle this once and for all."

It was the marquess, a drawn sword in his hand, his gray eyes like two pieces of stone.

"What! My dagger to your sword?" said Lord Ian,

looking around him desperately for escape. Lord Freddie and Hoskins came up at a run.

"Give Lord Ian your sword, Freddie," ordered the marquess.

"For heaven's sake," howled Freddie. "Drag the fellow off to the magistrates and have done."

"I have a score to settle," said the marquess quietly. He had found his dragon and he was out for blood.

"Oh, very well," said Freddie, handing Lord Ian his sword.

He and Hoskins drew back beside Jean as the two antagonists faced each other. Then the grim fight began. Sparks flew up from the swords into the stormy suffocating air and the marquess pressed Lord Ian back along the jetty. Jean watched in terror. She did not know the marquess was the finer swordsman and at any minute she expected to see him fall to his death. With a little whimper of terror, she picked up a rock and threw it full at Lord Ian.

It smashed him full in the face and he flew backward over the edge of the jetty and plunged into the water.

The marquess whipped around in a fury. "You stupid hell cat," he shouted. "Cannot you leave me to settle this honorably."

Freddie and Hoskins rushed to the jetty with Jean and looked over. The moon raced out of the storm clouds and Jean could see the body of Lord Ian Percy imprisoned in the glass curl of a wave like some grotesque insect sealed in a paperweight. Then the wave broke. The three men turned and looked at Jean in silence.

Freddie put his hand on the marquess's shoulder. "Go easy, John," he said. The marquess shrugged him off.

"This was an affair of honor which you have just made dishonorable . . . you stupid chit." The marquess was tired and overwrought and his voice dripped acid. What on earth was the point of slaying dragons if the fair maiden was determined to make him look foolish by slaying them herself? What would Perseus have felt if Andromeda had remarked, "Oh, excuse me," and killed the sea monster by shying a rock at it. The marquess's most vulnerable points were his pride and his honor and Miss Jean Lindsay had just offended both.

"What will we do with the body?" asked Freddie.

"Leave it," snapped the marquess. "No one else knows we have been here and I do not want this disgraceful affair dragged before the Brighton magistrates."

He took Jean firmly by the arm and pushed the frightened girl up the beach toward the waiting curricles and delivered himself of a blistering lecture on her behavior.

"Did it not occur to you that if I wished to be private with you, I would merely have requested Lady Frank's permission. It is a miracle you were not assaulted before you even met Lord Ian.

"Do you not know that it is unforgivable for *anyone* ... anyone at all to interfere in a duel? I had thought you were at last growing up and learning to behave like a lady instead of a hoyden but I take leave to tell you, Miss Lindsay, that you have worse conduct and manners than a scullery maid.

"You have embroiled me in one shameful episode after another but this time you have gone too far. I wish I had never met you."

The threatening storm burst about their heads and mercifully drowned out most of the marquess's tirade. Jean merely caught a few splutterings of "shameless" and "dishonor" as the curricle, drawn by its tired horses, arrived in Brighton.

There was the usual tedious effort to rouse Muggles who eventually opened the door and retreated before the marquess's glare to the shelter of the elephant.

"Now," said the marquess. "We will settle this matter once and for all."

But Jean felt on her home ground and that she had stood more than enough. With a choking sob, she pushed past him and fled to the safety of her bedchamber.

The marquess would have followed her but was forcibly restrained by Lord Freddie and Hoskins, who dragged him off to the drawing room.

The marquess was cooling down and beginning to feel that his temper had been excessive but Freddie's mild remark, "She was only tryin' to save your life, y'know," fanned his wrath anew.

"I'll take no criticism from you, Freddie," he said spitefully. "Don't tell me how to go on when you can't even manage your own household.

"I take leave to tell you," said the marquess, gathering the rags of his dignity about him, "that you've got a demned sloppy kitchen, demned sloppy servants and," his voice carried back from the hall, "a sloppy elephant."

"Demme, that's the last time that snobbish fellow sets foot in here," said Freddie. "Nothin' up with the elephant."

Muggles tactfully handed him the decanter. "May I suggest, my lord, that things will look different in the morning."

"No, you may not and no, they won't," said Freddie sulkily. "Listen to that demned storm. Hope Fleetwater drowns on the road home."

Things looked definitely worse in the morning. The storm still raged outside and Miss Taylor reported in a hushed whisper that Jean had a dangerously high fever and that a physician should be sent for immediately. Freddie had already told his sister about the goings-on of the night before and Frank had to be forcibly restrained from rushing out into the storm to give the marquess a piece of her mind.

The physician arrived and disappeared upstairs followed by Miss Taylor, leaving brother and sister on tenterhooks. He came back after half an hour with a grave face.

"I don't know what has been going on here," said the physician dryly. "But Miss Lindsay has a high fever and seems to be in the grip of a perpetual nightmare. I recommend absolute peace and quiet. I have taken some blood and will call this evening to check on my patient."

"Shouldn't we tell Fleetwater?" asked Frank after the doctor had left.

"Not me," said Freddie, shaking his curly head. "Called my elephant sloppy."

"Called your . . . honestly Freddie, you're all mad," said Frank.

By the next day, Jean's fever had abated, leaving her weak and listless. The doctor promised her that she would be up and about in no time, but his patient showed a marked disinterest in anything to do with the outside world. Even the news that the marquess had called to inquire after her health did little to rouse her.

After several days when Jean still kept to her room, Lady Frank began to despair of her ever getting well again. But Jean was young and resilient. The horrors of the drama on the beach gradually began to fade. The marquess, after all, must have been as upset and shocked as herself otherwise he would not have said any of those dreadful things. Finally, she moved to a daybed in the front parlor and the sparkling view of holiday Brighton repaired her spirits. The doctor advised sea bathing. Jean could swim like a seal and, unlike other fashionable young ladies, did not need the services of the burly bathing attendant to dip her in the water.

Accordingly, she soon set out accompanied by Miss Taylor to start her daily bathing schedule. The sun shone and the sea was as calm as glass with only a thin line of foam breaking gently on the pebbles. Jean breathed in the familiar air of the bathing machine, composed of salt-

190

water, seaweed and stale perfume and felt as if she were coming alive again.

The bathing woman helped her down the steps into the water and she floated off, enjoying the unconstricted freedom of a healthy swim.

Moving strongly, she had soon swum far out of range of the bathing machines and the noisy young ladies, shrieking and screaming every time they were "dipped" by the bathing attendant. She rolled over and floated lazily on her back, staring up into the vault of the heavens, dreaming of sailing to the Greek Islands on honeymoon with the marquess. In fact sailing anywhere, she thought, where the social conventions were not as tight and pinching and restricting as an over-small corset. A slight breeze crinkled the surface of the water and she shivered. The black thought that she had actually killed someone always seemed to be hovering on the edges of her mind. She decided to swim back.

Diving under the water, she blinked at the glittering shoals of tiny fish and wished she knew their names. A beautifully striped one zigzagged across her vision and she swam after it. Suddenly, she could see a dark mass moving under the blue water toward her. She surfaced, threw the water out of her eyes and dived again. Like the nightmare on the edge of her mind, the mass came slowly toward her, and all at once she saw a pair of white, bloated hands stretching out as if in mute appeal and before she broke for the surface, screaming and gasping, she saw, gazing at her through the summer window of the translucent sea, the hideous, swollen, dead face of Lord Ian Percy.

Swimming as if her life depended on it, she reached the safety of the bathing machine and fell gasping to the floor. The bathing attendant assumed she was still too weak after her illness and had a cramp and Jean had not the courage to enlighten her. Let Lord Ian Percy float around his watery grave for some other unfortunate to find and report to the magistrates.

Even afterward, she held back her grisly knowledge, shrinking from telling Freddie, Frank or Miss Taylor. If she could only stubbornly ignore the horror then it would surely go away.

Lady Frank eyed her pale face. "Freddie and I were going to take you to an assembly at the Ship Inn tonight. Are you sure you feel strong enough?"

"Of course," answered Jean quickly. A ball was just what she needed to cheer her spirits and remove her mind from death and disaster. A new ball gown had arrived that day from London—and what nightmare could stand up to the miracle of a white silk dress, light as a feather, with an enchanting overdress of silver gauze woven in a spider's web pattern?

Even Freddie gasped his appreciation as she came down the steps into the murky gloom of the hall that evening among the stuffed animals like some bright, ethereal goddess descending into the jungle.

The party decided to walk the short distance to the Ship Inn. The evening was clear and warm, sparkling with lights and voices and snatches of music. Underneath it all, Jean could hear the steady slurring sound of the gentle waves pulling at the pebbles on the beach and shivered uncontrollably.

"You're not catchin' a cold are you?" asked Freddie, all solicitation. "Never did think sea bathin' was a good idea. Get put in a little box, dragged out into the water, bathin' chap drops you in and fishes you out and you're all cold and wet and sticky. Ugh!"

Jean shivered again and said faintly, "I quite agree, Freddie. I am resolved not to have any more bathes so please let us not talk ab . . ."

"Could kill you, all that wet," continued Freddie cheerfully, "and then your corpse would be found floatin' in . . ."

"Stop your nonsense," snapped Lady Frank.

But the damage had been done. Fighting against the memory of Lord Ian's dead face, Jean walked determinedly on. But nothing felt real and everything around her seemed to be very far away as if she were looking down the wrong end of a telescope.

"Hope you're still not mad at John," she heard Freddie's voice say as if from a long way off. "Even the mildest of gentlemen gets very crotchety when it's a question of honor.

"Take one of m'old friends, Geoffrey Lancing. Very quiet, unassuming sort of chap. Well, one day we was both passin' this farm and Geoffrey sees these two ducks walking toward the pond. So he says, 'I'll lay you a monkey, the one with the black spot on its head makes it first.' So I agree 'cause I thought the other one was faster. Well, Geoffrey's bird is racin' away like it was in the races at Newmarket and just when it got to the pond—out comes the farmer's wife and wrings its neck! Well, Geoffrey, he was so mad, he ups and he's goin' to strangle the old girl and we has to pull him off.

"Wasn't because he lost his money, y'see. It was because the silly old frump had interfered in a gentleman's bet. *Now* do you understand? I say! You're lookin' under par."

But with a peculiar, waxen, fixed smile, Jean assured him that she was perfectly all right and they entered the Ship Inn together.

Jean was soon surrounded by admirers, clamoring for the first dance, including many of the young cavalry officers who were stationed nearby at barracks on the Lewes road. Automatically, she selected the nearest, a large officer she had met briefly before who had enormous sideburns and a terrifying military moustache.

193

It was a country dance and a very energetic one at that so for half an hour she was not obliged to make much conversation and the cavalry officer took her subdued replies as becoming maidenly modesty and fell head over heels for at least the third time that week.

Dance followed dance like some weird moving dream to Jean, the colorful figures bowing, curtsying, retreating and advancing, the dowagers and chaperones along the wall with their enormous turbans and jewels, nodding and gossiping and looking like some exotic Eastern guard of honor.

The Master of Ceremonies announced the waltz and suddenly the marquess's face swam up in front of her eyes, looking to her fevered brain, brooding and malevolent.

Deftly, he swung her onto the floor and she followed him like a clockwork toy.

"My behavior the other night was possibly much too harsh," he began. "But the provocation was great. Well, well. Let us put such distasteful thoughts from our minds. Lord Ian is probably wallowing around somewhere in his watery grave and I hope the fish have a very good dinner, although, if the truth be told he . . ."

He stopped in amazement as Jean wrenched herself out of his arms and stood a few feet away from him in the middle of the ballroom floor, her bosom heaving and two hectic spots of color on her cheeks. They faced each other in silence. Slowly the musicians faltered and stopped playing, the dowagers stopped gossiping, the dancers stopped dancing.

Jean finally addressed the marquess, her high, clear voice carrying to every corner of the room.

"Shut up . . . you . . . you silly, *silly* old fop!"

There was a long indrawn "Oh!" of shock as the elite of England's fashionable society witnessed Miss Jean Lindsay's downfall.

Another "Oh!" was expelled and died away among the

pretty lanterns and banks of flowers. It was a matter of seconds but to horrified Lady Frank the room and its company seemed to stay rigid with shock for hours.

The marquess was the first to break the spell. With a slight bow, he turned on his heel and walked off to the card room. Several debutantes fainted, more burst into tears, all anxious to convince the gentlemen that their delicate sensibilities had been rudely assaulted. Only the dowagers, relics of the more free-spoken eighteenth century, remained unmoved.

Lady Frank moved forward and tugged at Jean's arm, leading her toward the door. Jean's white face flushed crimson as she realized what she had done.

Like a field of corn changing color on the wind, back after back turned against her as she moved through the throng. When her slight figure had disappeared into the night, a great burst of sound arose from the ballroom as everyone started talking at once.

It was the biggest piece of scandal to come their way for some time so it accordingly had to be rolled on the tongue, masticated and spat out in various forms of shock and amazement.

Lady Frank tried to say something to the shivering, trembling girl on the road home but was, for once, beyond words.

Henry followed them a few paces behind, burning with curiosity. They did not have to rouse Muggles for the footman had taken the precaution of bringing the house keys with him.

The footman looked hopefully at the two silent women standing in the shadow of the elephant but, since neither seemed about to talk, he asked for permission to retire.

Lady Frank roused herself. "Bring us some brandy to the drawing room first."

"Brandy, my lady!" Henry raised his eyebrows superciliously. "Perhaps some negus or ratafia?"

"I said brandy. I want brandy. I need brandy," retorted Lady Frank curtly. "Hop to it."

In the drawing room, Lady Frank threw her heavy turban across the room where it hung at a rakish angle on the head of one of the many Buddhas and with an "Oof!" of relief, collapsed on the sofa.

When Henry returned with the decanter, she poured two measures with a liberal hand and turned to Jean.

"Want to talk about it?"

Faltering at first, with stumbling incoherent sentences, Jean told the story of Lord Ian's body.

"I felt so horrified and sick when I got to the ballroom, I think I must have been nearly insane," said Jean piteously.

"Then he . . . he . . . John, I mean . . . started to dance with me and talk in that cool, languid drawl of his about Lord Ian's body being eaten by the fishes as if it all didn't matter and then I felt ill and thought of all the humiliation he had caused me and I just wanted him to be quiet."

"Well, you certainly succeeded," said Lady Frank wryly. "But, my dear, you are socially ruined."

Jean coughed over her brandy and said in a whisper, "What on earth shall I do?"

"Rusticate," said Frank. "Come back North with me—or better still—why don't you go back to Scotland and look at your inheritance?

"Better to keep your mind occupied. Colqhoun said something about your uncle having left a house in Edinburgh. Go and visit there for a bit. Take a look around the place. Take the Taylor female with you for company. This scandal will be a seven-day wonder, I assure you. With Prinny in Brighton, there's bound to be a new one to take its place."

Secretly Lady Frank thought no such thing. She knew well that the report of Jean's outburst would race through polite society from Land's End to John O' Groats.

Jean meekly bent her head.

"Shall I ever see him again?'"

Lady Frank looked at her sadly. "If you mean Fleetwater—no. And a good thing too, if you ask me. What you need is a pleasant, sensible young man who hasn't the temper of a Turk or the morals of a tomcat.

"You're a rich woman remember. You can go to Scotland in easy stages and stay at the best inns and posting houses on the road. See some of the sights. I'll get Freddie to hire a traveling coach for you and take your gorilla, Hoskins, with you. The roads ain't safe these days."

"I wish to leave on the morrow," said Jean.

" 'Course you do. But you ain't packed and it ain't fair on Miss Taylor. Just keep indoors out of sight until we get everything arranged."

The next two days were weary and bitter for Jean. Not one person called. Tired of being cooped up in the house, she at last went for a walk on the Steyne with Miss Taylor. She could have been a ghost for all the notice the fashionable crowd gave her. They simply pretended she wasn't there.

Even Freddie shied like a startled hare when he met her in the house and fled off muttering that he was busy. He did not even show up at mealtimes, preferring to dine with his friends in the town.

Hoskins, Jean's bodyguard, had been reinstated, and Jean's eyes filled with tears as he accepted her apologies with a rough grace, tugged his forelock, and mumbled shyly that he would be "uncommon happy to go to furrin parts if Miss so desired." To a lot of English like Hoskins, the Union of the Crowns might never have taken place and they still regarded Scotland as a wild country inhabited solely by savage, hairy Highlanders.

Finally, Freddie announced that all was ready and on a bright, holiday morning, Jean and Miss Taylor climbed into the cumbersome traveling coach. Lady Frank hugged

Jean fiercely and turned away to hide an uncharacteristic burst of tears.

Hoskins climbed on the roof, the coachman cracked his whip and only Jean's new maid, Sarah, showed any signs of excitement. It had been unusually hard to find a girl to accompany her as the servant class had proved to be more rigid and snobbish than their masters. Sarah had been the Blackstone's between stairs maid and eagerly accepted the rise in status to lady's maid even though it meant leaving the country.

Brighton had never looked so gay or frivolous. Flags cracked and snapped in the breeze above the Pavilion, the bright dresses of the ladies, set off by the morning dress of the gentlemen decorated the walks.

Suddenly, Jean saw the marquess with Lord Freddie, who had not waited to see her off. Both were walking with Lady Sally and Lady Bess, chatting and laughing without a care in the world. As the coach rumbled past, Freddie caught a glimpse of Jean's white face at the window, half raised his hand in salute and dropped it again.

Jean snapped down the blind and the coach gradually left Brighton behind and made its ponderous way up the Lewes road.

Chapter Eleven

It was well into November before the weary party finally arrived in Edinburgh. They had stopped for several weeks in various places. Jean's obvious wealth always brought her to the notice of the polite world in each town but it only took a little time for her scandalous reputation to arrive hot on her heels.

They had stayed for some time in Harrogate in Yorkshire, visiting the excellent library and the pump room to try the waters. Jean had loved the placid, sedate town and had seriously considered making her home there until, one dreadful night at a ball in the Assembly Rooms, she had had the humiliation of seeing the familiar wave of gossip running through the room, the curious eyes turned in her direction, and the young man she was dancing with being called abruptly to heel by his mama as if he were a dog.

There was nothing left to do but terminate the lease of her pretty house, pack the trunks and take to the road again.

They arrived in Edinburgh on a lowering windy day with huge, ragged, black clouds tearing across the sky. Jean felt as if she had stepped back into the Middle Ages as the horses pulled up the hill toward the High Street and James Colqhoun's offices.

At the city's west end stood an ominous medieval castle crouched on top of a four-hundred-foot pile of black and broken rock. The High Street ran along a ridge from the Palace of Holyroodhouse to the castle and turned out to be a narrow canyon running between enormous black tenements, crowded with every sort of human life imaginable. Running off from the High Street was a maze of dark, smelly alleys and courtyards and it was in one of these that they discovered the lawyer's office. Jean had often heard of Edinburgh described as "the Athens of the North" and had assumed that it was the buildings and the appearance of the city which had earned it this name rather than its intellectual pursuits. It all seemed so incredibly grim and Gothic.

James Colqhoun's clerk ushered them into the lawyer's office with great ceremony, trying to resist Hoskins's efforts to follow his mistress without success.

Jean felt embarrassed by what appeared to her to be the dismal squalor of her surroundings. Perhaps Mr. Colqhoun had fallen on hard times?

After the welcomes were over, Jean tentatively suggested this, which amused the lawyer greatly.

"And you a Scotswoman! And not familiar with the capital of your country," he exclaimed.

"My quarters here are only just beginning to become unfashionable," he laughed. "Until recently all the aristocracy and gentry lived around the High Street in the Old Town, all crowded together in these tenements you see out of the window. Now, you would maybe get an aristocrat and a tailor sharing the same tenement, and in some cases it's still the same. We don't have the same social distinctions here that you have in London.

"But not very long ago, the New Town on the other side of Princes Street was completed and is as fair a place as the West End of London. So most of the rich folk and the aristocracy moved into the New Town and left people like myself high and dry.

"I like it here but business is after all business and I have been seriously thinking of following my clients. Some of the ladies who used to dwell in the tenements around the corner but a few years ago now turn up their noses at my office and demand that I visit them at their homes.

"Ah, well. For all that, it's still the most overcrowded city in Europe.

"Your uncle's house, however, is in Charlotte Square in the New Town and a very pretty residence it is too. Your poor Uncle Joseph. I bought it for him on his instructions sent from India and even hired the staff and chose the furnishings. He did so long to retire here after his days in the heat of India. But it was not to be. He died without ever having seen it. Come and I'll take you there myself."

When the coach came to a stop in Charlotte Square, the travelers gasped with pleasure and relief. The late Joseph Lindsay's residence stood in an elegant row of Georgian houses, facing a pretty circular park. The squalor of the Old Town seemed hundreds of years away.

Mr. Colqhoun opened the door and led them into an exquisitely furnished house. Unlike most nabobs, Uncle Joseph had not sent home any Eastern trophies or ornaments to decorate his home and Mr. Colqhoun had avoided the current fad for Etruscan rooms and Egyptian rooms. All was a gem of quiet simplicity in keeping with the Georgian architecture of James Craig, who had designed the whole of the New Town in the last century and had not lived to see its recent completion. On the ground floor, an extensive library had been built onto the back of the house.

"You will find a lot of your uncle's personal papers

here. Perhaps you would care to look through them when you have the time," said the lawyer.

He was interrupted in his guided tour by a much flustered housekeeper who came in bobbing and curtsying.

"I forgot to tell you, I kept on your uncle's staff until you came to some decision of what you want to do with the property. This is Mrs. Abernethy."

"You puir wee thing," said the housekeeper, beaming a welcome and thrusting Jean unceremoniously into a chair. "Sit yourself down and I'll bring you a dish of tea. You must be fair forfechit."

After she had hurried out, James Colquhoun coughed delicately. "In Edinburgh, more than in other parts of Scotland, there is a certain disrespect for rank. James Boswell once warned Rousseau about the shocking familiarity of Scotsmen. I hope it does not trouble you after your sojourn in London."

Jean shook her head in denial and then, emboldened by the young lawyer's kindly manner, she hesitantly began to tell him of her terrible social disgrace.

Despite her very obvious distress, Mr. Colquhoun could not refrain from laughing.

"You have come to the one place where Society will not be in the slightest concerned. Education, metaphysics, logic—they are the gods who rule this city. A well-informed mind is an entrée into the highest Society, not the turn of a hem or the setting of a cravat.

"For example, the Reverend Sydney Smith, that famous English wit, has a very funny story that sums it up. He overheard a young lady of his acquaintance at a dance in Edinburgh exclaim during a sudden pause in the music, 'What you say, my lord, of love is very true in the *abstract*, but . . .' and then the sound of the fiddlers drowned the rest of her words. Metaphysics, my dear Miss Lindsay, metaphysics are what concern fashionable ladies."

Jean sighed. "I shall fail there as well. I have only been tutored in the accomplishments deemed suitable to a young lady of rank."

"Then get yourself a tutor," said Mr. Colqhoun enthusiastically. "Expand the boundaries of your mind and then you will be able to put the petty snobberies of the English court behind you."

Life did not turn out to be exactly the halcyon state of affairs that the lawyer had predicted. The Edinburgh gentry were, in some respects, trying to ape the modes and manners of London and put a barrier of refinement between themselves and the bawdy squalor of the Old Town. But a surprising number of the town's Society left cards and, in no time at all, Jean found herself making morning calls, studying with her tutor, attending lectures on philosophy and attending balls at the Old Assembly Rooms around the corner.

For the first time, she began to enjoy being rich and started giving supper parties for her new group of friends. Miss Taylor was inclined to be shocked by the easy-going familiarity of the servants who were apt to join in the conversation at a moment's notice, but Jean simply found it refreshing, recognizing the underlying affection behind the rough manners which made even one Edinburgh scullery maid worth a room full of Henrys with their supercilious manners.

As Christmas approached, she realized that she had not yet taken a look at her uncle's papers so, on one particularly vile day when the gales from the North Sea funneled up the Firth of Forth and flung icy squalls of snow on the city, she took herself off to the library and began going through the desk.

There were piles of personal letters and, after some hesitation, she began to look through them, recognizing in some of them, her Uncle Hamish's crabbed hand.

The first letter was very much in Hamish's usual hectoring style, so she merely skimmed over it. The second, however, began with a reference to her father, Philip's marriage.

"She is a sweet and delicate thing and he is nothing but a wastral," Hamish had written. "I offered Venetia Harrington my hand and my heart. I told her she was throwing herself away on Philip and, I tell you, Joseph, she laughed at me. Were I not a man of God, I would see fit to murder them both, the mocking, feckless, cruel pair."

Several of the other letters were in the same strain. How happy he must have been when my parents died, thought Jean bitterly. But however wild and mad the letters were, they seemed to exude the very breath of thwarted passion and Jean's love for the marquess, which had settled down into a small dull ache, reanimated into a sudden, sharp, physical pain so that the sweat stood out on her forehead.

Would she never be free of that pestilent man? She was already being courted by several very suitable young gentlemen and had almost made up her mind to settle for companionship instead of love. Love was a wild, savage, unruly, hurtful beast, tearing at her innards and leaving her no peace of mind. It left her with so little dignity that the ranting letters of a twisted man who had repeatedly tried to murder her could move her to tears.

Snow was beginning to pile up on the window ledges of the library, thick, cold and suffocating. Edinburgh began to seem claustrophobic, the philosophical discourse of her friends, mere intellectual posturing, the assemblies with their wild Scottish reels and hectic gaiety, loud and boorish. Jean longed for the marquess with every fiber of her eighteen-year-old feminine being and was glad of a diversion when Hoskins, who acted as temporary footman, brought in the mail.

She flicked idly through the cards and invitations and

found herself looking at a long, heavy letter with the familiar Glenrandall seal.

It was from Lady Bess.

"My dearest friend," she read. "We are still in London for the Little Season. Mary was married last week at St. George's, Hanover Square and all Society was there. We did not send you a card since you are beyond the social pale but as I said to my beloved friend, John—you remember the Marquess of Fleetwater, do you not?—since the poor little thing cannot return to society, it behooves me to send her some little crumbs of gossip to soothe her exile.

"Lord Fleetwater's engagement to Lady Sally is, of course, imminent. Gentlemen do so love a well-conducted female! It does seem a pity you can never return to London although there are many ladies like you in the demimonde and I could always visit you—in secret, of course. Quite an adventure! My friend, Miss Stokes—do you know her—of the Stokeses of Huntingdon?—had a governess who disappeared and was found to be living under the protection of some Lord! But dear Miss Stokes was so fond of the poor, fallen woman that she used to go to visit her, heavily veiled, in a hack and she told me it was prodigiously exciting to see how these sort of women live.

"So at least you know, my dear Jean, that you still have one friend.

"Your name was mentioned among much laughter at the Courtlands a fortnight ago and I did not hear what was said but Lady Frances threw her glass of wine in the gentleman's face. It is not amusing? But Lady Frances was a friend of yours, I believe, and always has been a quiz. *Chacun á son gôut*—every man to his taste—as Miss Taylor was wont to say in teaching us French! Do let me know how you go on, dear friend, and I shall write you all the details of the marquess's wedding to Lady Sally!"

Jean slowly put down the letter and wiped her fingers

on her dress as if they had been soiled. Bess meant to be hurtful and spiteful of course, but she seemed to be very definite about the marquess's marriage. Jean laid her head down on the desk and wept. Bess was indeed malicious but what had prompted her to go this far?

Had Jean known the true facts of the matter, she would have been a great deal comforted.

The Marquess of Fleetwater had returned to his well-ordered existence and was finding it unaccountably flat. He had firmly put the episode of Jean Lindsay from his mind as being merely an embarrassing passage in his life. He was once again treated with all the delicacy and courtesy due to a man of his rank and fashion. Why did it not then soothe? Why did the simpering of his adoring court of debutantes seem so dull? Why were the clubs, the coffee houses, the gaming tables so stale? Why had visits to a certain charming opera dancer taken on a sordid tone?

The marquess sighed, allowed his valet to help him into his evening coat, and stuck a large ruby pin in his cravat.

"My lord!" gasped the valet.

"Eh. What's up man?"

"We have a ruby in our cravat—a large ruby—and we are wearing our sapphire ring."

"Demme, you're right," said the marquess. "Too vulgar by half."

His long fingers rummaged through his jewel box and came up with a small sapphire pin to match his ring. What on earth had come over him these days? He twisted and turned like a girl in front of the mirror to make sure he was guiltless of further fashionable lapse.

Walking over to the fireplace, he picked up a gold-embossed invitation and gave another heavy sigh. A ball at the Courtlands. Why! He hadn't been to their house since the beginning of the Season when he had walked in and seen the lonely figure of . . . His mind refused to continue, clamping down rigidly on the subject like a steel trap.

The rooms were not so crowded as they had been during the main season and the marquess's lackluster eyes took in the full beauty of Lady Sally as she dimpled at him across the ballroom and came forward to take his arm possessively. The marquess listened with half an ear to her chatter and suddenly noticed Lady Frank across the room. She had obviously "dropped" her baby, because her figure was once again returned to its narrow, muscular proportions. He gave her a friendly bow but received only the coldest of nods in return.

He led Lady Sally toward the double doors of the card room where there were several young bloods standing at the entrance, hoping to unload her onto one of her other admirers.

Lady Frank was also standing at the card room door and, for reasons he did not wish to fathom, he had a sudden urge to speak to her, despite her chilly looks.

"Lady Frank! You are indeed in looks. I believe you have been blessed with a daughter," bowed the marquess, turning the full battery of his charm on the unresponsive Frank.

Lady Frank studied the wine in her glass thoughtfully and, for one awful minute, the marquess thought she was going to give him the cut direct.

Then she said slowly. "Yes. She's a lovely spirited little thing. Goin' to call her . . . Jean."

The marquess's thin face flushed as if he had been struck. Lady Frank's voice had carried into the card room to the ears of a group of drunken young bloods. One was so far gone in his cups that he forgot his surroundings and raised his voice in a tipsy yell.

"Heard m'latest poem 'bout Jean Lindsay? Sing it for you. Thass what I'll do."

His voice carried in mocking song.

> "It's a bit of a stop
> To be called an old fop
> But a lot, lot more
> To leave the dance floor
> Designated a whore."

Majestically, Lady Frank swept into the card room and flung the contents of her glass, full into the young man's face.

"What you starin' at, puddin' face," she snarled at the marquess. "Probably wrote the song yourself."

She swept off, leaving the marquess, for once, speechless. A touch on his arm made him turn and he found Lady Bess flashing her china blue eyes up at him.

"Poor Miss Lindsay," she sighed in mock sympathy. "No person of the ton will ever dare to be seen talking to her again."

Suddenly in front of her vacuous face there seemed to the marquess's eyes to be superimposed another . . . a small, piquant face with wide green eyes and topped with a flaming head of hair.

"I can assure you," he said in a brisk loud voice, not at all like his customary drawl, "I for one would be very glad to see Miss Lindsay again. I found her a charming, amusing and intelligent girl," and leaving Lady Bess with her mouth hanging open, he followed in the wake of Lady Frank.

He stood irresolute in the street outside the Courtlands' mansion as he watched Lady Frank's carriage disappearing around a bend in the road.

The snow was beginning to blanket London with thorough democracy, falling on the elegant houses of the West End and the stews of Seven Dials alike.

The snow was beginning to seep through his thin evening slippers and he came to a sudden decision. Admit it, he said to himself, you're demned bored. Life will never be the same without that chit. He would go to Lady Frank and beg her to give him Jean's address. Of course, the girl's godmother would know, but Lady Frank was better placed to know how Jean felt about . . . well . . . about things.

He hailed a passing hack and gave him an address in South Audley Street.

The marquess was fortunate in that Lady Frank was eccentric enough to turn away unwanted guests instead of leaving that service to the butler.

Accordingly, she emerged into the hallway, looked at the marquess, remarked flatly, "Get out," and retreated back into the drawing room.

The marquess found himself with a case of metaphorical and physical cold feet. His sodden evening slippers made a small pool of water on the tiles of the hallway and he felt at that moment that he would rather face a regiment of the Lancers than Lady Frank in a bad mood. Summoning up his courage and deciding to be just as eccentric, he walked into the drawing room and slammed the door behind him.

Frank was fortunately alone, sitting in front of the fire, and did not look up as he came in.

The marquess hesitated and bravely walked forward. "Frank, I really must speak to you about Jean Lindsay."

Without turning around, Frank said to the blazing coal fire, "Oh, for God's sake, leave the girl alone. You nearly sent her out of her wits with your damned philandering."

"Frank, I assure you, I am most concerned about Miss Lindsay despite her strange behavior to me at Brighton. I . . ."

He turned with a muttered oath as the door opened and Freddie sailed in.

"Hullo, John. Thought you was squirin' Sally at the Courtlands."

"He's sniffin' around Jean Lindsay again," snorted Frank.

"Really, Frank!" said the marquess acidly. "I realize you are angry with me but spare me the language of the stables."

At this, Frank straightened up and turned around, giving the marquess the full benefit of a pair of very contempuous blue eyes. "Why should I show you any pretty manners, Fleetwater? The girl finds Lord Ian's body floatin' around and gets the shock of her life, and just when she's tryin' to forget it, you start prattlin' on about what a fine dinner he'd make for fish or some such fustian."

"What! She didn't tell us that!" exclaimed both the marquess and Lord Freddie in chorus.

"Don't see as how either of you gave her the chance. Let the poor thing leave Brighton in disgrace without so much as a friendly good-bye. 'Course I wasn't surprised at you, Fleetwater. I've always said you were a spoiled brat. But my own brother . . ."

Freddie wriggled uncomfortably. He had felt for a long time that he had behaved badly and had been haunted by the memory of Jean's pathetic white face at the coach window.

"Frank, I honestly didn't know about her finding Fleetwater's body," pleaded the marquess. "I simply thought she had taken leave of her senses."

"Oh, well. That does throw a different light on things," said Frank gruffly, much mollified. "Well, what do you want to do?"

The marquess felt like a schoolboy. He cleared his throat. "I thought if you could supply me with her address in Scotland, I could travel there and well . . ."

"Marriage, I trust?"

"Of course," said the marquess coldly.

"There's no need to put on your high and mighty airs with me, Fleetwater. It's a bit hard for me to take in at this time of night—the fact that Society's best-known rake is considering gettin' leg-shackled. Oh, well . . . I'll give you her direction. She's at her uncle's house in Edinburgh—not Hamish, the nabob."

The marquess laughed. "Miss Lindsay certainly has been used to Eastern trophies. Remember that terrible house in Brighton. All those stuffed heads and—oh, my God—that elephant and those bud . . ."

He broke off as he realized that both brother and sister were regarding him frostily. "There was nothin' up that place," said Freddie. "Snuggest house in all Brighton."

The marquess got to his feet and bowed. He had better leave before he offended his valuable source of information further. "I shall set out tomorrow."

"Tomorrow," shrieked Freddie. "You won't get as far as Islington. Look out of the window. You won't get up those roads to the North before spring."

He tugged the heavy curtains aside and revealed a world of white in the lamplight shining from the room.

"In fact you won't even get home tonight," said Freddie. "We'll put you up."

Acknowledging defeat, the marquess sank into an armchair and stared at the fire. What if she were married already? What if she had thrown herself away on some great Highland oaf? What a fool he had been to leave it all so long.

Lady Frank watched him covertly from the other chair and hoped fervently that she had done the right thing. But Jean had seemed to be so much in love with him. The marquess was undoubtedly a very good-looking man. She studied the still, white aristocratic face with the heavy-hooded lids masking the eyes and wondered what he was thinking.

211

Many pictures were flitting through the marquess's head . . . how she had looked when he had kissed her, the feel of her lips beneath his, the feel of her slim body. A violent flame of passion threatened to consume him and he stared into the tumbling castles the coals made in the fire and felt physically sick.

He voiced his main worry. "What if she is married, Frank?"

Lady Frank blinked at the naked pain revealed in the gray eyes and all her strong maternal instincts were aroused.

"I'm sure she would have written to me, John, and told me about it. She talks about a lot of beaus in her letters but she ain't mentioned anyone in particular. 'Course the mails are slow this weather," she added doubtfully. "Anyway, I can't see Jean gettin' herself married without wantin' me to be at the weddin'."

The marquess sighed. If only his pride had not been allowed to rule his heart, she could be sitting next to him now and the snow could fall all over the world forever for all he cared. His mind returned to nibbling away at the main problem: was she in love, was she married?

Several hundred miles away, his beloved's mind was running along much the same lines. Miss Jean Lindsay was also staring into the fire as the snow fell heavily outside and the wind screamed in the chimney. Was he married to Lady Sally? Or had he fallen in love with some completely different beauty who was now dazzling the London scene?

"Miss Lindsay," her lawyer admonished her. "You should pay attention. Young Lord Dalkelp is about to propose a counter argument to Mr. David Hume's views on skepticism."

Jean smiled her apologies and turned her attention back to the drawing room.

She had carefully made up the guest list for her supper

party, inviting mostly young people, in the hope of a frivolous evening. Alas, it seemed to be following the usual pattern.

Clutching his lapel, Lord Dalkelp began, "In his Essays Concerning Human Understanding, Mr. David Hume says thus, 'There is a species of skepticism, *antecedent* to all study and philosophy, which is much inculcated by Descartes and others, as a sovereign preservative against error and precipitate judgment. It recommends a universal doubt . . .'"

Doubt! Jean turned her attention back to the fire. If only she could be sure. Perhaps it would be better not to know and still be able to dream of seeing him again. Damn Sally and double-damn Bess!

There must be somewhere where she would feel at home. She had to admit she missed the frivolous London life and found these Scottish forays into tomes of philosophy very boring, although she was modest enough to put it down to the inadequacies of her brain.

Faith! She was becoming as much of a snob as the marquess, pining for the elegancies of life. She thought suddenly of how they had laughed together that enchanted evening at the Ship at Freddie's silly jokes and a smile curved her lips.

To her horror, she heard the speaker addressing her.

"Ah, you smile, Miss Lindsay. Obviously you are a skeptic yourself. Do you agree with my views on the Cartesian doubt?"

"Oh, absolutely," said Miss Lindsay mendaciously.

But this was not London. "Really! In what way?" asked the infuriating Lord Dalkelp.

Jean racked her brains. "I would prefer to withhold my opinion until I have heard the end of your discourse, my lord."

Obviously she had said the right thing, for the young lord beamed and continued his speech.

After the guests had left and Jean had neatly avoided a philosophical discussion with the speaker, James Colqhoun remained behind to share the tea tray, as was his custom, with Jean and Miss Taylor.

"Have you considered visiting the manse at Dunwearie?" he asked. "You will no doubt wish to keep some mementoes and arrange the future of your housekeeper."

Jean was conscience-stricken. "Oh, poor Agnes. I had forgotten all about her!"

Mr. Colqhoun said, "I took the liberty of continuing her wages until I discovered what your plans were for her future. Of course the Duke of Glenrandall will naturally want to find an incumbent for the living, so I am sure her future is secure in any case."

"I would rather have her here with me," said Jean firmly. "I will leave for Dunwearie as soon as possible!"

"You will need to wait for the spring at least before you can travel," said Mr. Colqhoun, unconsciously echoing Freddie.

After he had left, Jean sat staring at the fire. Yes, she would go back to Dunwearie—back to where it had all started and there perhaps she could find her identity, for she was still plagued by a nagging feeling of homelessness.

It was an exceptionally long, hard winter, icy, bitter and snow-laden. The trees in the park outside stretched their skeletal arms to the sky and showed no signs of ever sprouting a leaf again.

March came and went and still Jean found it impossible to move as savage gales swept the country and slashing rains turned the roads to rivers of mud and made travel impossible.

Gradually, the showers of April gave way to heavy, mist-laden mornings and clear tranquil afternoons as the medieval city lay spread out under a sky of pure cerulean. Jean felt as if her youth had been given back to her.

Her laughter began to echo around the house in Charlotte Square and she passed her days getting ready for the journey to Dunwearie, her head filled with rosy dreams. As each day passed and brought no news of the marquess's marriage to Lady Sally, she began to hope again. Surely he could not have forgotten her!

On the first of May when the lilac trees were beginning to droop with their heavy weight of blossom and the hawthorn trees bloomed pink and white by the hedgerows, Jean and her entourage took to the road again.

As the heavy coach rolled around the corner of the square and disappeared, the post boy handed the housekeeper, Mrs. Abernethy, the morning mail.

On the top of the pile was a heavy, important-looking letter with a large, impressive seal.

Mrs. Abernethy stared down at the Marquess of Fleetwater's crest and debated whether she should send a boy after the carriage.

Then coming to a decision, she took the letter into the study and placed it on the desk. Mistress Jean will be back soon enough, she said to herself. 'Tis probably nothing important.

And the letter containing the marquess's tender avowal of passion and love which had cost that young man many a weary night of writing, lay unopened.

Chapter Twelve

The motley crowd that thronged Edinburgh's High Street turned briefly from their midday routine of eating, drinking and bartering to stare at the magnificent coach with its scarlet-liveried outriders which rattled over the cobbles.

The marquess stared out of the coach at the crowd. Some gave him a mock cheer and several of the women waved. He drew back, remembering Lady Frank's words before he had left.

"Ever been to Edinburgh, Your Lordship?" Frank had asked with a gleam of mischief in her eyes.

"No, but I am sure it is an interesting metropolis."

Frank had given a bark of laughter. "Well, milord, you could call it that. But I'd give a monkey to see how you get along with the natives."

He searched in his pocket for his scented handkerchief and held it to his nostrils to try to escape from the terrible stench which rose from the streets. How tall and black the tenements stood. He stared upwards and observed with amazement, a housewife throwing the contents of a chamberpot into the street.

At last the coach came to a stop, and one of the grooms explained that he had found Mr. Colqhoun's direction but it would be necessary to walk. With a sigh, the marquess descended from the coach and signaled to his groom to lead the way. He started at the sight of an enormous, shaggy Highlander wielding a battle-ax who spat in the direction of his Hessians and was subsequently even more surprised to learn that the ferocious gentleman was part of the Edinburgh Civil Guard.

Mr. Colqhoun, however, looked reassuringly the same. "This is indeed an honor, Your Lordship. I was just about to have a bite of luncheon. Would you care to join me?"

The marquess suddenly realized that he was very hungry and readily accepted the invitation. He picked his way through the incredible filth of the High Street until Mr. Colqhoun led him into John Dowie's tavern. The smoke and the noise were overwhelming and the marquess wondered how he could raise the delicate question of how fared Jean Lindsay's heart, in the middle of this babble.

But the company of advocates and their clerks and various businessmen and men of letters seemed completely unconcerned by the presence of an English aristocrat, being too intent on their own arguments and discussions. The marquess, who was accustomed to creating a mild sensation wherever he went, found this democracy surprisingly pleasant and remembering that Robert Burns had claimed that "freedom and whisky gang tegither," he ordered and drank his first glass of the clear liquid and found it went down very well.

Feeling somewhat emboldened after a second glass, he broached the subject of Jean Lindsay. He had expected the lawyer to be gratified that his client should have the chance of making such an advantageous marriage. To his surprise the lawyer not only disliked the idea, he disapproved heartily.

217

"I do not think that people of such different background should be wed," said the lawyer.

"I had thought I was in the Athens of the North," drawled the marquess. "And the Athenians invented the word democracy."

"They also kept slaves," replied Mr. Colqhoun dryly. "You must remember, my lord, that Miss Lindsay has been brought up to be a kind of servant despite her ladylike education.

"Married to you, she would be in command of a very great establishment and she would be living in a foreign country."

The marquess blinked until he realized that Mr. Colqhoun's foreign country was England. He turned the full blast of his very considerable charm on the lawyer.

"Now, Mr. Colqhoun, I have been torturing myself with these very ideas since I met her and all I have done is to make myself miserable. Have you never heard of love in this 'foreign country' of yours?"

"Ah . . . I did not know we were talking of love, my lord. I thought . . ."

"I am an extremely rich man, Mr. Colqhoun," said the marquess briskly, divining his thought. "I have no need of Miss Lindsay's fortune to repair my estates."

Mr. Colqhoun smiled happily and settled down to a philosophical discussion on the subject of love. It was, he hoped His Lordship realized, not to be confused with lust or passion? "Well, well, just so . . . we will take the matter from there . . . ."

After three hours, the marquess reeled from the tavern having been subjected to one of the longest lectures in his life. He had obviously passed some test, because Mr. Colqhoun clapped him on the shoulder and furnished the information that Miss Lindsay was to be found at Dunwearie.

"Perhaps Your Lordship would care to reside the night